D1501023

ADAMA

Publisher's Note

Adama is the first book of Turki al-Hamad's coming-of-age trilogy, which continues with *Shumaisi* and concludes with *Karadib*. *Adama* is also the first of his novels to be translated into English.

Despite being officially banned in several countries throughout the Middle East, including the author's native Saudi Arabia, *Adama* attained bestseller status within one month of its initial printing in 1998. Its popularity has continued unabated.

Turki al-Hamad

ADAMA

Translated from the Arabic by
Robin Bray

SAQI

British Library Cataloguing-in-Publication Data
A catalogue record for this book is available from the
British Library

ISBN 0 86356 311 2

Saqi Books
26 Westbourne Grove
London W2 5RH
www.saqibooks.com

I

Through the window of the train from Dammam the buildings of
Riyadh began to appear, vague and indistinct like a dream on a
summer afternoon. The heat haze of that August day mingled with
sandstorms whipped up by the breath of genies from the al-Dahna
desert, giving Riyadh the appearance of a talisman from
Scheherazade's tales, or a demon at the command of King Solomon
or Sayf bin Dhi Yazn, the fabled ruler of ancient Yemen: a demon
of the kind that suddenly appears, only to slip away again; an
amulet that signifies much and yet nothing at all; an island from the
tale of Sindbad and the pool of the enchanted king.

The noise grew louder and the hustle and bustle of the
passengers more frantic as they gathered themselves and their
belongings together in readiness to disembark. This frenzied race
might have led an observer to think every minute mattered to these
people, whereas to most of them their entire lives meant nothing at
all. Seven tedious hours crossing the desert between Dammam and
Riyadh in a hot tin can had worked them up, and they were now
made more restless by the anticipation of imminent deliverance
from the magic bottle.

A relentless commotion ensued, here and there people laughing and shouting. One man yelled at his wife while searching for their children for the first time since boarding the train; another arranged his possessions anxiously; women began straightening themselves out, making sure wraps and veils were in place; others went digging for their handbags. Everyone was engrossed in activity but for a young man who remained in his seat, staring out the window through the dust rising from the exhalations of the desert genies. His gaze panned blankly over the view, as though he had no concerns; but despite this calm outward appearance, his heart was churning.

He was a slim, clean-shaven eighteen-year-old boy of average height, with skin the colour of pale wheat. His mouth was small and thin, his nose straight and his forehead broad. He had long, straight, jet-black hair which his skullcap and headdress could not completely conceal. From behind a pair of glasses his large, long-lashed eyes observed everything, but took no interest in anything in particular. These were the outward characteristics of a certain individual who had one day emerged into the world and been given the name of Hisham Ibrahim al-Abir.

❖ 2 ❖

As the train approached Riyadh Station, passengers began to crowd the doors. Hisham remained seated, roaming free in his imagination. He had just finished secondary school and received his diploma, with results that were neither among the lowest nor particularly outstanding – though by all accounts he was highly intelligent, and well-read despite his youth. His only passion had ever been reading anything and everything he could get hold of. Hisham excelled throughout primary and middle school, and had been promoted from third to fourth form in recognition of his ability. This was a source of pride to his parents, especially his father, who could talk of nothing but his only son and how clever he was, a habit that would infuriate certain acquaintances whose sons were not on the same level. Yet everyone recognised Hisham's ability and acknowledged the brilliant future that undoubtedly awaited him.

When he had just started secondary school, Hisham's interest was drawn to politics and philosophy after a friend of his father gave him a copy of *On the Nature of Tyranny*, by the 19th-century Arab nationalist Abd al-Rahman al-Kawakibi. That led directly to late nights reading Marxist, nationalist and existentialist texts, as well as works from other schools of philosophical and political thought. Local libraries were his suppliers, but Hisham soon learned to acquire books by other means when official censorship kept them from the shelves.

His mother often opened his bedroom door late at night to see her son buried in books; she would break into a loving smile, believing him to be engaged in earnest revision from his textbooks. 'That's enough reading, son,' she would tell him. 'Get some rest.' Hisham, too, would smile with undiluted affection and reply, 'In a bit, Mother – just a few more pages.' His mother would smile again and close the door behind her as she said a prayer for him. Before long, however, she would return with a glass of hot milk and place it on the little desk, insisting once more that he rest. 'Drink this milk and you'll begin to drop off in no time,' she would say. He would smile as though giving in and answer, 'How could I say no when you tell me to do something?' Hisham's mother would insist on staying until he drank the milk. He would submit, drinking it quickly, and she would leave convinced that he would soon be asleep. But Hisham inevitably continued reading, say, *The Story of Philosophy*, dazzled by the profusion of ideas and the men who dreamed them up. Only when the muezzin issued the call to the dawn prayer would he come round, roused from his thoughts.

❧ 3 ❧

The train drew into the station, spurring on the jostling and clamour of the passengers. The smell of human bodies packed together spread through the air and mixed with that fine dust found only in Riyadh; the children's screaming rose and with it the shouting of the men and the indignant huffing of the women at all the pushing and shoving that respected neither veils nor the sanctity of people's bodies. And still Hisham seemed far removed from his surroundings.

In secondary school he'd neglected his studies completely. Had it not been for the fear of wounding his father's pride and his mother's heart he would not have studied at all, but devoted himself exclusively to the ongoing study of forbidden texts. Instead, he would launch himself into revision a month or two before the end-of-year exams and memorise whole sections of textbooks, enabling him to scrape by. He did not, therefore, pass with distinction as he had used to do, but it was enough to protect the feelings of his parents and save face in front of them and others.

His parents were puzzled by the deterioration of their son's academic achievement, despite his constant reading and what seemed to them diligent studying. Deep down, their surprise was tinged with a kind of pain, but at any rate things were better than outright failure and the despair and embarrassment that would have gone with it. On one occasion, Hisham's father tried to discuss the reasons for the drop in performance, and Hisham responded with feeble excuses and justifications. His father was aware of the weakness of the arguments, and Hisham realised this; but his father reluctantly kept quiet, putting this state of affairs down to the changes that accompany the transition from childhood to adolescence. Seeing no alternative, he prayed to God to grant his only son success and guidance.

In secondary school Hisham especially loved history, and would hang on every word of the young history teacher newly returned from America, Rashid al-Khattar, with all the fervour and energy of a boy eager for action. Hisham remembered this teacher, who had reciprocated his affection, for years afterwards, although he had only remained at the school for one academic year before settling in one of the Gulf emirates. The greatest shock of Hisham's life came when he learned that this teacher had committed suicide in the wake of the Israeli forces' entry into Beirut in 1982. This event came fourteen years after they had last met, by which time Rashid had become an ambassador in Europe for his adopted country.

Hisham loved lessons about the Industrial Revolution, the French Revolution and the Napoleonic wars, the clash of ideas in Europe and their influence on the Arab world following the French campaign in Egypt and its effect on intellectual and political life. He loved political and ideological conflicts in general; the official textbook versions were not enough for him, and he took to searching everywhere for other books on these subjects to the point where he became a well-known figure in Dammam's few libraries. Mr al-Khattar would also let him have some of his many books on political and intellectual movements. Soon the local libraries were unable to satisfy Hisham's passion, and from every holiday with his parents to neighbouring Jordan, Syria or Lebanon he would bring back books that had been banned in his own country, and which subsequently became his principal source of knowledge. In those days no one had heard of London, Paris or New York; few people had even been to Cairo, which to them was more of a dream than a geographical location, a fantasy like the Baghdad of Haroun al-Rashid or the Damascus of the Umayyad caliph Abd al-Malik. Cairo was the capital of the Arabs then, and an object of longing for intellectuals, writers, politicians and society itself.

What upset Hisham, upon reflection, was the painful sense of having deceived his parents during those holidays. He would spend all his pocket money on books that were unavailable in his own country, especially the books of Ernesto 'Che' Guevara, Regis Debray and Frantz Fanon, as well as the works of Marx, Engels, Plekhanov, Lenin, Trotsky and Stalin, which formed his main intellectual references. What really shook him up were the works of Guevara; they stirred something inside him. These books, as well as literary works and classic world fiction, were sold cheaply in Amman, Damascus and Beirut, on the pavements and on wagons like vegetable carts. During his travels and thereafter, he would devour classic Russian novels. He read Tolstoy's *Anna Karenina* and *Resurrection*, Dostoevsky's *Crime and Punishment* and *The Karamazov Brothers* and *Quiet Flows the Don* by Mikhail Sholokhov. Maxim Gorky's novel *Mother* aroused intense, mixed emotions in him from anger to ardour, sorrow to sympathy and callousness to tenderness, all of which led him to re-read it several times. Frequently, he wept with Uncle Tom in his cabin; lived with Wang Lang and his wife in *The Good Earth* and pitied Madame Bovary as deeply as he loathed Scarlett O'Hara. He would steal moments to read Alberto Moravia, Honoré Balzac and Emile Zola, not always out of love for the works in and of themselves, but to find a sex scene here or the description of a torrid affair there, picturing himself in his daydreams as the hero of these

11

relationships. The fascinating depictions of social life in these books did not much interest him: he regarded Russian literature as unsurpassed in this area. He also read some of Dickens's novels and particularly enjoyed *A Tale of Two Cities* which, alongside *Mother*, he considered to be the finest work of fiction ever written.

Hisham would spend generous amounts of money, given to him by his parents, on books like these. When the time came to return to Dammam he would gather them together, allowing his parents the impression that he needed them for his studies if he were to pass with distinction. With love and admiration they would help him to pack, unaware of the explosive ideas contained in the books. Hisham was glad, but felt just as strongly that his behaviour was despicable: by any standards he was a liar and a cheat. This painful sensation only grew more acute when he reflected that he was doing this to the people who were dearest to him. But sometimes he would attempt to convince himself that what he was doing was neither lying nor cheating; after all, these books were made up of ideas, culture and learning, even if the subjects were not covered in the school textbooks that were in any case incapable of satisfying his thirst for knowledge.

❧ 4 ❦

His reading pushed him out into a wide world of excitement and passion, great open spaces where the entire globe became an object of interest for him without limits or restrictions. He became filled with a new spirit, eager to transform this world into an earthly paradise where everyone would live free from tyranny and prejudice, in complete fairness, equality and justice. The whole planet had become his new homeland, while his city was now a mere speck in the sea and his country simply one part of the great mass of mankind to which every true human being had to belong.

Hisham, formerly known to all but a small group of friends as a quiet and solitary boy, turned into an ardent and impetuous young man. He became a regular participant in the heated political and ideological student debates at school, now on one side and then on another, without ever becoming a card-carrying member of any party. The school itself was a microcosm of the ideological currents then sweeping the Arab world: Marxists and Baathists, Arab Nationalists and Nasserites, all openly arguing and debating. A Baathist pupil would pass another known to be a Communist and shout "Red!" at him, and the other would shout back "Aflaq!" as though they were insulting each other.[1]

Looking back, Hisham recalled an argument with his Religious Studies teacher about Darwin's theory of evolution. The teacher had cursed it as blasphemous and atheistic, calling Darwin a Jew and part of the Jewish conspiracy against all Muslims. Hisham told the teacher that Darwin's theory was the product of science, and that science was master of the age whether one liked it or not; as far as the origins of man and other species were concerned, Darwin might or might not be right, but evolution was a self-evident reality. In any case, he'd continued, Darwin was not Jewish, either on his father's or mother's side. From that day on the Religious Studies teacher adopted a hostile attitude towards him, thereafter referring to him as 'the sinner'. But it did not matter to Hisham at all, now that he had found a new world of energy and passion.

After the argument with his Religious Studies teacher Hisham became a school celebrity, and more so when the headmaster summoned him to his office one day and threatened to report him to the authorities for apostasy unless he immediately retracted what he had said. The other pupils began to take an interest in him, as well as some of the left-wing teachers; in a school where every pupil had to belong to one faction or another, every group wanted him to join their side in political and ideological disputes.

Hisham began writing feverishly for the bulletins displayed on the school walls: red-hot critiques calling for every radical solution imaginable. The headmaster summoned him again after two of Hisham's articles appeared in both Communist- and Baathist-run bulletins. (Everyone knew which was which, though no one ever officially claimed affiliation.) The first article was about the

---

1. The Baath Party was founded in Syria in 1947 by Michel Aflaq (1910–89), a Syrian writer and schoolteacher; it advocated a form of socialist, pan-Arab revolution, and eventually attained power in Syria and Iraq.

Setback of June 1967,[1] its causes and the role played in the war by the Western powers alongside Israel in destroying the progressive forces in the region; it argued that the aim of the war had been to put an end to any attempt by the Arab nation at revival. The second article condemned the English teachers at the school and their barbaric behaviour, despite the fact that they had come, so they said, to teach culture and civilisation. Back at the office, Hisham watched as the headmaster, without first asking anything, opened his desk drawer, took out a collection of papers and threw them on the desk in front of him.

"These pamphlets were distributed around the school today," he said, attempting to make his tone both calm and stern at the same time. "They call for opposition to the state, and they're signed 'The Democratic Front'." The headmaster remained silent for a moment as he watched Hisham to see the effect this news had on him. "They're written in a similar style to your articles in the wall bulletins." When he found that Hisham kept too quiet, apparently indifferent, the headmaster added, "It looks as though you've had a hand in this."

A shiver of fear passed through Hisham and his stomach clenched painfully. He wanted to say something in self-defence, but the headmaster leaped in first.

"Not one word," he said, raising his voice, "I don't want an answer. This is the second time I've summoned you here, and I swear by Almighty God that if you don't stop this suspicious activity of yours I'll report you, not just for apostasy, but for belonging to clandestine organisations as well."

Hisham tried to speak, but the headmaster brought the meeting to an end: "Not one word, I said. Go on, get out of my sight."

---

1. The Setback (*al-Naksa*) refers to Israel's victory in the Six-Day War of June 1967; it is both related to and distinguished from the Catastrophe (*al-Nakba*), an Arab term for the creation of the state of Israel in 1948.

Hisham stood up, feeling weak as though drained of blood, his face and hands in a cold sweat. He was hardly able to believe he had got off so lightly, even though he had no connection with the things the headmaster had accused him of. How many times had he heard that in cases like these a mere accusation was considered proof of guilt, so there was no need for evidence? "Damn the lot of you," he heard the headmaster muttering as he was leaving the room. "You want to get us into trouble ..."

On his way out Hisham almost bumped into the school monitor, Rashid Abd al-Jabbar, who had been in the headmaster's office all along without Hisham's having been aware of him. Rashid used to mix with the pupils a lot and was closer to them in appearance than he was to the teachers and the other people who worked at the school. He was a young man, no more than twenty-two years old, short in stature and thin to the point of skinniness, with a dark brown complexion and small, piercing eyes. His mouth was very small, with thin, dark lips and little, regular teeth that were slightly stained from smoking. He had a thick, jet-black moustache and a small, snub nose; his features earned him the nickname 'Goat-Face' amongst the pupils.

The monitor left the office with Hisham, a hand on his shoulder, and gave him words of encouragement. "Don't worry about what the headmaster says ... He's a good person, despite everything. If he really wanted to do you any harm he could, without summoning you to his office or threatening you. Anyway, don't let his threats get to you. You're a great guy and you've got a good future ahead of you. Just keep going. 'Keep on going and you'll get there in the end', as the saying goes." With this Rashid gave him a long look, smiling enigmatically.

Hisham did not pay much attention to what the monitor said, preoccupied as he was with the image of his mother and father in his mind's eye from the moment the headmaster had thrown the pamphlets in his face. He was filled with apprehension: if anything happened to him, how would his parents cope? He made up his mind to stop all his political activity and revert to his old solitary ways. These anxieties took hold of him on the way back to the classroom, and as he resumed his place he was completely unaware of a word uttered around him or the glances of the other pupils.

5

Hisham stopped writing for the wall bulletins, which became less active and less political after the episode of the pamphlets and the introduction of strict censorship by the headmaster's office. Instead he decided it was enough to have debates with his classmates, especially those who took part in the history society set up and supervised by Rashid al-Khattar, the history teacher. The rest of his time he spent either reading or in the company of his childhood friends, Adnan al-Ali and Abd al-Karim al-Duhaimani. The three of them used to meet up every afternoon with several other friends at Abd al-Karim's house, drink his mother's mint tea and talk or play cards until just before sunset or later. Hisham's whole world consisted of reading and friendships, especially with these two.

On Fridays, or whenever they felt the need to get away, they would make quick trips to the nearby beach or the desert by the Dhahran road, with its soft sands and gentle breeze in late autumn and early winter, which on long summer days changed into a searing blast of steam. Even in summer they would go, lighting a fire using the dry palm leaves they found lying about and sitting around it chatting until after sunset. They spoke about ideas, politics and art – Adnan had a remarkable gift for drawing. But what they liked best was to talk about sex and girls; occasionally they would get hold of some contraband pornographic stories and one of them would read aloud while the others listened attentively, ears pricked up, eyes gleaming, limbs tense and imagination in keen activity.

Sometimes the boys would bring a metal pot and a jug to make black tea; it was almost undrinkable, but they would knock it back all the same. They might also cook *kabsa* stew, each of them bringing whatever ingredients he could from home. The only thing it had in common with real *kabsa* was its name: it was always either too salty or not salty enough, the rice undercooked or overcooked and the meat never properly done, when indeed they had any at all. But none of that mattered: they would wolf it all down with relish, licking their fingers noisily once finished and laughing together as they cleaned their hands by rubbing them in the sand. Then they would collect their things and head home, usually walking or, if pressed for time, taking a taxi for a quarter of a riyal each. (This they would do reluctantly, as it meant spending money and having to deny themselves something else they could have bought. Later, the transport problem was solved when Abd al-Aziz and two other 'gang' regulars, Saud and Salim, were able to convince their parents to buy them bicycles.)

✤ 6 ✦

The day soon arrived that would prove to be a turning point in Hisham's life. During the break, he was leaning against a wall on the second floor of the school overlooking the main courtyard, waiting for Adnan so they could eat together as usual. Mansur Abd al-Ghani, one of his classmates and also a member of the history society, approached him. Hisham had had no special affinity for this boy since meeting him for the first time at one of the society sessions and discussing Marxism. Later, Mansur would behave amicably towards him, trying to strike up some kind of relationship. Even then Hisham had felt an aversion to him. Mansur was generally mild-mannered, despite his stern features and somewhat lordly gait, which gave an impression of arrogance and superiority. He appeared over-confident, fixing anyone who looked at him with a piercing gaze. Mansur was undeniably good-looking, despite the hardness in his features, and was tall and athletic. He did not wear the skullcap and headdress; in fact, he did not even wear the traditional *thob* robes, preferring a shirt and trousers instead.

He approached Hisham, a broad smile playing on his lips and revealing large, white teeth. Mansur would not keep his smile up for long, however.

"Morning, Hisham."

"Morning," Hisham answered curtly, trying to convey that he had no desire for conversation.

"I hope I'm not disturbing you?"

"Not remotely, but I'm waiting for a friend. Sorry."

Hisham moved away in an attempt to bring to an end this little exchange, but Mansur caught him by the elbow and forced another smile, which again vanished quickly.

"I know you don't want to be friends with me," he said. "Every time I try to get close to you, you turn away, even though I really like and admire you. I don't know why."

Hisham stopped in his tracks, then turned to face Mansur, trying to smile. "Not at all. It's not like you think. But I haven't got time, and what with so much studying to do, you know," he said, filled with an intense wish to end the conversation in whatever way necessary. But Mansur kept hold of his elbow.

"No, it is like I think." For a moment Mansur was silent. "But I don't blame you: you're free to behave however you like. It's just that I want to talk to you about something important. When would be a good time for you?"

'He's such a pain,' Hisham said to himself. He looked Mansur straight in his stern little eyes. "I really am waiting for a friend, and I don't know when circumstances will allow −"

"Cut out the excuses and pleasantries," Mansur said, interrupting him sharply. "It's genuinely important: we have to meet."

The look in Mansur's eyes hardened and his lower lip began trembling, sending a strange shiver through Hisham's body and forcing him to agree. "All right, all right," he said, nodding. "When?"

"Tomorrow, during break."

"Tomorrow it is, then."

Mansur took his leave, walking purposefully in the direction of the courtyard. Hisham watched him go, confused, suspicious and so lost in reflection that when Adnan arrived he did not even feel his touch nor hear his voice.

⇒ 7 ⇐

The next day at school, Hisham counted the hours and minutes until break time. The physics lesson ended and the biology and history lessons followed, all passing without Hisham's taking in a word said in any of them; even the history lesson, in which he usually paid undivided attention, was far from his mind that day. 'What could Mansur want?' Hisham asked himself, 'And anyway, what is there between him and me?'

At last the bell rang, marking the beginning of the break: it was time for some answers. The pupils began making their way out, clustering together in groups and calling out to one another cheerfully. Adnan came up to Hisham with his innocent smile and placid expression, ready to proceed to the canteen together for a snack, followed by their usual unwinding in a remote corner of the courtyard where they sometimes met with the rest of the 'gang', far from the crowds. But Hisham excused himself gently, trying to force a friendly smile to his lips, and quickly left his best friend, who was taken aback at this strange and unprecedented behaviour.

Hisham made for the school courtyard, where he began wandering about in no particular direction until he saw Mansur standing in a corner, looking quite calm and superior. He approached and greeted him, dragging the words out:

"Morning, Mansur."

"Good morning. Let's go for a walk around the courtyard."

Mansur set off without waiting for him to answer, and Hisham followed automatically, as though he were bound to Mansur by an invisible chain. They walked a short distance without speaking, when suddenly Mansur said, calmly and without looking at him,

"What do you think of the government, Hisham?"

It was a surprising question, one Hisham had not expected, and felt like a sudden bomb dropped on him. He felt uneasy and did not answer. But Mansur dropped another bomb, turning his piercing eyes directly on Hisham.

"There's no need to answer – I'll answer for you. The government's corrupt. All it cares about is its own interests and plundering the resources of the people, who have no rights. The people are just slaves or subjects; at best they're no more than –"

Mansur stopped speaking and fell silent, but continued staring at Hisham, his face now sterner and his veins bulging conspicuously. Hisham, who likewise remained silent, was overwhelmed by surprise and agitation, a mass of questions spinning around in his head. What did this person want? Was he one of those spies his father had warned him about, trying to trap him? Or perhaps he was just a naive idiot who thought he had discovered something new? But Mansur broke the silence.

"I know what's going through your head," he said, softly and confidently. "You're suspicious of this person who's approached you without any introduction and started speaking to you directly and openly about things no one's supposed to discuss. You're right. Your reaction is perfectly healthy and proper. But believe me, I admire and trust you completely, so I'm going to speak to you frankly in complete confidence." Mansur paused for a few moments before continuing. "I'm inviting you to join an organisation dedicated to resisting oppression and establishing justice and freedom."

Mansur paused again, leaving Hisham feeling acutely embarrassed, suspicious and afraid all at once. What was this person on about? This time he had dropped a nuclear bomb. Was he being sincere? Where had he got this nerve from? Where had he learned to read people's minds? Was he really only twenty years old, as he had told the history teacher once, or were appearances deceptive?

Mansur's voice broke in on the swarm of queries in Hisham's mind. "Why so silent?" he said, his voice somehow sounding as though it came from far away. "Perhaps it's that you're scared. Still feeling suspicious? I told you that was only natural. But since I've shown that I trust you, you can trust me too."

Hisham looked at him foolishly. 'There he goes reading my mind again,' he said to himself. "What do you want me to say?" he said aloud, stammering noticeably. "Do you expect me to react any other way?"

"Not really," said Mansur calmly. "You're not the first person I've spoken to about this, and you won't be the last. They almost all have the same reaction. I'll leave you to think it over for a few days and then meet up with you again. Till then." Mansur strutted off without looking at him or waiting for a reply, leaving him rooted to the spot in a kind of vacuum, for how long he was unable to tell. That day he did not go to any more lessons.

❥ 8 ❧

During the following days Hisham was unable to sleep and withdrew from his friends. All he could think about was what Mansur had said to him ... An organisation? Against the government?! God, this was serious. The government was merciless when it came to that sort of thing. How often had he heard about people who disappeared without a trace the moment they merely breathed a word of criticism of it? He had frequently heard stories like that from his mother, warning him what would come of talking politics, and from his father and his friends and Adnan's grandmother, with her endless tales about 'the ancestors' and what had happened to them. But what Mansur was proposing was not just talk, it was action – and serious action at that. True, Hisham loved reading about politics, but he loved philosophy and literature, too. Loving something did not necessarily mean acting on it, especially when that thing was politics, the clandestine sort in particular. When his thoughts – or, rather, his misgivings – reached this point, the image of his mother and father came to his mind. Why had he not considered them before, he wondered ... What would become of them if their only son were sent to prison, the son in whom they had placed all their hopes, their entire future?

A shudder went through him and he had a painful sinking feeling in his stomach. He was terrified; afraid of prison, afraid of what could happen to his parents if anything were to happen to him: his mother might die from the shock, his father would be shattered. No, he would never agree to Mansur's proposal. He would tell him he was sorry, he wanted to be a free thinker, not a political activist in any organisation. His mind was made up, and he was determined to tell Mansur his decision at the first opportunity the following day.

He set off early the next day: perhaps he would meet Mansur before the register was taken and be able to get all this off his chest. He looked for him everywhere he could think of, but did not find him and decided to put off his search until the break. At break time he set off once more to look for Mansur, to the surprise of Adnan and the rest of the gang, but again he could not find him. He began to feel a little frightened. Could he have been put in prison? But surely if anything like that had happened the whole school would know by now. No, no doubt he was absent for some mundane reason. Hisham smiled ironically to himself. Amazing! Was this really the same person he'd been completely indifferent to, the person who only the day before he couldn't stand? Yet here he was today, worried to bits about him. How strange!

The bell rang, marking the end of the seventh and final lesson of the day, and still there was no sign of Mansur. Hisham gathered his books together and made his way out of the classroom, paying no attention to Adnan, who was trying to keep up with him so they could walk home together as usual. As he was walking along the pathway to the exit gate he heard a voice whispering to him from a distance: "Hisham, Hisham … over here." There was Mansur, standing behind one of the trees planted along the path. Once again he shuddered and felt his stomach contract painfully. He looked at Adnan walking beside him and asked him not to wait as he went over to Mansur, ignoring Adnan's inquiring glances.

"Let's wait while the pupils leave," Mansur said in a near-whisper when Hisham got to where he was standing, far from the path. They remained quiet, eyes darting about in expectation and anxiety, watching the groups of schoolboys surging from the gate. When at last the chattering and laughter of the pupils were out of earshot Mansur jumped up, taking Hisham by the hand, and without a word the two of them headed towards the exit gate which the porter was about to lock, having made sure everyone had left.

Walking down Education Department Street, the one that led to his house, Hisham's resolve slowly began to melt under the burning rays of the sun and the stifling humidity found only in Dammam during the summer months. Summer really began there halfway through spring and went on until mid-autumn, according to the sequence of seasons in the rest of the world. The sweat brought on by his nervousness mingled with his perspiration from the heat and the stickiness of the humidity to give his body a distinctive smell like a fresh, slimy fish; he felt a wave of nausea and wished he could somehow be free of his body.

"Well, what do you think?" Mansur asked quietly and firmly, after they had walked in silence for several minutes.

Hisham did not need the question spelled out. He stammered a little, not knowing where to begin, even though he had made up his mind to reject Mansur's proposal.

"No doubt you're still afraid," Mansur went on, without waiting for an answer to his question. "Like I said, that's perfectly natural. But there's really nothing to be afraid of." Mansur gave him one of those penetrating looks, but then quickly looked straight ahead again, saying, "If we patriots don't fight for our country, who will?"

"Yes, but ..."

"It isn't just our people who'll be liberated by our efforts: the whole Arab nation will; in fact, the whole world."

"True, but ..."

"The only way the slave will be liberated is through revolution. The only way the oppressed will be liberated is through revolution. History itself consists of revolution and the work of revolutionaries."

"Sure, but ..."

"We mustn't fear death or anything else. All of us are going to die one day, but there's a world of difference between dying for a cause and dying like a dumb animal."

"You're right, but ..."

"Believing in a cause or an idea doesn't mean simply being convinced of it, it means fighting for a better world. Haven't you read Marx? 'What matters is not to explain the world, but to change it.'"

"Yes, I have read him, but ..."

Mansur had spoken quickly and passionately, the words shooting from his mouth like bullets. Suddenly he stopped walking and looked at Hisham, a furious expression on his face and an even harder look in his eyes than usual.

"What's the matter with you?" he said harshly, taking Hisham by the shoulders. "I'm sick of all your 'buts'. What are you trying to say? Are you so indecisive and cowardly that you'd deny your duty when it calls you? I thought you were much better than that! Intellectual, sharp, enthusiastic you may be, but the most useless worker, the lowliest peasant is better than you. You're just a sham only interested in getting a reputation for yourself – you haven't got a single idea or a single principle, not one cause. We don't want you. I had the wrong impression of you. Just forget everything – we don't need the likes of you."

Mansur finished speaking and, glancing left and right, let go of Hisham's shoulders and strode off without looking back, leaving Hisham stirred up by his remarks. Was he really a coward? Was he really just a sham who didn't believe in what he said? Mansur's comments had touched a nerve, making him sweat even more profusely and accelerating his heartbeat. No, he began telling himself, he wasn't a coward, he wasn't all appearances and he would prove it to this conceited prig. In the heat of the moment he began running after him, calling, "Mansur, Mansur … Wait." But Mansur did not wait, and instead walked on without paying the slightest attention. Finally Hisham caught up with him and took him by the elbow; Mansur stopped and looked at him icily, his face a picture of pure cruelty.

"I'm sorry, Mansur," he said, his voice quavering. He swallowed with difficulty and went on, "You didn't get what I meant. I wasn't hesitating or afraid or being cowardly, I just had a few questions –"

"In revolution there are no questions, only action," said Mansur, interrupting him sharply.

Hisham swallowed again. "Anyway, you know where I stand; there's nothing I want more than to work with you."

For the first time since they had left the school grounds Mansur smiled, showing his white teeth, and put his hand on Hisham's elbow and squeezed it hard. "Now that's more like the young man I admired so much," he said enthusiastically, his voice ringing with pleasure. "I was sure you were a patriot and that you believed in the cause of the people and the Arab nation. But you provoked me with all your dithering."

They continued walking in silence until they reached Hisham's house, which was not far from the school. Hisham stopped and pointed out his home, inviting Mansur in and trying to tempt him with the prospect of his mother's cooking. But Mansur declined, saying he had to catch the bus to Qatif.

"Why do you want to go there?" asked Hisham, surprised by the explanation.

"For the simple reason," replied Mansur sarcastically, "that I'm from the area, my family lives there and so do I."

"So you're a Shi'ite?"[1] said Hisham without thinking, his astonishment plain to see on his face. He instantly regretted asking the question so hastily and was about to apologise, but Mansur answered quickly with an ironic smile.

"So they say. But I don't consider myself Shi'ite or Sunni."

"So what are you, then?" Hisham's second question was both impulsive and foolish.

"You'll find out later," said Mansur, smiling and waving goodbye. "See you tomorrow." And off he went towards the centre of town, leaving Hisham swimming in a sea of questions.

As he entered his room he heard his mother's voice coming from the kitchen.

"Is that you, Hisham?"

"Yes, Mother," he answered automatically; and at that moment the image of a bird he had long ago trapped in the garden passed through his mind.

---

1. Adherents of the Shi'i sect of Islam ('Shi'ites') are followers of the descendants of Imam Ali, the Prophet's cousin and son-in-law. Historically tensions have existed between Shi'ites and Sunni Muslims. Sunnis constitute the majority in Saudi Arabia.

❯ 9 ❮

"Excuse me ... Excuse me ..."

Hisham woke from his doze to a hand tapping him on the shoulder. He looked around and found that the train had come to a complete stop; one of the station attendants was standing in front of him, asking casually, "Excuse me, don't you want to get off?"

"Have we arrived at Riyadh?"

"Ages ago. Everyone's got off. Except you, obviously."

"I'm so sorry," Hisham said, getting up in haste. "I was completely exhausted. I must have dropped off just before we got in."

"Never mind. But please get off quickly." The attendant thus concluded a conversation that did not interest him and, giving Hisham a quick glance with no particular meaning, he made his way towards the front of the train. Hisham rubbed his eyes and wiped his glasses, then adjusted his robe and headdress. He gathered together the newspapers and magazines he had brought to amuse himself, though they were still exactly as they had been when he had boarded, and headed towards the exit.

He descended from the train and began getting his bearings. No sooner had his feet touched the ground than he was hit by a blast of hot air, filled with fine specks of dust that had a peculiar smell. 'My God, have we really just exchanged the humidity of Dammam for the dust of Riyadh?' he asked himself as he made his way into the main station. No one was there except another attendant, who was sitting on a dilapidated wooden chair drinking a large cup of tea and smoking a cigarette, swatting the flies that had come in to escape the heat. Hisham smiled as he remembered one of Abdullah al-Qusaimi's articles, with a title that went something like 'These Flies Kill Me Twice A Day.' He found his huge, black suitcase lying in a corner with some well-worn others and pulled it out, wheezing towards the exit as the attendant sat, still fighting off the flies.

Nothing in Station Street was moving except the hot wind, laden with that fine, red, irritating dust. Hisham sat down on his suitcase, waiting for a taxi to take him to his uncle's house, but nothing appeared on the horizon; it looked as though the passengers who had got off the train before him had claimed all the taxis. The wind blew harder. Hisham began drying his sweat with his headdress, which was soon covered in red blotches: the grains of sand had run down his face, mixing with the sweat to make an unpleasant soup. 'The humidity in Dammam's more bearable than this,' he repeated to himself as he continued to wipe away the soup, which would suddenly dry and leave behind specks of dust embedded in the fabric of his once-white headdress. And still there was no sign of hope on the horizon, until at last a car appeared in the distance sending up a cloud of red dust. Hisham jumped up and waved it down. The driver stopped, and Hisham approached and poked his head through the front window.

"I want to go to Old Shumaisi Street," he said, trying to sound authoritative, though a hopeful note crept into his voice. "It's not far from the al-Muqaibira souk."

The driver looked at him, stroking his beard thoughtfully. "It's a long way," he said. "It'll cost you three riyals."

"Three riyals! That's a lot for a journey like that. I'll give you two – that's the going rate."

"It's up to you. I'm not taking less than three," said the driver, getting ready to move on.

Hisham crossly agreed to his price, afraid that he would be unable to find another taxi. He put his suitcase in the boot and slipped into the front seat beside the driver.

"It's a long way: it could take more than half an hour with the traffic like this," the driver said. His skin was dark brown and dry, his face gaunt; he had a small, pointed beard and a thick, black moustache that arched over his mouth. His hair hung down over his shoulders in long plaits.

"Where are you from?" the driver asked, trying to strike up a conversation.

"Dammam," replied Hisham indifferently, staring out of the window.

"From the Eastern Province."

"Yes."

"You a *Rafidhi*, then?" the driver asked, using a derogatory term for a Shi'ite and giving Hisham a grin that showed his teeth: some were missing, others were dark from smoking, and a single gold tooth gleamed at the front of his mouth. But Hisham simply looked at him with a half-smile, without answering, and the driver realised that his customer did not want to make conversation. After repeating "There is no God but Allah" several times he also fell silent, and as the taxi crossed Dhahran Street in al-Mulizz, Hisham withdrew into himself. The taxi went to al-Mulizz via Railway Street, then proceeded to University Street and al-Assarat, passing by the Central Hospital to finally reach Old Shumaisi Street.

❧ 10 ❦

The night of his acceptance of Mansur's offer, Hisham did not sleep: the excitement had worn off and it was time for some serious reflection. His fear had returned. Once again the image of his parents became fixed in his imagination. 'What an idiot I am,' he began saying to himself. 'He told me himself to leave it alone, but I ignored him. I ran after him, begging him to accept me. He took me in with all his comments and accusations and made me chase after him as if I'd had a spell put on me. Me, the intellectual that people always sit up and listen to, paying attention to that stuck-up so-and-so! I'll show him tomorrow! "You can accuse me of whatever you want," I'll tell him. "I've got plenty of confidence in myself; your accusations don't fool me. And you can't make me doubt my ideals either, or my principles or my patriotism. Say what you like, you're not going to hurt the people I care about." Yes, that's what I'll tell him, and I don't care what happens.'

While standing in the queue the next morning his eyes met Mansur's; Mansur smiled at him, but he looked away. During the break he looked for someplace out of the way to eat his lunch, far from anywhere Mansur might be. Adnan, who had been finding his friend's behaviour of the last few days odd and perplexing, watched him. As Hisham was taking a bite of his jam and cheese sandwich and joking with Adnan, Mansur suddenly appeared, standing in front of him with that athletic figure of his and a faint smile on his lips like one of Solomon's demons just loosed from his bottle. Hisham stopped eating, feelings of trepidation overwhelming him once again. He tried to keep his composure, determined that this time he would refuse Mansur's proposal unequivocally.

"Hello Mansur," he said, looking at him steadily. "Do join us."

Mansur smiled. "*Bon appétit.* I've already eaten, thanks. If you don't mind, Hisham," he continued, "I'd like to have a word with you in private."

Mansur glanced at Adnan and looked at Hisham again. Hisham felt a growing sense of unease, but could only agree. He put his Coke and sandwich to one side and excused himself to Adnan with an unaffected smile before walking off with Mansur in the direction of the courtyard. Adnan watched them in astonishment.

They walked in silence for a while, Hisham almost too agitated to contain himself.

"What's up?" he said, trying to break the silence and suppress his nerves at the same time, while keeping his eyes fixed on the ground as though he were searching for something. "Haven't you got anything to say?"

"No, nothing," said Mansur with a smirk, looking at him calmly. "I was just thinking about what you said yesterday." He paused before continuing. "Why did you think it was strange I was a Shi'ite? Or rather, from a Shi'ite family?"

Hisham had not been expecting this question and stammered a little as he answered. "I didn't ... I didn't think it was strange, so much as an unexpected surprise."

"A surprise! In what way?"

"I don't know ... You can usually tell Shi'ites from their first names, or their surnames. But you, neither your first name nor your surname would make one think you were a Shi'ite. Sorry – I mean, that you belonged to a Shi'ite family."

Mansur smiled and cracked his knuckles. "You're right," he said. "My first name's just an ordinary one. It hasn't got anything to do with the Imams or mullahs. There are Sunnis and Shi'ites with it, even Christians and Jews. As for my surname, I'm from a little village; I'm a *barrani*, not from the *qal'a* – so my family name isn't well known. In fact, I'm not really from an old family at all."

"The *qal'a*? *Barrani*? What do you mean? I've lived all my life in Dammam and been to Qatif several times, but I've never heard of anything like that before."

Mansur's smile broadened. "Of course you haven't," he said. "You'd have to be a Shi'ite to have heard of them, not a Sunni." Mansur laughed nervously as he spoke. "By the way," he went on, "what do you think about the Sunni-Shi'ite issue?"

"It doesn't matter to me much, to tell the truth," Hisham replied without hesitation. "In fact, not even remotely. I see it as a remnant of the past. What have Ali and Uthman and Muawiya and the succession of the caliphs after Muhammad's death got to do with us? We're living in the present, and we've got enough to worry about as it is."

"That's true. But I want to explain for the sake of your social enlightenment and to make you more aware of the class struggle. The people of the *qal'a*, the *qal'awis*, are the city people, members of the leading families, people in authority and landowners. The *barranis* are the peasants who live in the villages, the *nakhlawis*, as the city people call them; they're the ones who serve the masters. And boasting aside," said Mansur, after a few moments' silence, "I'm a peasant."

This was all news to Hisham. "Strange," he said in amazement, "I thought you were all the same."

"There's no such thing as a homogeneous society, comrade. Everywhere there are different classes and the class struggle, whether it's Shi'ites you're talking about or Sunnis, Christians or Jews."

It sounded odd to Hisham the way the word 'comrade' tripped off Mansur's tongue, but he did not let himself get hung up on it for long. For a short while the two of them walked along slowly in silence as Hisham thought of the best way to tell Mansur that he had changed his mind about what he had agreed to the day before. But Mansur interrupted his thoughts:

"Anyway," he said, "I put your name forward to the comrades and they've agreed for you to join the organisation. In fact," he went on in a reassuring tone of voice, looking at Hisham and smiling, "they were thrilled to have a good element like you joining."

Hisham wanted to say something about what he had decided the night before, but was unable to. He had felt a kind of elation spread through him when he heard Mansur say how the comrades were delighted he was joining, a strange pleasure, a sudden enthusiasm coursing through his veins. The images of his mother and father and the bird vanished; he forgot all about his anxieties of the previous days, and all that was left was a single sensation: that he was someone important, someone wanted, someone sought after. He was full of this feeling as he said,

"I'm fully prepared to begin the struggle." He spoke fervently, but not with the same fervour that the words of Guevara or Fanon made him feel.

Mansur stopped walking and looked at him sternly. "In that case, my connection with you ends today," he said, as though giving an order. "Another comrade will come and see you to enrol you in your cell. The password is 'Ashrawi sends his regards'. Don't forget: 'Ashrawi sends his regards.'"

Mansur turned around and headed towards the school building, but Hisham caught up with him. "Who is this comrade?" he asked. "Where will he come to see me? And how?"

"Don't worry about it. Everything's been arranged. Don't forget: 'Ashrawi sends his regards.'" Mansur took a few steps, and then doubled back as though he had forgotten something. "By the way," he said, "your friend who was sitting with you; his name's Adnan al-Ali, isn't it?"

"Yes … why?"

"Nothing. Just curious. Don't forget: 'Ashrawi sends his regards,'" said Mansur, the shadow of a smile playing on his lips. Then he strode off, leaving Hisham confused and gazing into the distance.

❧ II ❦

It was about ten o'clock in the morning and the whole class was listening intently to Mr Haqqi, the biology teacher, as he explained single-cell organisms using the amoeba as an example. Suddenly the door of the classroom opened and Rashid, the school monitor, put his head round, a smile peeping through the thick moustache on that delicate face of his. The teacher stopped and everyone looked towards the door.

"Hisham Ibrahim al-Abir's wanted in the headmaster's office," Rashid announced. A shot of fear went through Hisham and he felt a cramp in his stomach again. This was the third time he had been summoned by the headmaster, whose threats were still within vivid memory. What could he want this time? Did he know about Hisham's meeting with Mansur and what they had talked about? 'Damn you, Mansur, I knew you were bad news,' he said to himself as he got up wearily, the other pupils watching him curiously, the teacher with a look of dismay. Dragging his feet, Hisham walked to the door where the monitor stood, still smiling. Hisham went on talking to himself. 'This time it's prison, no doubt about it. But what have I done? No, it isn't a question of what you've done, it's what you're going to do: it's your intentions they're interested in, not your actions. Well to hell with the lot of them: Mansur, the headmaster and Goat-Face here.'

Hisham and Rashid walked quietly along the hall that led to the headmaster's office, the silence broken only by the sound of their footsteps.

"So, what does the headmaster want?" Hisham asked, without expecting to get a reply: he knew the monitor was no more than a slave obeying orders.

"Nothing important," said Rashid. "He just wanted to tell you that … Ashrawi sends his regards."

Hisham stopped suddenly, rooted to the spot. His heart began to pound, his head felt hot and he began sweating from every pore. "You … you," he said, turning towards Goat-Face, his face drained of colour and his eyes bulging.

Rashid's smile, managing to get through his thick moustache this time, broadened as though he were enjoying the moment. "Yes, me. We haven't got much time," he went on abruptly, his clownish smile vanishing as he glanced in all directions. "I'll see you this afternoon in front of the municipal park. You know where I mean, obviously?"

Hisham nodded as Rashid walked on to the headmaster's office. "Go back to your classroom. I'll see you later."

For several moments Hisham remained transfixed as he watched Rashid hurry away and disappear down one of the corridors without looking round. In a state of complete bewilderment he dragged himself back to the classroom. 'Rashid Abd al-Jabbar,' he said to himself, 'the monitor. Goat-Face. He's the comrade! I can hardly believe it.'

He walked into the classroom without first asking the teacher's permission and threw himself into his seat as teacher and pupils alike looked on inquisitively.

"What did the headmaster want?" asked Mr Haqqi.

"Nothing. He just had a question about something," said Hisham, feeling as though he had bells ringing in his head. The teacher glanced at him and then went on with the lesson, looking over at Hisham from time to time.

"Everything all right?" One last attempt by Mr Haqqi to satisfy his curiosity.

"Perfectly all right, sir. Perfectly all right."

The class came to an end and still Hisham felt as though he were drowning, oblivious to the pupils crowding around him and bombarding him with questions.

❧ 12 ❧

All the way home Hisham was spinning in a vortex of conflicting thoughts. He felt completely dejected, oblivious even to Adnan walking beside him and talking away. He was confused by this new world he suddenly found himself in, without any prior warning. The faces of pale phantoms kept recurring: Mansur, Rashid, the headmaster ... Suddenly a vision of a police officer sprang up, followed by another of crossed bars, and in the distance a coarse rope swinging ... Hisham's heart was thumping so hard it seemed about to burst from his chest.

"Hisham, Hisham! You haven't moved house, have you?" Adnan's voice reached him from another dimension.

"No ... No, why?" he answered in a voice that seemed not to belong to him.

"Because we've already passed your place and you're still going!" said Adnan, clearly astonished.

Hisham came to his senses and looked around. Indeed, he had gone much further than his house. "You're right," he said. "I'm sorry. I've got a lot on my mind at the moment."

"Mansur, obviously," said Adnan with a jealous edge to his voice. "You haven't been yourself since you started going around with him."

"Don't be silly," said Hisham, looking at him calmly. "It's got nothing to do with Mansur or anyone else. We really have gone way past my place," he went on with a smile. "We're almost at your house. Why didn't you say something before?"

"I tried, but you carried on walking regardless and I thought perhaps you were going somewhere else."

"Never mind, never mind. I'll see you tomorrow."

"Aren't we meeting at Abd al-Karim's place this afternoon, then?"

"I don't think so … My father's got me doing a few things I have to finish today. Bye."

Adnan watched Hisham set off, perplexed, jealousy eating him up inside. 'He often doesn't turn up when the gang meets these days. What's going on?' Adnan wondered to himself, watching his friend disappear down the alley leading to his house.

❧ 13 ❦

At home Hisham still felt as though he were spinning, and neither his mother's smile nor the feast of a lunch she had made – a large dish of potatoes with lamb – could dispel the images that kept flashing in his mind's eye.

"And how's the best son in the world?" his father said to him as usual when he returned from work. But instead of answering, "He kisses the hands of the best father in the world," as Hisham normally did, he gave a listless traditional reply without conviction. He ate his food with none of the pleasure and relish he would otherwise feel when his mother made one of her special dishes as a surprise. As he ate he wondered what would happen if they knew what he was up to. Was this what their love and their pride had been for? He was throwing himself into something most people would be afraid even to mention. A clandestine organisation; the government; politics: his involvement with one of these alone would be enough to shatter them. 'I'm such a disobedient son,' Hisham agonised. 'The only thing I think about, the only person I've got any time for, is myself.' Wasn't it just the same making sacrifices for these two as making them for the Islamic community, for the people, for the homeland? He couldn't be bothered with the latter, but he could kiss his mother, and he saw his father every day. He only had to look at them to see the pride in their eyes. Was he going to throw all that away for the sake of a few things someone he didn't know or like had said? Was he going to abandon genuine love for the sake of a supposed duty? Didn't love itself bring with it its own kind of duty? No, he wouldn't go to the meeting. Goat-Face would turn up and not find him there. And then they would leave him be.

When Hisham came to this decision his face lit up and he gave a grin. "You've done a great job, Mother," he said, smiling. "The food was absolutely wonderful."

His parents looked at one another, completely bewildered. "Praise be to the Changer of Circumstances," his father said, getting up to wash his hands before his afternoon rest. Meanwhile his mother cleared the table, washed up and came back with a pot of tea. She and Hisham would drink it while she attended to her knitting until it was time to wake Hisham's father.

"You're in a funny mood today, Hisham," his mother said, looking at him without a pause in her handiwork. "While we were eating your father and I were wondering what was the matter with you, sitting there silent and distracted, and all of a sudden you come back to life and start telling me how good the food is when you'd hardly even tasted it. What's the matter? Is something bothering you?"

"Everything's fine, Mother," he said, looking at her affectionately, with a genuine smile. "I'd never do anything you'd disapprove of. I'm sorry if I upset you earlier."

His mother looked at him lovingly, putting down her crochet. "We just want you to be happy," she said. "We were blessed when God gave you to us."

Hisham felt a lump in his throat, and he made up his mind once and for all not to go to his meeting with Rashid. His mother carried on with her knitting while he picked up a copy of 'The New Public' magazine and flicked through the photos of society women in Beirut.

❧ 14 ❦

It was coming up on four o'clock. Hisham's mother was still in her favourite place in the sitting-room, absorbed in her never-ending needlework directly opposite the television, and his father was still resting. A few minutes hence his mother would get up to make more tea and wake his father, and the television would begin to broadcast the cartoons, Hisham's favourite programmes. He never claimed them as favourites, but his mother knew they were and would smile when he made a show of not liking them in front of other people; in reality he was usually glued to them. Hisham looked at the clock on the sitting room wall in the corner opposite his mother, and it seemed to him as though the hands had turned into real hands and the minutes ticking by faintly had become drops of water, dripping onto his head. The closer it got to four o'clock the more depressed he felt. He began sweating profusely all over, despite the freon air-conditioner his father had spent months saving for. All their neighbours coveted it, privately accusing the family of being rich while pretending to be poor. But Hisham knew his parents were middle-class, neither poor nor wealthy. Dammam's rich people were well known and could be counted on the fingers of one hand. Even then Hisham's family had only become comfortable through his parents' hard work, since they were not notables and had not inherited any property. His father was just a civil servant, paid one thousand riyals a month. It was, in fact, a substantial salary, but he was still only an official with a limited income. However, with the help of his mother's thrift, his father had managed to build the house they lived in as well as another house which they let for one hundred and fifty riyals a month.

Just five minutes to go before four o'clock. Hisham was becoming increasingly nervous. He picked up 'Arab Week' magazine and tried to read an article by Yasser Hawari about the Palestinian resistance, but found himself passing over the words without taking anything in. He tossed the magazine aside and turned on the television. The broadcast had not begun yet, the screen still filled with the Aramco Television logo and the picture of that Red Indian. Hisham sighed irritably.

"Good old Mickey Mouse," his mother said with a smile.

Hisham looked at her without comment, then picked up a copy of 'Al-Jadid' magazine and began reading a report about youth camps in the Soviet Union, full of pictures of girls of all races in their bathing costumes, in all kinds of poses. Hisham gazed at the photographs, trying to make out the bodies under those bikinis.

His mother got up from her chair. "Time to wake your father up," she said. "It's four o'clock exactly. I'll put the kettle on, too."

Hisham shuddered and threw down the magazine. 'Boy, you're strange,' he said to himself. 'Haven't you decided not to go? So why are you so nervous, then?' For a few moments he remained quite still as though paralysed, absently watching the green flag waving on the television screen. Suddenly, as though in a dream, he heard the whistle of the kettle boiling. He sprang up as though an electric charge had shot through him and dashed out, passing the kitchen on his way. "I'm off to Abd al-Karim's house, if that's all right with you, Mother," he said hurriedly. With this he took off; in the

49

distance, he heard his mother asking, "Isn't it a bit early for that?" Her voice blended with the sound of the Qur'an reciter Abd al-Basit Abd al-Samad reciting part of the Sura of Joseph.

❧ 15 ❦

Hisham had no idea what had made him rush out like that. Almost without noticing he found himself walking down Thamantash Street towards the primary school, not far from the fish and vegetable market in al-Adama, the area where he lived. When the school appeared in the distance he noticed the skinny figure of Abd al-Jabbar in his white robes and headdress. He looked so tiny that it was almost impossible to make him out, but the thick cloud of smoke coming from his mouth showed he was there. Hisham thought of turning back; he had been hoping he would not find Rashid waiting for him, but some indefinable urge pushed him onwards. Rashid was tense and agitated when he reached him, looking in all directions and drawing heavily on his cigarette, his hand trembling slightly.

"You're late. It's a quarter past four. I'd almost gone," Rashid said quickly, manifestly nervous and exhaling the last drag of his cigarette in Hisham's face; he threw the butt on the ground and trod on it with his plastic sandal.

"I wish you had," muttered Hisham, looking at the stubbed-out cigarette. "The truth is I had a few things to do for my father," he went on, raising his voice. "I finished them and came here as quickly as I could."

"Let's go, then. We're already late as it is."

Rashid walked ahead briskly, lighting another cigarette from his packet of Abu Bass and drawing on it voraciously while checking behind him from time to time. They headed in the direction of the beach via al-Hubb Street, al-Dawasir and the old city souks. Hisham walked alongside Rashid as though stripped of his will, thinking of nothing, like an automaton.

They emerged into al-Imara Street and continued until they reached the al-Dawasir area, where Rashid took the first turn right, Hisham following him like his shadow. After about two minutes they entered a very narrow alleyway near the end of which Rashid looked at Hisham, his face now relaxed and a broad smile visible under his moustache.

"Here we are at last," he said, calmly enjoying another cigarette. "Please, you go first." He pointed to a house at the end of the alley. Hisham looked around; he was in a part of the city he had never been to before, full of small houses packed together and giving off a smell of fried food and raw and cooked fish. The house Rashid had pointed out was a little larger than those around it, though built from the same materials.

"We're considered rich here," said Rashid, with a certain pride.

"Yes," Hisham answered mechanically, mentally comparing his family's house in al-Adama with this one by the coast. Their house was built of bricks and mortar, whereas these houses were made of sea stone. It was the first time he had seen this kind of house close up, though he had spent his entire life in Dammam. He had only seen homes like these occasionally, in some of the areas he and his parents used to pass through on their outings to Qatif, Saihat and Safwa in the Eastern Province, or when he and his friends came to the beach. For the first time he realised that he did not know his city inside out, or rather for the first time realised that it was not one but several cities. He looked at Rashid and without thinking, asked,

"By the way, Mr Rashid, are you a Shi'ite?"

Rashid stiffened. "Not at all," he said sharply. "Why?"

"Nothing, nothing. Sorry." Hisham wished he had not asked the question. "Please don't get me wrong. For me there's no difference between one sect and another. In fact, I don't care about any of them. It just crossed my mind. Again, I'm sorry."

Rashid looked at him and smiled. "Don't worry about it. But for your information I'm a Sunni. I mean, I come from a pure Sunni family."

Hisham was surprised by his use of the word 'pure' and the way he pronounced it, stressing the syllable and clenching his fist at the same time: it made him smile for the first time since they had met by the school. Rashid invited him to enter the house.

"Please go ahead. And by the way, don't call me 'Mr Rashid' from now on. Save the 'Mr' for school: here we're all comrades. Call me 'comrade'.."

Hisham nodded and entered with Rashid through the front door, which led directly up a steep flight of stairs to a room furnished in a simple style, with a red and blue striped carpet covering the floor and a few red cushions stuffed with straw around the edges. At the end of the room there was a small door which led to the rest of the house. Rashid pointed to a particular place in the room, inviting Hisham to sit down.

"Excuse me," he said. "I'll be back in a minute."

Rashid went out through the small door without closing it behind him, so that Hisham was able to steal a glimpse through it. He saw a narrow passage ending in a half-open door, behind which a woman was standing wearing a loose-fitting green dress with a shiny black veil over her face and a black scarf covering her head and chest. 'She must be his mother,' Hisham thought. Rashid walked up to the woman and the two of them disappeared beyond the door. Along the sides of the passage there were three other doors, one on the right-hand side and two on the left. The house was permeated with a distinctive smell of fried food and cheap incense, mingling with the smell of the sea and the stifling humidity. From the ceiling hung down an old fan that had once been white, but was now covered all over with the innumerable small black marks of flies' droppings. The heat and the humidity were unbearable: Hisham felt as though he were suffocating. He got up and turned on the fan, which began revolving sluggishly, emitting a high-pitched squeaking sound as it circulated the damp and the smell of the place without doing anything to alleviate the heat.

The house was also smaller than, and very different from, those of Hisham's family or acquaintances. In Hisham's house the front door led to a small garden area, at the end of which four steps led to the main entrance, opening onto a small passage. On the right-hand side of the passage was the men's sitting room and on the left-hand side the dining room. At the end another door led to a wide hall off which four rooms were distributed: his parents' bedroom, his own bedroom, the family room and the women's sitting room, as well as the kitchen and the family bathroom. The men's bathroom was located outside the house, in the garden. At the end of the hall was a doorway leading to the back of the house, where the women had a door that gave onto a side street. Everyone he knew, Adnan and Abd al-Karim and others, lived in houses like theirs. But this house looked strange, even though its owners were apparently middle class like them; it reminded him of the poor people's shacks he had seen in the 'Bedouin camp' on the outskirts of the city going towards Dhahran.

"Sorry," said Rashid, interrupting his thoughts, "I hope I wasn't too long?" He was carrying a silver-coloured tray with a huge, red and green striped teapot, two teacups and a plastic container with something red, shiny and wobbly inside that Hisham could not identify. Under his arm he had a collection of books. Rashid had taken off his robe, headdress and skullcap and put on a loincloth with blue and green stripes, firmly tied at the waist, and a white short-sleeved vest. For the first time he saw Rashid with his head bare and found that among the many uses of the headdress, the most minor was to cover those barren expanses of the head: he was surprised to see that Rashid was bald, even though he was young.

Rashid set the tray in front of Hisham, who was leaning on a cushion, and sat down opposite him.

"No, not at all," said Hisham, sitting up. "Take your time."

Hisham began looking curiously at the red, wobbly substance in the plastic container. Rashid poured the tea and picked up the container, dipped three fingers in it and scooped up a large helping, which he put in his mouth and began chewing with visible relish.

"Go ahead," he said, offering the container to Hisham. "It's a Bahraini pudding. There's nothing like it."

Hisham dipped his fingers in the container and took a small piece, which he began chewing for a while, nodding to show his approval. "It's delicious," he said. "What's it made of?"

"Actually I don't know exactly. But it doesn't matter; the important thing's just that it's delicious."

"You're right. It's how it tastes that counts."

"It's funny that you're from Dammam and you've never had Bahraini pudding before!"

"No one we know has had it either, to tell the truth."

"You're definitely not originally from Dammam!"

"Is anyone?"

They both laughed and chewed the pudding. "Some people insist that it's originally from Oman," said Rashid, as he dipped his fingers in again, "but there's a difference between the Omani version and the Bahraini one: the Omani pudding's greasier and has more cardamom in it. The Bahraini one's better."

Hisham nodded in a mechanical, meaningless way. They both began drinking their tea quietly and dipping their fingers in the container from time to time. Each of them was looking at the other, and when their eyes met they would dip their fingers in again or take a sip of their tea.

"It tastes even better with coffee," Rashid said finally. "Or so my mother says. But I don't like Turkish coffee; I prefer instant. I drink it a lot at the house of a relative of mine who works at Aramco and lives in al-Munira. Especially with milk. Wow …"

"I don't like Turkish coffee either," Hisham replied. "But my father loves it. He'll only go to work in the morning once he's had a whole pot."

They both laughed again briefly but then once more fell quiet, the silence broken only by the sound of sipping tea as they glanced at one another.

"By the way," said Rashid, "why did you ask me if I was a Shi'ite? Do Shi'ites have some special mark that distinguishes them from other people?"

How embarrassing, thought Hisham; here he was, bringing up the subject again. "I told you, it was just something that crossed my mind," he said. "I was comparing the houses and thought that – I don't think I can make you see what I mean. No offence."

"I don't understand."

"Please, forget about it."

"All right. Anyway, we're originally from Bahrain. We came to Dammam ages ago, but most of our relations are still there, and they're all Sunnis. My grandfather says we're distantly related to the al-Khalifa family," he said, referring to Bahrain's ruling dynasty with obvious pride in his voice. He lit a cigarette and took a sip of tea. "And you," he said, "you're evidently not from the Eastern Province."

"Not exactly. I was born here. My mother and father were both born in Qusaim, but they've lived here in Dammam for most of their lives."

There was another pause as Rashid began looking through the books he had brought in. "Have you read these?" he said, looking at Hisham. He handed him the books and Hisham began looking at the titles: *The Communist Manifesto* by Marx; Lenin's *What is to Be Done?* and *Imperialism, the Highest Stage of Capitalism*; *The Origins of Marxist Philosophy* by George Pulitzer; Engels' *The Origin of the Family, Private Property and the State*; three novels by Yasin al-Hafiz and a booklet called 'The Theoretical Principles of the Arab Socialist Baath Party', brought out by the party's sixth national conference in 1963. Hisham had read all of them, except the works of al-Hafiz and the Baath Party Theoretical Principles. He gave the books back to Rashid, keeping back the ones he had not read and leafing through them.

"I've read all of them before, except the al-Hafiz and the Principles ... I prefer Marxist thought, actually."

"Great, that's wonderful," Rashid cried enthusiastically. "But you must read the al-Hafiz books and the 'Principles'; those are very important. The next time we meet we'll discuss what you've read. You can keep those books until our next meeting."

"And when will that be?"

"Same day, same time every week, here in this house. But I don't want you to be late again. A freedom fighter must be punctual," Rashid said, as though giving him an order. For the first time Rashid's tone provoked him, but even though his blood was boiling Hisham kept quiet, flicking through the books to suppress his reaction.

"From now on I'm responsible for you," Rashid went on. "Anything I say you must do immediately, without discussion. Act first, talk later – that's the first lesson the organisation teaches you."

Another provocation! Hisham was more used to giving orders himself and having them obeyed: he would speak and everyone else would keep quiet; that was how things were at home and with his friends, as well. "All right, all right," he replied irritably, fired up inside like an oven as he began to regret what he had let himself in for. There was a long silence, broken only by the buzzing of the flies around them and the faint, sleepy squeaking coming from the fan.

"The session's over," said Rashid. "We'll meet again next week." Rashid got up quickly, as though throwing him out; at least that was how it seemed to Hisham, who was not used to this kind of behaviour. Hisham in turn got up, humiliation eating him up inside. He, who had abandoned his friends so that Goat-Face could kick him out! 'I deserve better than that. "I've done myself wrong," as the song goes,' he said to himself as he descended the stairs on his way out, with Rashid leading the way.

"I'm sorry," Rashid said to him as they parted company by the front door, as though he had realised what was going through Hisham's mind. "Maybe you think me rude or bad-mannered. But I'm just trying to train you in the tough ways of the organisation. We're not friends; our relationship is not a purely social one. We're comrades. The relationship of comrades is far superior to any other, but it has its own limitations and restrictions. You might not realise that now, but later on you'll come to understand them."

Rashid shook Hisham's hand vigorously while patting him on the shoulder with his other hand. Hisham smiled wanly, feeling slightly better, and quickly slipped outside. When he reached the turn into al-Imara Street he looked back one last time and saw Rashid still standing at the door. Rashid waved to him and closed the door, and Hisham disappeared down the winding route back to his house.

❧ 16 ❦

On the way home it seemed to Hisham that everyone he passed was looking at him and knew where he had come from and what he had been doing. He took the books Rashid had lent him and slipped them under his vest where they stuck to his skin, sticky from the humidity. As soon as he arrived home he slunk into his room, locked the door behind him and hastily put the books in his desk drawer, which he locked. He threw himself on the bed, trying to catch his breath and give his heart a chance to slow down. His whole body was perspiring and damp from the humidity outside. Moments later the doorknob turned, and his mother's voice called from the other side of the door.

"Hisham, open the door."

He jumped up and went to the door, trying to look as calm as possible. His mother stood there with a worried look on her delicate features.

"What's the matter, son? Is everything all right?"

"It's nothing, Mother. I'm just a bit tired today," Hisham replied.

"You don't usually come in without saying hello, and anyway you normally go straight to watch television. Aren't you feeling well?"

"Yes, it's just that I'd rather have a rest. I'm sorry if I worried you." His mother calmed down a little, but retained a somewhat suspicious expression. "And locking the door!" she said. "That isn't like you."

Hisham felt as though he were about to collapse, but kept his cool as he said, "Did I really? I hadn't realised. Maybe it was because I'm so tired. Believe me, Mother, everything's fine."

His mother looked at him tenderly, a smile returning to her lips, and she kissed him on the cheek. "Did something happen at Abd al-Karim's house?"

"No, nothing, nothing at all. Just the usual. Having a laugh and a few games of Kiram and Plot. The same as always."

"How's his mother, by the way?"

"Fine, fine. She sends her regards."

At last his mother left. Hisham heaved a sigh of relief, while at the same time feeling a pang of guilt: it was the first time he had lied to her since childhood. He lay back on the bed, crossing his hands behind his head. Why was he so afraid, so nervous? The books he had brought with him were no more dangerous than the ones he had acquired in Amman, Damascus and Beirut. Was it the meeting with Rashid, then? But the gang would meet at Abd al-Karim's house almost every day and talk about things that were far more serious than anything Rashid had said. So why this fear? It was a clandestine organisation ... Hisham shuddered. It was just talking and reading, which was what he always did in any case; the only difference was that now he had comrades as well as friends. But that imperious tone Rashid had used with him! Hisham felt the bitterness of the insult again. For a long time he remained lying down, until he felt it growing dark around him and heard the sound of the television along with his parents' voices in the family room. He got up and turned on the light, then went to the sitting room where he greeted his father. Hisham sat in his usual place, watching television without taking anything in while his parents chatted and drank Turkish coffee. A presenter was introducing a programme called 'The Three Provinces Culture Contest' when he jumped up and went back to his room. His parents watched him go without comment. He locked the door, removed the books from the desk drawer, sat on the floor and began to read.

❧ 17 ☙

He was impressed by al-Hafiz's books and the 'Principles'. They were a fascinating combination of Marxism and Arab nationalism. He found in them something he had felt was lacking in the Marxist texts and the various nationalist works he had read. He had read Michel Aflaq's *On the Path To Revival* and some of the works of the Jordanian writer and guerrilla leader Munif al-Razzaz and Salah al-Bitar, co-founder with Aflaq of the Baath movement, as well as a few Nasserite texts such as *The Philosophy of the Revolution* by Nasser himself and books by Anwar al-Sadat on Nasser and the Egyptian Revolution of 1952. He also knew Muhammad Hasanayn Haykal's column 'Frankly Speaking', published in the Egyptian newspaper *Al-Ahram* every Friday; he would listen to it broadcast on the 'Voice of the Arabs' from Cairo, as *Al-Ahram* itself was banned in Saudi Arabia. The Marxist texts were mainly concerned with social and international questions, ending the capitalist mode of production and the advance of the world communist revolution; but whereas he passionately believed in the importance of the former, Hisham was less sure about the latter. He felt he was an Arab nationalist to the core: it flowed in his veins. Nasser's speeches would shake him up, and the nationalist slogans used by Baathists, Nasserites and Arab nationalists alike had an intoxicating effect on him. Still, he felt something was missing, that these people did not attach the importance to social issues that they warranted, especially concerning such matters as the class struggle, scientific socialism and historical inevitability. And so, despite his reservations, he came to believe that Marxist thought could light the way and offer a comprehensive philosophy of life. He admired the writings of al-Hafiz and the 'Principles' because they combined nationalist and social issues, bringing together in a single philosophy the ideas to which he felt the strongest affinity. He was impressed by his new discovery and looked forward to discussing it with Rashid.

Hisham kept his rendezvous with Rashid, returned the books and asked for more, relating the strong impressions they had made on him. Rashid responded generously, giving him more books by Yasin al-Hafiz as well as works by the Iraqi Baath politician Ali Salih al-Saadi, the Lebanese Baathist ideologist Elias Farah and others. Hisham read them all with great enthusiasm, discussing the theories contained in them with Rashid during their subsequent meetings and forgetting his initial fear of the organisation. It transpired that all it was about was sessions organised around reading and discussion. What more could he want?

One day he was sitting with Rashid at one of their usual meetings, discussing the failure of the petty bourgeoisie in the aftermath of the Setback; they agreed on the need for a new revolutionary project to express the thoughts and hopes of the oppressed classes of workers, peasants and allied intellectuals. Hisham spoke passionately on this point; Rashid was listening intently, it seemed, sitting with his left leg bent and his hands crossed over his knee, his other leg stretched out; his loincloth had fallen away from his skinny thighs and he was unaware that part of his pubic area was exposed. Hisham, who was facing him, felt slightly embarrassed, but could not say anything without causing embarrassment himself. He continued talking, trying to look Rashid in the eyes, when suddenly Rashid sat up and spread his loincloth over his legs.

"Hisham," said Rashid, interrupting him, "what's your opinion of the Arab Socialist Baath Party?"

Hisham stopped talking, taken by surprise like a car crashing into a wall that suddenly appears from nowhere. "I think you know my position," he replied after a moment's hesitation. "We've talked about nationalist ideology before."

"True, but I want a more specific answer. Tell me frankly, what's your view of the party?"

Hisham thought for a while. "To be honest, I don't have much time for Aflaq and al-Bitar and al-Razzaz's ideas. I think they're too sentimental, though I do agree with their general argument. What we need is an all-embracing philosophy. And I think that Marxism is the solution, even if it does lack a few things that would need to be added to perfect it."

"Who's talking about the likes of Aflaq?" said Rashid with a smile.

Hisham looked bewildered. "How can you talk about the Baath without talking about Aflaq?" he said. "The two go together, don't they?"

"Haven't you read the 'Principles'?" answered Rashid, exhaling cigarette smoke. "Haven't you read Yasin al-Hafiz? What do you think of all that?"

'What an idiot I am,' Hisham reproached himself, feeling embarrassed. 'Everything was clear in the "Principles".' "I told you before how impressed I was with all that," he said aloud, stammering noticeably and slightly blushing.

"That's the new Baath ideology," said Rashid, crossing his legs. "And as you know, it has no connection with Aflaq, except for the fact that he was the founder of the party – and not the only one, either. But apart from that they're different things. So, what's your opinion of the Baath Party?"

Hisham paused for a moment before speaking. "If what's in the 'Principles' is the Baath ideology, it appeals to me: it combines nationalism with Marxism, and that's what I believe in."

"So what would you think about joining the party, as long as its ideology was the same as yours?" Rashid said, leaning forward and looking Hisham in the eyes.

This time Hisham felt afraid, but his fear was nothing like what he had felt the first time Rashid spoke to him about the organisation. In fact, when he thought about it he doubted his intelligence; he ought not to be surprised by this kind of proposal, considering that the books Rashid had given him and their discussions had all distantly revolved around the Baath. Admittedly Aflaq and his associates were out of the picture, but it looked as though this was all about the other Baathists. 'What a fool,' he thought, 'I should have understood.'

"You haven't said. What do you think?" said Rashid, hurrying him on.

Hisham looked at him with a half-smile. "I knew from the start that all this had something to do with the Baath, Yasin al-Hafiz and the 'Principles' and all that. But I didn't want to discuss it till you brought the subject up."

Rashid gave him a searching look for a while and then grinned. "I knew from the start you were a clever guy who wouldn't miss that sort of thing. So, now, are you going to join the party?"

"Why not? I haven't found anything that goes against my convictions. And anyway, I'm already a member of the organisation," Hisham answered without much enthusiasm, but without hesitation either. Rashid smiled broadly again, and lit another cigarette from his packet of Abu Bass. He took a deep drag, then blew the smoke up to the ceiling out of the corner of his mouth, adding to the odours of fish, incense, smoke and damp that the fan spread throughout the room.

"Great, great," he began repeating over and over in a near-whisper as he continued smoking voraciously, looking even more wide-eyed at Hisham. "In that case, this time next week another comrade will join us: he'll be in charge of you from now on. He'll take you to the cell you'll belong to." Rashid paused briefly as Hisham crossed his hands over his knees, listening in obedient silence. "And from now on you must also have a movement name that your comrades will know you by."

"A movement name?" asked Hisham. "What does that mean?"

Rashid gave a brief, arrogant laugh, and Hisham's feelings of humiliation returned. "Your movement name," said Rashid, "is like a mask that you wear so as not to be recognised. We use them for reasons of security, as comrades are not allowed to call one another by their real names. Now, do you want to choose your name, or shall I?"

"No, I'll choose," cried Hisham.

"All right. What's it to be?" asked Rashid, trying not to laugh while Hisham began thinking of a name, his sense of mortification growing ever stronger.

"Abu Huraira," he blurted out, a name that for some unknown reason had just popped into his head. "Yes, Abu Huraira. That'll be my movement name."

"Why 'Abu Huraira'?" Rashid laughed out loud. Why not choose the name of a freedom fighter, like Guevara or Castro? Or do you just like 'Abu Huraira'?"

Hisham felt as though a knife were cutting through his insides and blood rushed to his head, but he kept his cool and tried to sound as calm as possible. "I think it's a good name. Have you got anything against it?" he asked, with an edge to his voice.

"Not in the slightest, Comrade Abu Huraira," replied Rashid with a scowl before standing up, bringing the session to an end in his usual way. Hisham got up too, and they went out towards the stairs.

"Next week will be our last meeting," Rashid said by the front door.

"Your help has been a godsend," said Hisham, automatically using a traditional expression as he set off without looking back; treading on the salty patches of sand in the road he felt an obscure pleasure as he heard them crumble, a sound that to his ears might have been a symphony.

⇒ 18 ⇐

"This is Old Shumaisi Street. Where did you want exactly?" The taxi driver's voice seemed to be coming from far away, jolting Hisham out of the imaginary film that had been unreeling in his mind like an afternoon siesta dream.

Hisham looked around. "Do you see that mosque?" he said, pointing to one about halfway between the al-Muqaibira cemetery and the central hospital. "Take the street immediately opposite it on the left."

The driver set off accordingly and turned into a dusty, narrow street. Hisham was trying to remember where his uncle's house was; he had only ever been there twice before with his parents, on their way to visit his grandmother in Qusaim. A few children began running after the car, laughing and revelling in the dust storm it stirred up in its wake. In the distance, a shop selling gas canisters appeared, above which Hisham remembered his uncle lived.

"You see that gas shop?" Hisham pointed it out to the driver. "Stop just there, please."

The driver braked by the house, sending up even more dust. Hisham got out, followed by the driver, who opened the boot but left his passenger to struggle with the suitcase himself. Annoyed,

Hisham paid the driver, who took the money and returned to his seat, muttering, "God, a job like that's worth four riyals. God sustain us …" As the car drove off, Hisham heaved his suitcase through the dust over to a little iron door near the shop. He knocked and waited, then knocked again, harder this time, but still no one answered. 'It'll be a disaster if they've gone away,' he thought to himself as anxiety began creeping over him. Before he had a chance to knock a third time he heard a faint voice from behind the door.

"Who is it? Who's there?"

"Me."

"Who are you?"

"Hisham al-Abir."

The door opened a crack, emitting a high-pitched squeak. A dark brown boy, about eleven years old with short, curly hair and a fine, handsome face, put his head round. 'He must be Said,' Hisham thought. 'How he's grown.' Said was his uncle's Eritrean 'boy', who had come from Asmara with his own uncle, the owner of the gas shop. Hisham's uncle had adopted him when the shop owner was unable to care for the boy, who was then no more than five years old. The last time Hisham had seen him was on his most recent visit to Riyadh three years earlier.

"I'm Hisham, the son of your 'uncle's' sister. Don't you recognise me?"

Said looked at him indifferently. "Come in," he said, the door squeaking again loudly as he opened it wide. "My uncle's not at home at the moment."

Said led him into the sitting room, to the right of the corridor that led to a courtyard off which the bedrooms of the boys, Muhammad, Hamad, Ahmad and Abd al-Rahman, were located. The bedrooms of their parents and the girls, Munira and Moudhi, were on the second floor overlooking the courtyard where the whole family would gather on various occasions. On cold winter days, anyone could go there to sit in the sun for warmth; if Ramadan fell during spring or summer, the male members of the family would meet here each day for the *iftar*, when they broke their fast after sunset. If Ramadan fell during winter, the men would have their *iftar* in the sitting room where Hisham was standing, and the women would have theirs in his aunt's room on the second floor or in the large kitchen at the back of the courtyard. Occasionally his uncle and aunt would share dates and coffee together in one of their rooms, but main meals were always taken separately; this custom was familar to Hisham, though he had never followed it with his parents.

Hisham sat down near the door, resting on one of the plush cushions elegantly arranged in a row around the walls of the sitting room and laid on top of a red carpet from Isfahan, with blue and yellow designs, that covered the whole floor. With the breeze from the three white fans suspended from the ceiling Hisham began to relax; here the fans refreshed the air, unlike in Dammam. Riyadh was dry, and its houses built of mud bricks which were a natural form of insulation. During the scorching summers they kept the heat out, and in the bitter cold winters they kept it in. Hisham felt a sense of languor spreading through his body, and dozed off for a little while, waking when he heard someone welcoming him.

"Look who's here! Thanks be to God you've arrived safely. God preserve you, cousin."

He opened his eyes, looked drowsily at the smiling face bent over him and smiled back. He was very fond of Abd al-Rahman, his youngest cousin. They were about the same age, although Abd al-Rahman was taller and more handsome, with lighter-coloured skin; but he was not as well read as Hisham was, nor as interested in current affairs. It was this difference that made Hisham feel superior when he compared himself to his cousin and found that, overall, the result was not in Abd al-Rahman's favour. He had no interest in culture whatsoever; he loved life and just wanted to get on with it. All he cared about was having fun, going on trips to the desert with his friends, playing Plot and flirting with girls in Suwaiqa and al-Wazir Street. He was not interested in studying and so only just managed to pass his exams, when he passed them at all, which would infuriate his father to the extent that Hisham's uncle would occasionally come close to beating the boy; but Abd al-Rahman's mother would intervene, and his father – who was too good-natured a person in any case – never actually hit him.

"God preserve you too, cousin. How are things? How is everyone?" asked Hisham happily with a big smile. He and his cousin embraced and then sat down again next to one another.

"Where's Uncle?"

"At the mosque."

"The mosque! But it's not prayer time?"

"You know your uncle: he loves going to the mosque. He goes every prayer time and then stays behind afterwards."

"He's a good man, no doubt about it. I've never met anyone like him."

Hisham's uncle, Abd al-Aziz al-Mubaraki, was truly unique. His mother's only brother and older than her, he had spent his life travelling extensively, finally settling in Riyadh. He could not bear to live in Qusaim, where Hisham's maternal grandfather had lived out the last of his days, and had left first of all for Kuwait, where he spent several years before returning to Qusaim. Soon after the death of his father, Abd al-Aziz had resumed his travels, going to Egypt, Iraq, Syria, Jordan and Palestine as a merchant. Eventually he came to rest in Qusaim again, where he married and had Muhammad and Hamad. When his wife was expecting their daughter Munira they moved to Riyadh, where he had acquired a good position working for the government. When his family grew and his responsibilities with it, he stopped travelling altogether. In Riyadh Ahmad had been born, then Moudhi and finally Abd al-Rahman.

Hisham and Abd al-Rahman continued chatting for a while when a young woman came in, covering her head and face with a black veil.

"God preserve you, after coming all this way," she said rapidly, in a high-pitched and rather loud voice. "And I was just saying to myself, 'Why is it Riyadh looks brighter today?' It's because you're here."

Hisham realised this was his cousin Moudhi. He had not seen her face for years, as she had worn the veil since reaching puberty and in any case had always worn it in his presence since he had come of age himself. In the past, Abd al-Aziz would sometimes bring his family to Dammam during the Eid al-Fitr holiday at the end of Ramadan and occasionally at Eid al-Adha and during the summer whenever they did not go to Qusaim or Taif. Abd al-Aziz used to travel to those cities throughout the summer months when the government moved there. Hisham remembered how happy he was when they came to Dammam to visit. Moudhi, Abd al-Rahman and he would play together and watch Aramco Television, the broadcasts from the American air base and, when the humidity was high, even Iranian television. They would go swimming in the shallow waters at 'Half Moon Bay' (or 'Half Bombay' as they used to pronounce it) and Aziziya. But their favourite outings were to al-Shabak in Dhahran, where they would gaze at the wide, clean streets, towering trees, elegant buildings and the American women driving sleek cars and wearing tight shorts. He could still remember Moudhi's comments as she had looked at those women with a sigh: "So," she had said, "these are their women; they're not a bit like us. Shame on us!" With that she had covered her face with her hands.

After all those years Hisham could still remember what she looked like. Moudhi was not a dazzling beauty, but there was something undeniably attractive about her. She was the least fair-skinned of her brothers and sisters; in fact, she was positively dark.

When she came into the room Hisham recognised her despite her veil, from her slim figure, voice and manner of speaking. He jumped to his feet when he saw her and took her hand as she held it out to him.

"Hello, cousin," he said. "How are you, Moudhi?"

"Well. And how's the family back in the Eastern Province?"

"They're well. They send their love to everyone."

"The tea will be ready in a moment," said Moudhi, going back into the house once the exchange of pleasantries was over. She vanished beyond the doorway, leaving behind the faint trace of perfume as proof of a recent female presence.

"Where are the others?" Hisham asked, Moudhi's scent lingering in his nostrils. "Where are Muhammad, Hamad, Ahmad and Munira?"

"Muhammad's doing overtime at the ministry, Hamad's with his friends as usual and Ahmad's asleep in his room."

"Asleep! At this time of day?"

"That's Ahmad for you. He can never get enough of anything."

"And what about Munira?"

"Didn't I tell you?" said Abd al-Rahman, sitting up straight and smiling. "Munira got married. She's gone to live with her husband in Jeddah. You know her husband; he's my cousin Nasir al-Suwayfi."

"Yes … yes. How long ago was that?"

"About two months ago."

"And none of you told us, as though we weren't part of the family."

"It was a quick wedding. There wasn't a big reception. It was all done in a rush. You know your uncle, he doesn't like extravagance or ostentation. We tried to convince him that a wedding reception wasn't like that, but he insisted on having a small dinner just for the bride and groom's immediate families."

'Lucky man who married you, Munira,' Hisham thought to himself. He could still remember her: that oval face; those big, black eyes; those full, crimson lips that would reveal her pearly teeth when she smiled; her tender, voluptuous body, eye-catching despite her short stature, and the jet-black hair that reached down to her bottom in two long plaits. All that he remembered from the time when he had still been allowed to mix with the 'harem'. So Munira had got married … What a lucky man Nasir was!

"But never mind all that. What about your news?" said Abd al-Rahman, with a strange smile and an enigmatic twinkle in his eye.

"Well, I finished secondary school and got my diploma. Tomorrow I'll go and apply for a place at the Faculty of Commerce. I'll be staying with you for the first year of my course until I can get things sorted out. Nothing worth mentioning apart from that, really."

"But why don't you stay with us for the whole of your course? It's a big house, and it would be fun for all of us. You know what I mean," said Abd al-Rahman, grinning even more and giving Hisham a wink.

Hisham felt embarrassed. He knew all about Abd al-Rahman's exploits. "Yes … yes. By the way, where's your mother?" he said, trying to change the subject. "I want to say hello to her."

"She's in Qusaim, visiting my sick uncle," Abd al-Rahman said casually, before suddenly changing his position quickly, as though he had been stung by a scorpion. "Speaking of my mother," he said enthusiastically, "I made her pressure my father into buying me a car. OK, it's second-hand, but it's better than nothing. Ahmad's no better than I am. Now I can go wherever I want," he continued, eyes shining. "Having a car really is a blessing. Last week," he said, drawing so close to Hisham that their heads were almost touching, "I was sitting on the doorstep of the …"

But before he could finish what he was saying, Said came in with the tea. Abd al-Rahman broke off and took the tray from him, telling him to leave, and then continued talking in a whisper as he hastily poured out the tea and offered a cup to Hisham.

"Last week I was sitting on the doorstep of the house in the afternoon. I had nothing to do and I wasn't in the mood to do anything, either. Suddenly a girl passed by; I started looking at her, and when she passed directly in front of me she looked at me from behind her veil, which was very thin: it hardly hid her face at all. She was very pretty. She smiled at me and without realising what I was doing I followed her, watching her arse shake as she walked. Oh, Hisham, it was a sight to make your heart bleed."

Abd al-Rahman paused, his breath coming more quickly, and sipped his tea. "To get to the point," he went on, "I carried on walking behind her until she got to a house not far from here. She opened the door and went inside, then closed the door behind her. I was disappointed, but a moment later when I was just about to leave she put her head round the door and beckoned to me to come near, calling my name in a hushed voice, 'Abd al-Rahman, Abd al-Rahman,' and looking left and right and back inside the house. I went up to her and she said in a hurry, 'Today, after the evening prayers. I'll leave the door open a bit; come inside and you'll find me waiting for you. Goodbye for now.' And she shut the door."

Abd al-Rahman paused to pour himself another cup of tea. Hisham was on the edge of his seat and urged him to finish the story. His own cup was still about half full. "After the evening prayers," said Abd al-Rahman, "I went to her house. The truth is I was in two minds about it at the beginning, but in the end I decided to go and put my trust in God. I found the door open like she'd said and I went in, shaking all over and drenched in sweat. I shut the door behind me and then all of a sudden I felt something pulling me inside. I nearly passed out, but then I heard her voice saying, 'Over here,' and I came to again."

Abd al-Rahman drank some more tea and went on breathlessly, "She took me to a very small room and closed the door, saying,

"Everyone's watching television on the other side of the house. Now's our chance." Then she threw her arms around me and I felt the softness of her body, so hot it almost burned me. She pressed her lips to my mouth and then drew me further into the room. All my fear and nerves dissolved and the only thing I felt was that furnace I had in my hands."

"But how did she know your name?" asked Hisham, rather doubtfully.

"You doubt what I'm telling you, don't you? Well, in that case I'm not telling you the rest."

Hisham apologised and asked Abd al-Rahman to go on: he was all ears. Abd al-Rahman refused at first, but soon continued, one of his hands planted between his thighs. "I asked her the same thing myself. She said everyone in the neighbourhood knew the sheikh Abd al-Aziz al-Mubaraki and his children, and that she had been waiting for the opportunity to get to know me, until the chance had come along that afternoon." Abd al-Rahman's tone betrayed his pride. "Anyway, the point is, I felt as though my whole body was so tense it was going to explode. My clothes didn't feel like they could contain so much tension. She stripped and lay down on an old carpet on the floor. Hisham, what can I tell you? I started looking at every part of her, trying to make out her body in the dim light from the window high up on the wall. My eyes fixed on that dark triangle of hers. I started getting tenser. I took my clothes off and lay down on top of her, but I couldn't do a thing. She chuckled and whispered, 'He must be a virgin … and there he was, making himself out to be a right ladies' man!' Then she made me lie on my back and got on top of me. And all of a sudden I felt like I was drowning in a sea of moistness and heat and pleasure I can't describe. I felt myself coming several times before we parted. Oh, Hisham, it was an indescribable moment."

By the time Abd al-Rahman finished his story, Hisham was worked up to an unimaginable pitch of excitement. He felt as though he had a cauldron boiling inside him. "There's one thing I find confusing," he said, when he had calmed down a little. "How could you have had sex with her if she was still a virgin? I gather from what you said that she still lives with her family, so she must have been a virgin?"

"You don't believe what I told you!" Abd al-Rahman shouted at him, flying into a temper. "Who said every girl who lives with her family is a virgin? And anyway, in her case she's divorced but still young, and she needs the money. I'm seeing her again the day after tomorrow. I'll show her to you just so you believe me."

"No, man, don't show me anything and I won't show you anything either. I believe you; she's a blessing sent to you by God. But you haven't told me, how could you –"

Hisham did not finish his sentence, as just then he heard his uncle returning from the mosque and uttering ritual expressions of piety: "Praise be to God, thanks be to God, God is great … God forgive me for my sins." A moment later his face appeared around the door. He was a tall, thin man with a kindly face and a neat, short white beard; his moustache had been twisted with conspicuous care, and his forehead was broad, with a round, dark mark in the middle. Hisham jumped to his feet as soon as he saw his uncle, rushed over to him and kissed him on the forehead. Abd al-Rahman got up too and greeted him, bowing his head and saying, "Good evening, Father," with the utmost politeness. "Good evening," he mumbled back, and then stood there for a few moments asking Hisham all the conventional questions about his mother and father, their health and how they were generally.

"Did you both pray the sunset prayers?" Hisham's uncle asked, looking at Abd al-Rahman, who was still standing politely with his head bowed and his hands folded over his chest.

"The truth is we weren't able to go to the mosque, Father, so we prayed here," stammered Abd al-Rahman in reply.

"There's nothing wrong with praying at home if you have to," said Hisham's uncle, his irritation showing on his face, "but praying in the mosque is better and more appropriate and worthier in God's eyes. I hope it doesn't happen again."

Without waiting for an answer Hisham's uncle turned and went into the main part of the house, where he would read the section of the Qur'an designated for the day before returning to the mosque again.

Hisham and Abd al-Rahman sat back down. "Everything about my father is good except this mosque lark," said Abd al-Rahman, clearly fed up. "It's always, 'No matter what, the dawn prayers must come first.'"

"Don't get upset," said Hisham. "My uncle's one of the best people around. Try another father and you'll soon realise just how good he is." This remark had occurred quite spontaneously to Hisham.

The two young men continued talking, and the conversation drifted from one topic to another. They were joined by Ahmad, who had woken up from his long siesta without Hisham's uncle seeing him. Ahmad was extremely cunning in his relationship with his father. When the latter asked why he had not seen him in the mosque, he would take advantage of the unpredictable nature of his work at the electric company to convince the older man that he had prayed here or there, in one of Riyadh's numerous other mosques or at work. He also treated his father with utmost courtesy, which made Abd al-Aziz so fond of this son that he was willing to believe him even when he suspected he was not telling the truth.

The three of them continued talking until Hisham's uncle returned to tell them to go to the mosque for evening prayers. They did as he said, feeling slightly irritated as it was not yet prayer time.

❧ 19 ❧

When they returned from the mosque, Moudhi had prepared supper and laid the table with a large plate of *saliq*, grain cooked with cinnamon and fennel, in the middle of which she had placed two great chickens. There were also small plates of hot mixed salad dotted around the dish of *saliq*. The men took their places at the table: Abd al-Aziz at its head, Ahmad on his right and Hisham and then Abd al-Rahman on his left. They all remained silent around the table until Hisham's uncle mumbled, "In the name of God, the Merciful, the Compassionate," and reached for the food, after which everyone else followed suit.

Everyone was helping themselves to the *saliq*, with their eyes on the chicken. Hisham's uncle tore a leg off one of the chickens and put it on Hisham's plate, and he began eating it quietly as Ahmad and Abd al-Rahman glared at him. Before long his uncle cut another leg and put it in front of him; he did the same thing again, as the glances of the others grew even more enraged. Then his uncle took a piece of breast meat and began chewing it softly, and at that point the others reached for the rest of the chicken, tearing off pieces and quietly eating them. A little while later Hisham's uncle stood up, licking his fingers and muttering, "Thanks be to God,

Lord of the Worlds" as he made his way to the washbasin and then from there to his room, where he would read a little of the Qur'an before saying the night prayers and going to sleep.

No sooner had Ahmad and Abd al-Rahman made sure that their father had left than they pounced on the remains of the chicken and began fighting over them. Hisham watched them, dumbfounded; later he realised that if he wanted any meat to eat in this house he had to behave like a wolf at the dining table.

They finished their supper, with nothing left of the two chickens but a few little bones, and washed their hands in the bathroom next to the sitting room. Then they went upstairs to the roof terrace to have tea and talk into the evening and enjoy the light breeze. The tea tray had already been prepared; it had been set down between four mattresses facing each other, spread with fine clean, fresh-smelling sheets. They all undressed and put their clothes neatly aside, keeping on their undergarments, which were long white shorts and vests. Lying on the mattresses, they propped themselves up on their elbows with their heads cupped in their hands and the tea in the middle waiting for someone to pour it.

After a while Ahmad got up and poured himself a cup. "I'm not responsible for anyone else," he said. "Whoever wants some tea can pour it themselves." He retraced his steps to his mattress and began slurping his tea, leaning on his elbow and looking at his brother.

Abd al-Rahman heaved himself to his feet and poured a cup of tea for himself and another for Hisham. "Some people have no shame; they don't even have respect for their guests," he said, holding Hisham's cup out to him and looking at Ahmad out of the corner of his eye. But Ahmad paid no attention to his brother's comment and continued drinking his tea.

"If you're referring to me," he said, "you're wrong. Hisham's a member of the family."

Abd al-Rahman went back to his mattress, grumbling something that no one caught. The two brothers were curious in that they were alike in almost every respect but their personalities. Ahmad was the opposite of Abd al-Rahman: he was calm and collected to the point of coldness, and loved making money with a passion. Abd al-Rahman, in contrast, would fly off the handle at the slightest thing and never managed to hold onto his riyals for longer than the twinkling of an eye.

Hisham leaned on his pillow, drinking his tea and savouring the breeze, which one did not always find on such clear nights. Meanwhile the brothers were arguing over who was going to accompany their father to the market the next day to buy household supplies.

"Brother, make the most of the car Father bought you," said Ahmad frigidly, paying no attention to Abd al-Rahman's edginess. "Go to the market with him and take him wherever he wants. It's the least you can do."

"Oh God," Abd al-Rahman replied tersely, "as if he wasn't your father too. Why don't you take him in your car? Or is it too precious for that?"

"I paid for my car with my own hard-earned cash, unlike some people."

"I know you," said Abd al-Rahman, raising his voice. "You'd sell your own mother and father if the price was right."

"Of course I like money," said Ahmad, unperturbed. "Haven't I earned it by the sweat of my brow?" He smirked at Abd al-Rahman.

"You've got the grace of God to thank for that, not yourself. I'll go with Father, and I hope your stinginess does you good."

"Look, you're just talking nonsense. It's time you stopped acting like such a baby."

"It's not your fault you're such a pain," muttered Abd al-Rahman, covering himself with his sheet, "it's other people's fault, for even trying to talk to you."

Peace and quiet returned again, and Hisham went back to gazing at the clear sky teeming with stars. Moudhi came to his mind. What a fetching girl she was, and an excellent housekeeper, too. It was she who had prepared the supper and laid it out, spread the mattresses on the roof terrace, made the tea and did all the housework. She certainly had enough on her hands with the demands of all her brothers. No doubt whoever married her would be a lucky man. Moudhi was less than a year older than Abd al-Rahman and less than a year younger than Ahmad. Their mother had had her first three children, Muhammad, Hamad and Munira, one after the other, and then had no more for about five years. After she had Ahmad, Moudhi and Abd al-Rahman in succession, she stopped having children for good.

"You haven't said what you are going to read at university," Ahmad's voice came from the other side of the roof terrace, interrupting Hisham's musings.

"Economics and political sciences, at the Faculty of Commerce," he answered, taking a sip of his tea, which had gone cold.

"Politics and economics!" said Ahmad, pouring himself a fourth cup. "Why don't you study something useful, like engineering or medicine? Politics? What does that mean? It's a load of rubbish."

"Politics is important," cried Hisham. "It teaches you about systems of government and international relations and political philosophy and all kinds of things."

"Systems of government? And what's government got to do with you? The traditional rulers are the ones who know all about that. You mind your own business. Do you really want to get yourself into serious trouble? Eat, drink and be merry and forget about politics; leave that to the people it really concerns."

"Politics concerns all of us," said Hisham with feeling, sitting up. "I don't want to bring about a revolution. I just want to understand."

Ahmad huffed dismissively. "Do as you like. It's got nothing to do with me. Talking to you could land a person in jail … You've always been stubborn, but I thought you'd come to your senses."

Ahmad fell silent and sipped his tea while Hisham lay back down, convinced that there was no point in talking to this cousin of his.

"Why can't you keep your mouth shut?" he heard Abd al-Rahman say, addressing his brother. "What would you know about it, anyway? You don't know anything. You left before you'd even finished primary school to work as a debt collector, you love money so much. An ignoramus arguing with an educated person: how ridiculous! And Hisham," he added, addressing his cousin, "you're to blame as well for talking about things like that."

Abd al-Rahman looked at his brother out of the corner of his eye, but his comments had no effect on Ahmad, who remained leaning on his pillow. "Knowledge and understanding have nothing to do with diplomas, fart-face," said Ahmad. "But that's you all over: in secondary school, but stupid as an ox."

Abd al-Rahman flew into a temper and jumped up, looking daggers at his brother and ready for whatever might happen next. "Me, an ox? That's rich coming from you, thicker than a donkey! At least I'm a student, whereas you, you … You're just a pathetic little clerk in a pathetic little company."

"If you weren't such an ox, you wouldn't still be in the first year of secondary school. Look at Hisham: he's the same age as you and he's about to go to university. Yes, you're a stupid ox, and unfortunately you're my brother as well. God knows where they found you."

Abd al-Rahman hurled himself at Ahmad and would have hit him, but Hisham intervened to break up the scuffle. Just as this was going on they heard the sound of footsteps coming up the stairs; everyone stopped fighting and went back to their mattresses, thinking it was Abd al-Aziz coming after overhearing their row. They all pretended to be asleep until a familiar voice broke the silence:

"Greetings, all ye faithful."

Whoever it was guffawed and then clapped his hand over his mouth, looking over at the other side of the terrace. All the others jumped up from their mattresses, throwing off their sheets.

"Damn you, Hamad," said Ahmad angrily. "You gave us a fright. And you've been at the *coffee* as well."

"Good evening, Hamad," said Hisham, as Ahmad lay back down and covered his head with his sheet.

Hamad pricked up his ears at the sound of this unfamiliar voice and looked over in Hisham's direction, squinting in the darkness. "Hisham!" he cried ecstatically. "What brings you here? I mean, what good fortune is it that brings you here?" he added, laughing. He went over to Hisham, who got up from his mattress, and they embraced.

"It'll be good to have a fresh face among all the cows we see every day," said Hamad, sniggering at his two brothers.

"What about him who always turns up in the middle of the night? He's the cow," said Ahmad quietly from under his sheet.

"Why are you such a pain, brother? Can't you take a joke?" said Hamad, going over to his mattress and throwing himself down on it without taking off his clothes. There was no reply from Ahmad. Hamad yawned deeply and gave a loud groan, and moments later the sound of his snoring rose into the night sky. Hisham went back to his bed, lay down and looked at Abd al-Rahman, whose mattress was next to his.

"Abd al-Rahman … Abd al-Rahman, are you asleep?"

"No one can get any sleep in this house," said Abd al-Rahman.

"Hamad doesn't look normal. His eyes were red and he was slurring his speech. And he wasn't walking straight and his breath smelled bad, like burnt plastic. Is he ill?"

Abd al-Rahman chuckled. "No, he's not ill or anything. He's like a genie … Just a bit of a coffee man."

"A coffee man! What does that mean? He drinks coffee?"

Abd al-Rahman laughed again. "No, silly! He drinks arrack."

"What kind? Western arrack? Sadiqi arrack?"

"No, the local stuff. It looks like piss, tastes like sick and smells like shit, if you'll pardon my language."

"Where does he get it? I thought there wasn't any alcohol in Riyadh!"

"Everything's possible in Riyadh. Some people make it locally for profit. Did you know that one bottle can go for twenty-five riyals?" Hisham whistled, and Abd al-Rahman continued to enlighten him. "Yes, and I'll tell you another thing: foreign drink can fetch even more; you can sell one bottle of whisky for fifty riyals!"

Hisham whistled again, louder this time. "But who brings it?" he said.

"I don't know. It must be smugglers and other people with their own ways. Who knows?"

"Are you a coffee man too?"

"No way. I don't like it. But I can get you some, if you want," he went on. "You can buy it in the neighbourhoods behind al-Wazir Street and by the Umm Salim roundabout, and in Hillat al-Abid and al-Atayef, and the lanes in al-Batha, and a few other places."

"Don't get me anything and I won't get you anything, either," said Hisham, turning over onto his other side and throwing the sheet over his head. "Twenty-five riyals! Fifty riyals! I could live on that for a month …! Good night."

They were so tired that within moments a cacophony of snoring could be heard.

❧ 20 ❦

Ghosts passed before Hisham in a fitful series of dreams. Faint images appeared, some with distinct faces, others shrinking away and unrecognisable. He saw Mansur and Rashid, Rashid and Adnan and Moudhi and that girl Abd al-Rahman told him about, calling him to her and laughing; no sooner would he approach her than she would run away, giggling. At one moment he found himself in Dammam, at another walking down al-Salat Street in Amman. Suddenly he was whisked away to al-Marja in Damascus, which in turn transformed into Martyrs' Square in Beirut. In al-Safat Square in Riyadh, Ivan Karamazov came into view; then the head of Jean Valjean from *Les Misérables* emerged, Cosette behind him with her golden hair stealing glances at him. He heard Ahmad Abd al-Jawad from Naguib Mahfouz's *Cairo Trilogy* reproaching someone, Zubayda giggling in front of him and Kamal dancing between them both as Yasin bit Zanuba's bottom. The images became jumbled up, and suddenly there was Amina from the *Trilogy* dancing and Christine Keeler praying and in the distance Hisham's mother, anxiously biting her fingers like Jacob warning Joseph not to go near Zuleika. He saw Noura, his young love, pouting; he went towards her, holding out his hands, but when he tried to embrace her she was not there. On top of the Empire State Building, he sensed someone standing behind him and looked round and saw Fahd, his superior in the party, hurtling towards him; he tried to duck but Fahd pushed him over and he fell, screaming as he went down.

Hisham awoke with a shout, his face wet with sweat. Everything was quiet. 'Thank God, I haven't woken anyone up,' he thought. He lay back down and looked up at the mass of stars in a flawless, tranquil sky that was never as clear in Dammam. There were a great many more stars too, shining more brightly than over his home town. Dammam stars were a dull grey colour, while these in Riyadh sparkled silver. A refreshing breeze blew, and Hisham's body drank it up as a parched man would water. Hisham looked over towards the other side of the terrace, from which they were divided by a high mud-brick wall. Over there Moudhi and the other female members of the family were sleeping and nearby, separated by another wall, slept Muhammad, his wife and their children Abd al-Aziz and Faisal. As for his uncle, he only ever slept in his room, summer or winter.

That Moudhi was sleeping just across was an exciting thought. Hisham wished he could see her asleep. How did she sleep? Did she take her clothes off like her brothers, or sleep with them on? At the thought of her taking off her clothes he trembled and felt a hot sensation flowing through his veins.

Hisham looked around again and saw Hamad with his mouth gaping open like a dead person's, lying on his back with his sheet off, robe pulled back. Ahmad was sleeping quietly, with one hand clutching his sheet and the other under his head. Abd al-Rahman was on his right side; his head had fallen away from his pillow and some saliva was dribbling down the side of his mouth. He was curled up, with his hands between his thighs and his sheet scrunched up under his feet. Hisham got up from his mattress and covered up Hamad, who gave a loud snore, and Abd al-Rahman, who mumbled something incoherently and then stretched and turned over. Hisham returned to his mattress and tried to doze off for a while, enjoying the dawn breezes unique to this place. His mattress was cool and dry, which made him smile; when they slept on the roof terrace in Dammam they could hardly breathe – the humidity would soak you through, as though you had wet yourself in your sleep. They used to struggle to find even a waft of fresh air, but when the humidity became unbearable, especially in July and August, they would be forced to sleep inside and turn on the air conditioning despite the expense. The electricity bill for that period would almost exceed fifty riyals a month, a huge amount that the family budget could never have stretched to all year round, even with Hisham's father's high salary.

But notwithstanding the Nejd east wind, Dammam was still more pleasant than Riyadh; people were gentler and kinder there. Perhaps it was just that he was used to them. Perhaps.

Moudhi came to mind once more, and he remembered Noura in Dammam and then thought of Abd al-Rahman's girl ... The heat and tension returned. Hisham turned over first onto his right side, pressing his thighs together, and then onto his left. It felt as though Hell itself were burning inside him. He lay on his back and opened his legs, his breathing growing more audible. Suddenly he jumped up with a start as he heard his uncle under the stairs, calling:

"Prayers, prayers. All of you pray, and may God grant you guidance. Morning has come and all power is in the hands of God, the One and Only," he continued in a murmur. "There is no god but Allah. I am glad of Allah as my Lord, of Islam as my religion and of Muhammad as my Prophet."

Hisham looked about, and finding that no one had stirred, remained lying down; but a moment later his uncle appeared. He was wearing a white, flowing robe with the sleeves turned up and a white skullcap. His hands and face were still dripping water from his ritual ablutions. Hisham leaped up and greeted Abd al-Aziz.

"Good morning, Uncle."

His uncle smiled. "Good morning, son," he replied cheerfully. "God bless you. You're up already?"

"Yes, long may you live," Hisham answered formally, as his uncle folded the sleeves of his robe back down and looked around the terrace at his sleeping progeny.

"What's the matter with these layabouts? Why don't they get up?" he muttered. "God curse the Devil: he stops people from waking up and doing what is due to the Lord. Hamad," he went on, raising his voice, "Ahmad, Abd al-Rahman. Wake up, and may God grant you guidance. Time for prayers, time for prayers."

Hamad stirred sluggishly when he heard his father's voice, while Ahmad nimbly sprang from his bed and kissed his father on the forehead. Abd al-Aziz could not help smiling and repeated, "God bless you, son, God bless you." Abd al-Rahman got up yawning and stretching as he said good morning to his father. But instead of replying, his father simply glanced at him and turned towards the stairs, reminding them, "Prayers, prayers: don't miss prayer time." With that, the stairwell swallowed him up and the rhythmical sound of his footsteps clicked into the distance.

As soon as Hisham's uncle disappeared Hamad went back to bed, muttering something incomprehensible, and moments later began to snore. Ahmad, who had stretched pleasurably, soon went back to bed too. Abd al-Rahman likewise dived back onto his mattress. "God save us," he said. "Every day the same thing ... Can't they postpone the prayer until later in the morning?" He threw the sheet over his face and began dribbling again. Hisham was left standing there, not knowing what to do: should he go to the mosque with his uncle, or return to sleep like his cousins? Eventually he decided on sleep; his cousins were bound to know best how things were run in the house. He lay down on his mattress, and the cool breeze and the dawn humidity began to make him feel sleepy; by the time the muezzin began chanting,

"Prayer is better than sleep … Prayer is better than sleep," he had dozed off completely.

⇒ 21 ⇐

Everyone gathered around the breakfast table, and for the first time since he had arrived, Hisham met Muhammad. They embraced and exchanged the traditional greetings and questions, then joined the others who were already eating. There was complete silence, except for the sound of their chewing hot, white unleavened *tamis* bread and stewed beans with tomatoes, and sipping tea with 'Abu Qaws' milk. Moudhi was standing by the door; she had lowered her veil over her face and was asking, as she did every day, whether they needed anything else. When no one answered she made to leave.

"Fine," she said, "then I'll go and milk the cow and churn the milk."

"Churn it well," Muhammad yelled after her, bits of tomato flying from his mouth. "Yesterday's milk was no good. It was too watery and didn't have any flavour or enough cream."

At this Moudhi putting her head back round the door and adjusted her veil. "Why don't you tell that to your wife?" she said, with a mixture of anger and sarcasm. "Why don't you tell that to that little princess al-Anoud of yours?"

"Al-Anoud has enough on her hands with the children and their problems," replied Muhammad calmly, paying no attention to his sister's scorn. "She spends all day hard at work."

"The children!" retorted Moudhi. "And 'all day hard at work'! Poor little darling. What children, what work are you talking about, my fine fellow? I'm the one who cooks and does the laundry and sweeps the house and does the milking and churning, while her ladyship sits in her room doing I don't know what, apart from making herself nice and pretty for his lordship."

The derisive force of Moudhi's tone embarrassed Muhammad in front of his father and brothers and particularly the new member of the family, Hisham. All eyes were on him, and Ahmad was smirking. Abd al-Aziz could sense his son's embarrassment. "Moudhi," he said, looking at her, "don't go too far."

Muhammad seized the opportunity and would have beaten his sister, who ran off, but his father told him to sit down. "Calm down, Muhammad," he said. "Calm down. Women have neither sense nor religion."

"You're right, Father, you're right," said Muhammad, sitting back down.

Everyone went back to tearing the bread into pieces and dipping it in the stewed beans and drinking their tea. Once the storm had subsided, Abd al-Aziz addressed Muhammad again, mildly reproaching him this time. "Your sister's right, Muhammad: your wife doesn't pull her weight in this house. She's become a great burden on Moudhi since Munira got married."

"Al-Anoud has great burdens of her own. The children and –"

"Don't make excuses," his father said firmly, interrupting him. "I'm warning you, that's all. You know I don't like interfering in your private affairs, so don't make me."

"Yes, Father, yes," answered Muhammad, who stole a glance at Hisham as he bowed his head. His handsome face was blushing. Everyone busied themselves with eating, but Ahmad and Abd al-

Rahman looked at one another and then at the food, trying not to laugh. Hamad drank his tea remarkably quickly but scarcely ate anything as he observed the proceedings with indifference. Of all of them, Muhammad was the one who most resembled his father, but he had not inherited the personality along with the physical appearance.

Hisham watched in astonishment; these family dynamics were new to him. In Dammam his mother, father and he would eat together at the same table and sometimes his father would joke with them. He would also occasionally cook lunch when he came back from work early, even though both his parents were pure Nejdis. His father left Qusaim before he was fourteen years old and went away with the *aqilat*, the itinerant traders of Nejd, just as their era was drawing to a close. He settled in Kuwait for a while, before eventually making his home in Dammam. There he found a steady income, initially with Aramco and later with the government. Aramco paid better, but the company 'sucked one's life away,' as his father used to say. But the customs of Hisham's family and those of his friends' families were completely different from anything that went on in this house, despite the fact that they were all from the same place and proud of Nejd and its people to the point of chauvinism, even if not one of them had ever set eyes on Nejd in his entire life. ("We love Nejd and we're proud to belong to it," Hisham's father once said to him, "but we wouldn't like to live there. Nejd has many children, but it doesn't feed them.")

"I didn't see you at dawn prayers today." Hisham's uncle addressed everyone at the table without looking at any one of them in particular. For a few moments there was quiet.

"We were there, Father," Ahmad said, breaking the silence with amazing audacity. "We were praying immediately behind you. But we came straight home after the prayers were over." The father looked at his son with a certain mistrust, but then looked away at his teacup which still had a drop left in it. "God bless you all," he said, drinking the remains of his tea. "What is due to God must never be neglected." Abd al-Aziz then left for his room on the second floor, where he would put on his work clothes – a pure white robe and headdress, brown cloak and shiny black shoes – and go to the ministry where he worked as an under-secretary. Hisham's uncle did not wear the *iqal* cord[1] around his headdress unlike most other civil servants, preferring to wear only the head kerchief itself as did older men and young boys.

"What a lying hypocrite you are," said Abd al-Rahman to Ahmad when their father had gone. "I don't know how Father can believe all your lies and hypocrisy."

Ahmad smiled calmly and took a large gulp of tea, which he held in his mouth for a moment before swallowing. "And what would you like me to have said?" he asked. "'We didn't say our prayers?' You're naive, brother." Abd al-Rahman was silent. He knew his brother was right, and he, too, found his father's religious zeal trying, as much as he appreciated that Abd al-Aziz did not keep a sharp, spying eye on his children like some other fathers he knew of. He was also aware that their father was a good and tolerant person: Abd al-Aziz knew that they sometimes did not pray, and that they played Kiram and Plot and listened to music, but he turned a blind eye to all that. However, his sense of religious obligation and duty as a father compelled him to encourage them to pray, to wake them for the dawn prayers in particular and comment when he did not see them in the mosque. When they answered, "Yes, we were there, we said our prayers," he would feel relieved at having done that duty. But he tried to appear severe in order to prevent them from becoming any more lax than they already were, even though his favourite aphorism was, "All we can

---

1. The *iqal* cords are ropes used to hold men's headdresses in place. Standard accessories for public wear, they are sometimes left off in more informal circumstances.

control are outward appearances, for the secrets of men's souls are known to God alone."

"It's time to go, I'm almost late," said Muhammad, getting up and heading for his room on the other side of the house. Then Ahmad got up, cup still in hand. Finally Hamad heaved himself to his feet, grumbling; he had not said a word throughout the entire meal.

Abd al-Rahman and Hisham were left alone, and no sooner had Hisham made sure of that fact than he addressed his cousin. "Abd al-Rahman," he said, "there was something I wanted to ask you last night."

"Go ahead, ask whatever you like," replied Abd al-Rahman, trying to extract the last drop of tea from the pot.

"Doesn't my uncle suspect Hamad? I mean … I mean …"

"You mean about the arrack, don't you?"

"Yes."

Abd al-Rahman put the teapot down and laughed, having given up hope of getting any more tea out. "Your uncle doesn't even suspect that there's any alcohol in this country to start with, so how would he suspect it in his own house, his own son? Even if he saw Hamad staggering along he wouldn't suspect anything like that."

They both fell silent when Moudhi came in with Said in tow to take away the leftover food and clean the room. She folded the tablecloth after Said had collected the crockery. "I hope you liked our breakfast," she said to Hisham.

"It was wonderful; God bless the hands that made it," he replied, smiling and looking in her eyes, which somehow defied her veil.

Moudhi laughed and looked at her brother. "That's a nice way to talk, really. God bless you too," she said, and then left with Said following her. Hisham kept smiling and watching her until she disappeared from sight.

"That sister of mine's got a sharp tongue on her," said Abd al-Rahman bitterly.

"You shouldn't all be so hard on her," remarked Hisham with a smile. "Anyway, what have you got planned for today?"

"Nothing special," said Abd al-Rahman, his face brightening as he spoke. "I'm going to meet some friends and we might go to the Suwaiqa market together, or to one of their houses and play Kiram. Won't you come with us? You'd have a good time."

"Not today," replied Hisham. "I've got to go to the Faculty of Commerce to hand in my application. Term starts in a fortnight."

"Damn term! Do you have to remind me? Let me enjoy the holiday without anything spoiling it," grumbled Abd al-Rahman. "Fine," he went on, "today you'll finish your business at the faculty. What about the rest of the days you've got left? What are you going to do with the two weeks you've got left?"

"I don't really know. I might go back to the Eastern Province. Or read. Or see the sights in Riyadh: you know I don't know it well, this city where I'm going to live for four whole years. Who knows?"

"Forget about the Eastern Province and all that other rubbish. I'll get you to know Riyadh like you've never known anywhere else before. I'll show you another Riyadh, another world."

Hisham smiled. "Goodbye," he said. He went to his suitcase, still in the sitting room, took out some clean clothes and went to have a shower before going out.

✤ 22 ✤

Having asked Abd al-Rahman how he could locate the Faculty of Commerce, Hisham was furnished with clear directions to the building, which was situated in Alisha. He was surprised his cousin knew the way, given that he was not interested in that sort of thing, but Abd al-Rahman told him he often passed it on his way to see some friends who lived in the area.

Hisham left the house with his papers in his hand and Moudhi's voice in his ears, telling Said to do something or other. He turned right towards the dusty road that divided Old and New Shumaisi Streets. It was not a long way, but far enough for him to get dirt all over the new Nejdi shoes his father had bought him as a going-away present. New Shumaisi Street was one of the smartest streets in Riyadh, newly paved with two lanes divided by a row of trees. On either side there were shops of every description: greengrocers, butchers, tailors, barbers, estate agencies and restaurants. But above all the street was known, along with Asir Street nearby, as the place where the best camel calf meat in Riyadh was sold. The only place with anything like its reputation was Hillat al-Abid, where one could buy the finest, most famous camel calf's liver in the city.

Hisham stood at the top of the street, waiting for the 'City Line' bus to al-Assarat Street. The bus came quickly and the driver stopped without Hisham's having to wave. The bus, a small Volkswagen, was packed. Hisham pushed his way to a small seat at the rear; at first he was almost knocked out by the smell of sweat from the other passengers, who were mostly Yemeni labourers plus a few locals, but he soon got used to it. The bus drove west towards al-Assarat Street and, once there, turned right to go north. When it reached the junction of al-Assarat and al-Khazzan Streets, Hisham waved to the driver to stop, fought his way off the bus as the other passengers grumbled around him, and paid the driver four fils.

He stood still on the pavement for a few moments to take in some fresh air and get his bearings, as he recalled Abd al-Rahman's description of the place. He saw the Television Building not far off to the east and an enormous abandoned palace to the west, and headed in that direction with the palace on his right. After several minutes and a few more turns he came to a small, ugly building marked 'Riyadh Water Department, Alisha Branch'. He continued until he reached a building surrounded by soldiers with a forest of transmission masts on the roof, but without any sign identifying it. He knew from Abd al-Rahman's description that this was the Secret Police building and as he passed it his heartbeat quickened along with his steps and he shivered as he remembered how Abd al-Rahman had described the place: "They think no one has any idea what the building is, but everyone knows it's their headquarters. God protect us from evil."

Hisham kept walking until he reached the Faculty of Engineering nearby. Soon he caught sight of some high walls with a magnificent palace set between them. 'From the way Abd al-Rahman described it, this must be the Faculty of Commerce,' Hisham thought as he approached the building. On the huge, green gateway made of beautiful wrought iron two signs indicated

'Faculty of Agriculture' on one side and 'Faculty of Commerce' on the other. Inside, Hisham found himself before a vast expanse of green planted with all kinds of flowers and trees, bisected by an elegant paved avenue leading to the doorway of the palace. Slowly, quietly, he followed the avenue and climbed the seven broad marble steps to the palace's main door.

Hisham entered the palace through a large wooden door flanked by two vast columns of white marble. It led to a spacious hall in which everything was also made of marble, sparklingly clean and so quiet one could hear the slightest movement. The hall ended in a marble flight of stairs that led up to the second floor, and a back door that opened onto a number of animal pens, from which cows' lowing and the bleating of sheep could be heard. Numerous rooms with gleaming ebony doors were located in a circle around the hall. Hisham did not know where to begin. The hall was completely empty and silent but for the echoes of voices coming from somewhere he could not make out. The vacation period had not quite ended, which greatly reduced the chances that any students or professors would be about. Eventually he decided to go through the rooms one by one in a circle, starting on the right. The doors were marked 'Dean of the Faculty of Commerce'; 'Director of the Faculty of Commerce'; 'Head of the Department of Accounting and Business Administration'; 'Head of the Department of Economics and Political Sciences'; 'Accounts'; and 'Registrar'.

Hisham knocked on the last door and entered without waiting for permission. He found himself in a large room with black leather chairs at the sides and a black, semicircular desk with a glass-covered top at the end. Behind the desk sat a grossly overweight man in a white robe and a white headdress without *iqal* cords. He had a nose like a hawk's beak and a tiny moustache with a very sparse beard that was barely more than a scattering of little hairs. On the wall directly above the desk there was an enormous portrait of the king, standing, in a cream-coloured cloak, white headdress and *iqal* cords decorated with gold thread.

"Peace be upon you," Hisham said as he approached the desk.

"And also on you, with God's mercy and His blessings," mumbled the man sitting behind the desk, without looking up from his papers. "What can I do for you?"

Without sitting or being invited to do so, Hisham held out his file. "I would like to join the faculty ... and these are my papers," he said.

"The deadline for registration has already passed," the registrar said, as he took the file. Hisham's heart began to sink. "But never mind," the registrar continued, smiling, "the faculty isn't full yet."

The last comment raised Hisham's hopes. The registrar leafed through the papers in the file, nodding from time to time, and then closed it and looked at Hisham.

"Your average is sixty-four per cent," he said, "and you had to retake two subjects." He paused for a moment. "But it doesn't matter. Please, do sit down." He pointed to a chair opposite. Hisham sat down as the registrar opened a drawer and took out a printed sheet of paper, which he held out. "Your papers are all in order; the only thing missing is your application form to join the faculty. Fill this out, and good luck to you."

Hisham took the form and did as asked, leaning on the table in front of him. The registrar added the completed file to the rest of his papers.

"The course starts in two weeks, God willing," said the registrar, as he began shuffling the papers in front of him to indicate that the interview was over.

"Thank you," Hisham murmured. He got up from his chair and walked rather hesitantly to the door, but when he reached it he turned with his hand on the doorknob and looked at the registrar again. "Excuse me," he said.

"Yes?" muttered the registrar distantly, looking up.

"Are you sure I've been accepted by the faculty?"

The registrar smiled and went back to his papers. "Don't worry," he said. "Just come along in two weeks' time."

"But my grades aren't good, and I'm concerned that –"

"Don't fret," the registrar said. "The main thing is that you've got your high school diploma; that's all that's required. God be with you."

"And also with you," replied Hisham, and left.

The world was scarcely big enough to contain his joy: at last he would achieve his aim of studying economics and politics as he wanted. He would be able to read *Das Kapital* and understand it properly (he had tried before, but all those equations and abstractions proved impenetrable). He would learn more in depth about how states rose and fell; more about systems of government and their different forms; he would learn *all* about Marxism, starting with its fundamental principles, and other political philosophies.

These were the tantalising thoughts Hisham had on his way home. He looked out at the surrounding gardens and smiled. Four whole years to enjoy this beautiful place! And they would be giving him a grant of three hundred and twenty riyals a month – what a fortune! He would be able to buy whatever he wanted: books, magazines, meals in restaurants ... But one question occurred to him as he walked through the gardens. Why had they built the faculty like this? It was more of a palace than a normal college building. Why had they not made it like the Faculty of Engineering he had passed earlier? He made up his mind to ask someone about it at a later date.

❧ 23 ❧

On his way home Hisham passed by a small bookshop on New Shumaisi Street and bought a few magazines: 'Arab Week', 'The New Public', 'al-Jadid' and of course 'Superman'. He still loved the comic, and had been reading it for years. He and Adnan were two of Superman's greatest fans. Week after week they would amass copies, boasting to their friends of their collection. But about two years earlier Hisham had begun reading it in secret, embarrassed to be seen with it – he, the young intellectual who read Marx and Mao Tse-Tung, Dostoevsky and Naguib Mahfouz, interested in Superman! But what could he do? He enjoyed it, and could see no alternative!

It was about twelve o'clock when he reached his uncle's house; the men were still at work, except for Abd al-Rahman, who was off somewhere in the city. Hisham knocked and heard Moudhi's voice in the distance calling out, "All right, all right." She opened the door. "Hello, cousin. Come in," she said cheerfully, drawing her veil when she saw him, but not before he managed to catch a glimpse of her face. She was quite pretty, he noticed, in fact even prettier than before, despite an outbreak of acne. He went into the sitting room, and noticed that his suitcase was no longer there.

"We've taken it up to your room on the second floor," said Moudhi before he could ask. "It's the only free room in the house. It's big and airy. Please have a seat; I'll bring you some tea straight away." She turned to go back into the main part of the house, but Hisham called her back.

"Moudhi, if it's all right with you, I'd like you to show me my room. I want to rest for a bit."

"Fine, fine," she said, returning. "Follow me." She began climbing the stairs opposite the sitting room, with Hisham behind her. He could not help noticing the erotic sight of her buttocks as she walked in front of him, but averted his gaze as they swung back and forth with every step she climbed.

"Where's Said today?" he said, trying to distract himself. "Why didn't he open the door?"

"I sent him to get a few things from the shop next door," she replied, panting. "Did you want him for anything in particular?"

"No, just asking."

Before they got to the second part of the staircase that led up to the roof terrace, Moudhi passed through a door between them that opened onto a small, narrow landing with a room on each side overlooking the courtyard. Moudhi opened the door to one of the rooms and invited him to go in. The room really was big. It had a very high ceiling from which a huge fan hung, and two small windows. He noticed that his suitcase had been placed carefully at the far end of the room and a smart, clean mattress laid on a clean yellow rug, beside which was an elegant if inexpensive carpet.

"This is your room; I hope you like it," said Moudhi as she opened a window.

"It's excellent. But … what about the room next to it?"

"It's empty. We sometimes use it for guests, but you're not a guest. And also," she said, looking at him, "this room is bigger and airier. And it faces my room on the other side. You'll only have to call me if you need anything. I'll leave you to rest now," she said,

104

moving quickly towards the door. "I've got to start getting lunch ready. You'll have your tea in a moment."

"Thank you, Moudhi. I don't want anything more, just to rest for a little while," he called out to her as she closed the door and disappeared, leaving a trace of that distinctive scent of hers. He picked up his magazines and went over to the mattress, but before he could lie down the door opened and Moudhi looked round again.

"I forgot to tell you. Lunch is at about three o'clock. I'll call you when it's time." As she closed the door again it seemed to him that he saw the shadow of a smile behind her veil.

Hisham looked around. He really did like the room. It was large, private and clean; all it needed were a few essentials, but he would provide those: a bed, a desk, a clothes rail and a small stove for making tea. It did not make sense to ask Moudhi for tea every time he wanted some – she had enough to do already. He stripped to his underwear and threw the rest of his clothes carelessly on top of his suitcase. Then he turned on the fan and sat down on the mattress, leaning against the wall, and began reading a story about Superman on one of his journeys into the past. Hisham looked up after awhile, and as he did the film in his mind began again.

❊ 24 ❊

When Hisham arrived at Rashid's house for their next meeting he found someone else there he had not met before, a young man of about twenty-six who was as white as a ghost and grossly overweight with a conspicuous paunch. He had short, curly black hair, a huge moustache and a wide mouth with thick, dark lips and large, regular teeth stained dark yellow. He was wearing a white robe and the cheap sort of trousers used by Aramco labourers. When Hisham entered, the man was smoking a Jordanian 'Reem' cigarette, the square packet lying beside him. He struggled to his feet when Hisham and Rashid came in.

"Comrade Fahd, Comrade Abu Huraira," said Rashid, stepping forward to make the introduction. They shook hands and all sat down around the empty teapot. When Rashid picked it up to pour Hisham a cup, the lid fell off and only a few drops of tea spilled out.

"I'll ask for another pot," said Rashid, getting up.

"There's no need," Fahd said in a domineering tone of voice, catching Rashid by his loincloth so that it nearly slipped off. "We'll be leaving in a moment."

Rashid sat down, retying the loincloth. He lit a cigarette and calmly began smoking without uttering a word; at the same time Fahd took the last drag on his own cigarette and, as Rashid watched wide-eyed, stubbed it out on the tea tray despite the fact that the ashtray was next to him.

Fahd looked at Hisham with little, bloodshot eyes. "Comrade Khalid has told me about you and says you're ready to join the party. I'm in charge of the cell you'll belong to."

'So Khalid is Rashid's movement name,' Hisham thought. 'But I know Rashid by his real name, so why bother with a movement name?' "Who is this Comrade Khalid?" he said, plucking up courage. "I don't know him, so how come he knows me?"

Rashid smiled. "No, you do know him," said Fahd, giving Hisham a nasty look. "He's Comrade Rashid. But I want to train you to use the movement names. I know your real name's Hisham, and Khalid is Rashid. But you don't know my real name, and nor should you."

"But what's the point of having movement names if we all know each other anyway?" asked Hisham in surprise.

"You were bound to know Rashid from your school," said Fahd, "and I had to know your real name in order to make inquiries about you when you were nominated to join the organisation. But you must only know me and any other comrade you haven't met before by our movement names."

"And Mansur …" Hisham said without thinking.

"What?" said Fahd, looking at him sternly.

"Nothing … Sorry."

"You have nothing to do with anyone except me, is that understood?" said Fahd angrily, as Hisham began to feel a loathing for this person in front of him.

"But you know Rashid – sorry, I mean Comrade Khalid," said Hisham after a short silence, "without the two of you having been acquainted before?"

"So what? And anyway, I have to know everyone I'm in charge of."

"So what's the point of movement names?"

"Security, comrade! If one of us gets arrested, he won't be able to give away the other comrades' names."

"But you know everyone's real names; what if you got arrested?"

"It won't happen. Only the comrades who joined the struggle before me know my real name. And there would be nothing to fear from them, even if they were arrested. In any case, the chances of that happening are very remote, because no one knows who they are."

"So the little people will be the ones to be sacrificed?"

"Who said that? No one can get arrested unless the comrades in the leadership get arrested, and there's no reason to be afraid either for them or of them."

"But what if —"

"You ask a lot of questions," said Fahd, interrupting him sharply, "and I've put up with enough from you already. In our work it's not allowed to ask a lot of questions. The important thing is action. Didn't Comrade Khalid explain that to you?" Fahd looked at Rashid. "Didn't you explain that to him?" he asked angrily. "You said he was quite ready."

Rashid was caught unawares and gave such a jump that he almost choked on his cigarette, scattering ash onto the carpet. "He is ready," he replied, stammering, "but he's the kind that asks a lot of questions. I mentioned all that in my report about him."

Fahd looked at Hisham. "Look, comrade," he said, his anger having abated a little, "if he didn't tell you, I'm telling you now: asking a lot of questions is forbidden in our line of work. Now let's go. It's time for our meeting with the other comrades."

Fahd got up and Rashid and Hisham followed. Together they went down to the front door. Fahd looked at the other two. "After today you two don't know each other," he said peremptorily, wagging his finger. "The connection between you is over, even if you happen to meet anywhere, at school or anywhere else. I hope that's understood."

They both nodded without saying anything, and as Rashid shut the door Fahd and Hisham set off towards al-Hubb Street.

❧ 25 ❧

It was approaching five o'clock when they arrived at an old house built, like Rashid's, out of sea stone in one of the narrow, sandy alleys off al-Hubb Street. Fahd took a key out of his pocket and opened the dilapidated wooden door, which they passed through into a tiny, bare room. At the far end stood a small gas stove, and a wooden chest covered with a piece of grease-stained material atop which stood a teapot, cups, a small cooking pot and some utensils. Nearby, various items of food had been left in a mess, including packets of tea and sugar, a few tins of sauce and a small bag of rice. Halfway along one of the walls there was a small sink filled with water in which some plates and spoons had been left to soak. There were two more doors, one on either side of the sink, leading to two other rooms; in one of them Hisham noticed a metal bed covered with a red and blue striped sheet and next to it a clothes rack with some garments casually thrown over it. Fahd pointed towards the other room, inviting Hisham to go in.

A shabby blue carpet dotted with burn marks was spread on the floor, and on top of it was a row of old, red cushions. Several metal ashtrays were also scattered about on the carpet, and not far from the door was a faded green fan peppered with flies' droppings.

Fahd gestured to Hisham to sit, which he did, in a corner as far away as possible. Hisham drew his knees up, feet on the ground, and leaned against one of the cushions. Fahd turned on the fan, then walked out of the room.

"I'll go and make some tea," he said as he left. "The comrades will be here any minute now."

Fahd left Hisham on his own staring at the walls of the room, which had begun to crumble in the damp sea air, and trying to adjust to the odours of decay, damp and cigarette smoke. Shortly afterwards he heard a knock on the door, followed by the sound of the bolt being slid back and then the door being closed again. A moment later someone entered the room. Hisham jumped up to greet him and they shook hands. Hisham returned to his place while the person who had just arrived sat down cross-legged opposite him, leaning forward with his hands in his lap. His complexion was dark and he had fine, handsome features, straight, black hair and a small, black, arch-shaped moustache. He was tall and thin and was wearing an old black suit with a white shirt and sandals without socks. He and Hisham smiled at one another, then gazed at the ceiling without speaking.

After that there were two more knocks on the door. The first heralded the arrival of a clean-shaven man of average height and build; his curly hair was uncovered and white robe open at the neck. Everyone shook hands, and the new arrival sat down next to the first man. Then a short, thin person arrived; he had a pale complexion and a huge moustache that was doubly conspicuous because he was obviously no more than nineteen years old. His appearance was all the more remarkable for his enormous head, bulging eyes and jutting ears. He too shook hands with everyone and sat down not far from Hisham. Shortly thereafter Fahd returned, carrying a large tray with a huge, oval-shaped teapot. He had changed his clothes and put on a red loincloth with white checks and a white, short-sleeved vest.

"Welcome, comrades," he greeted everyone, setting the tray down on the floor in the middle of the room and sitting down behind it. "The rest of you already know each other," he said, indicating Hisham, "but let me introduce you to Comrade Abu Huraira; Comrade Abu Huraira, this is Comrade Hudaijan, our representative in the desert." With this he pointed to the dark, handsome young man and chuckled; Hudaijan's face betrayed his irritation, which he tried to conceal with a faint smile that quickly faded. "Comrade Abu Dharr," Fahd went on, indicating the clean-shaven man; then, pointing to the pop-eyed youngster, "Comrade Hasan al-Sabah."

Once the introductions had been made, Fahd asked everyone to stand and repeat the party slogan to mark the beginning of the cell's meeting. They all got to their feet, including Hisham, who did not yet know his role, and bowed their heads.

"One Arab Nation," said Fahd solemnly.

"With an Eternal Mission," the others repeated after him in the same tone.

Afterwards they all sat back down and Fahd began pouring the tea and handing it out to the comrades. Hisham was watching with all the astonishment of someone who has said prayers for the first time after embracing a new religion.

Fahd lit a cigarette, inhaled deeply and blew the smoke high up into the air. He took a sip of his hot black tea, slurping as he did so, while the others remained silent, waiting for him to begin the discussion.

"Comrades," he said, "our nation is passing through dire straits and a difficult phase of our glorious history. The Setback has proven that the petty bourgeoisie is incapable of leading the nation. The project of the petty bourgeoisie fell with the defeat of '67, just as the project of the feudalists and the rotten compradorist bourgeoisie fell with the defeat of '48. Now it is the turn of the working classes, the proletariat, to put forward a progressive project that will express the aspirations of the struggling masses and the oppressed classes. The hope of our nation hangs on the project of the working class and its allies, which through its own liberation will liberate all society and the entire nation. Our party, the Arab Socialist Baath Party, and its revolution against the opportunists and vacillating petty bourgeoisie and all those who benefited from the compradorist bourgeoisie and the feudalists, has come to express the project of the working class and all the deprived classes in society. It is the sole nationalist party that represents the aspirations of the nation and the working classes of society. The forces of reaction, feudalism and the bourgeoisie, and behind them imperialism, colonialism and world capitalism with its protégé, Zionism, are standing in the way of our great party and fighting to sabotage its progressive project. But historical inevitability is on our side! We shall be victorious in the end, the nation will return to its glory and its natural role in history and scientific socialism will become a reality in the unified Arab State. History is on our side. This is what makes us fight, certain of victory over all our enemies."

Fahd finished speaking and paused to catch his breath. He took a few sips of his tea, lit another cigarette and with his lips pursed looked at the others to see the effect his words had on them.

Hisham had been listening carefully, but remained worried by the question of Nasser's position on all of this. He was the Orchestrator of the July Revolution, the Destroyer of the Tripartite Aggression of Israel, France and Britain in '56, the Creator of the United Arab Republic between Egypt and Syria and the Socialist Laws of '61 ... Yes, he had been defeated in June '67, but that was the result of a global conspiracy, and in any case the conspiracy had not succeeded. Its aim had been to bring Nasser down, and he had not fallen. Nasser, for whom the Arab streets would empty when he gave one of his speeches, whose words had the power to make listeners tremble: what would he think about all of this? Was he part of the reactionary groups Fahd had mentioned, or what?

Hisham steeled himself and looked at Fahd. "Comrade Fahd …" he said, stammering a little.

Fahd looked at him indifferently, nodding his permission for Hisham to speak.

"Comrade Fahd, how should we categorise Nasser, and how should we evaluate him in this historic phase of the nation's journey?"

Fahd gave a half-smile and nodded several times. "Nasser is certainly an important nationalist figure," he said, "but this phase has gone beyond him. He represents the petty bourgeoisie that fell with the defeat. We need an organised party, not an individual leader; a party with a comprehensive, scientific project, not just the exertions of one person. Nasser's mistake from the very beginning was that he didn't establish a party, and did not co-operate with ours. If he had done, the picture would be different now. The Setback wouldn't have happened. In any case, he couldn't have done anything; he belonged to the weak-willed, opportunistic, petty bourgeoisie that fell with the Setback, and he with it. The present phase is the phase of the party, and only the party."

Fahd fell silent and lit another cigarette. An air of despondency had descended over the others, who began nodding their heads in agreement. Hisham also agreed more or less with Fahd's analysis: it was this that had attracted him to Marxism in the first place. Yet another question began going round in his mind, although he was reluctant to ask it, particularly given that this was his first meeting with these people.

"But Comrade Fahd," he said after hesitating for a while, "wasn't the Baath party in power in Syria before the Setback? How come it happened when the party was in government?"

For a few moments Fahd was silent, frowning and looking into the distance with his chin between his middle finger and his thumb and his index finger on his cheek. "It was not the party that was in power in Syria," he said, "it was that group of reactionary Aflaqites. The party has only been in power since 1966, that's to say from less than a year before the Setback, and one year isn't enough to put right the mess created by the previous opportunistic governments, which from March 1963 had used the party's name as a fig leaf. And the conspiracy was greater than the party as well. All the reactionary forces and their agents were ranged against the party to bring it down, but in the end the party proved stronger than the conspiracy and managed to beat it – even though it had only recently come to power – only because the masses rallied round it. From another point of view, comrade, the rapid collapse of the Egyptian front and the treachery committed there, as well as the collaboration of the Jordanian regime with the Zionist entity, led to greater pressure on the Syrian front. Everyone wanted to bring about the downfall of the party in Syria. But it fought against all that and won, and this is proof that it is the party of the masses. Can you find an example of any other regime in the world, ancient or modern, able to struggle against Zionism, colonialism, imperialism, capitalism, the forces of reaction, treachery and conspiracies, and still remain firm, defiant and even victorious? This is our mighty party, and you will see, comrades, how Syria will transform itself into a model for all the Arab world to follow. It will be the Syria of the Baath, the region from which will come the spark of Arab unity, freedom and socialism."

Fahd went on talking almost throughout the session about the party and the nationalist and historic duties on its shoulders. He then read out several declarations and pamphlets from the regional and national leaderships for internal distribution among the cells, all on the same subjects.

Once all that was over, Fahd asked the comrades whether they had any view or question they wanted to put to him. "You all know that the party is based on the principle of centralised democracy. Any opinion or query that you have you must raise, but once a decision has been taken it is binding on everyone, even those who may happen to disagree with it. For this reason our internal discussions must be completely free. Are there any questions?" Fahd began looking around at those present until he reached Hudaijan, who asked, "Comrade Fahd, we've talked a lot about the Arab nation, but what about our own part of it? How is it to be liberated? Isn't the best thing for us to concentrate on our own country, rather than discussing the entire Arab nation with all its different regions, which their patriots are sure to take on themselves to liberate?"

Fahd's anger showed plainly on his face, and his expression one of utter repugnance. "This regional approach is completely unacceptable," he snapped, spitting as he spoke. "We are one nation and we operate on that basis. The liberation of the whole will mean the liberation of every part, while the liberation of a part is only a single step towards the liberation of the whole. We must operate within the framework of the entire nation. For that reason we have a national leadership that co-ordinates our efforts and from which we derive the guidelines of our struggle. Our goal is the entire Arab nation, comrade, not any one particular country to the exclusion of another. And besides, they're all false entities with artificial borders imposed by the colonialists. The truth is the Arab nation alone."

Fahd calmed down and Hudaijan bowed his head as Fahd asked again whether there were any other questions, once more looking round at the comrades' faces. "Fine," he said, when met with complete silence, "in that case today's session is over. We meet again at the same time next week." He got up and the others stood up after him, ending their meeting with another repetition of the slogan.

"One Arab Nation."

"With an Eternal Mission."

For a few seconds they remained standing. Fahd addressed Hisham. "When leaving the building after a meeting," he said, "we mustn't go out all at once. Comrade by comrade." They all sat down again while Hudaijan went out. A minute later Hasan al-Sabah followed, then Abu Dharr and finally Abu Huraira.

❧ 26 ❧

It was about six o'clock in the evening when Hisham left Fahd's house. He headed towards al-Hubb Street and then to the centre of town, to Sheikh Mousa's Mosque via the al-Adama clinic and finally Thamantash Street and then home. For some reason he had chosen this long way round, during which he considered his new experience and these unwillingly made acquaintances: he did not like any of them, least of all Fahd; he had felt annoyed upon first meeting him at Rashid's house. The only one he had warmed to at all was Hudaijan; he had an endearing look about him and a good-hearted nature one could sense easily. There was an underlying innocence in his face that was absent from the others.

When Hisham got home he went straight to his room and threw himself down on his bed, still reflecting on the events of the day. He was not scared. His fear had almost gone, and there was nothing to be afraid of after all: it was all just reading and talking, as he had concluded, with comrades instead of friends. The people he had met seemed unlikely to be capable of changing anything, especially when one took into account the power of their opponent, the government. He went on pondering until the sound of the doorknob turning brought him round and his mother's face appeared in the crack of the door.

"Hisham," she said, staying by the door with her hand still on the doorknob, "where have you been for the last few hours?"

He got up and sat on the edge of the bed. "Good evening, Mother," he said, after a moment's hesitation. "I was at Abd al-Karim's house as usual."

"No you weren't. He and Adnan came by and asked for you. They said they don't see much of you these days. Where were you, Hisham?"

He was at a loss. What could he say? His nerve threatened to fail him. "Really, Mother," he stammered, after a short pause, "I dropped by Abd al-Karim's house but I didn't find him there, so I went round to some of the bookshops and after that to the public library, where I stayed until now."

His mother gave him a look full of doubt and suspicion. "And why didn't you say so in the first place?"

"I didn't think it mattered to you that much. What difference does it make whether I went to Abd al-Karim's house or the public library?"

"I want you to be honest in everything you say. We've brought you up to be frank and truthful no matter what. Don't let us down."

Hisham had a lump in his throat and felt unable to speak, but he pulled himself together and said, "That is what happened. Believe me, Mother."

She stood there scrutinizing him for a while, still holding on to the doorknob, then turned away. "I hope that's the truth," she murmured before leaving. "God preserve you, my child."

Hisham's mother trusted and admired him at the same time. "There's no one else like Hisham," she often said. But she was afraid that at his age he might go astray, falling in with 'bad boys', becoming deviant himself and ruining his future. She trusted Adnan and Abd al-Karim because she knew their mothers, as well as the fact that they were Hisham's peers. But Hisham could remember her instructions, when he was little and first going to primary school, not to make friends with children who were older than himself. She also used to forbid him to go on school trips on which the pupils spent a night or two away and likewise, later on, to go to sports clubs, because she had heard a lot about the 'bad things' that went on in those sorts of places.

When Hisham was little she was not simply afraid that he would go wrong; she used to worry that he would be kidnapped and sold into slavery somewhere else. (In those days kidnapping was one of the ways of maintaining supply for the slave market.) Hisham's mother forbade him to accept a lift from anyone on his way home from school, even though the distance to the house was no more than two hundred metres. He remembered her warnings not to enter anyone's car, even if it was his own father who asked, and that had actually happened: one day he was returning from school when suddenly his father stopped beside him in his white Volkswagen with its distinctive sound. He called to Hisham to get in, but the boy stubbornly refused out of obedience to his mother's orders. His father smiled and drove off. When Hisham got home his mother praised him for the way he had behaved; his father was standing next to her with a pleased and loving smile on his face, and Hisham realised that his parents had planned the incident as a test to see how far he would obey their instructions. He, in turn, was delighted at having passed the test, and his reward was a copy of 'Magic Carpet' magazine which his father went out and bought.

Hisham felt unhappy at having to lie, to his mother in particular; his relationship with her had always been extremely frank. When he reached puberty he had gone running to tell her without hesitation, instead of keeping it to himself or going to his father. He smiled as he thought of it, remembering what a fright he had got. He had returned from school on a stifling day, removed his clothes and had gone to have a quick shower to cool down a little. The shower head was broken and the water came down in a sudden jet, by chance hitting him hard in the groin; he felt a slight pain accompanied by a great deal of pleasure. He fought against the pain and stayed under the water until he was aroused; the pain – so like the sensation of needing to urinate – became so intense that he could no longer bear it. He moved away out of the water and discovered, to his horror, the mysterious white flow from his genitals. He was terrified, and quickly dried himself, put on his underwear and ran to his mother to tell her everything (except that he had deliberately sought to continue the pleasure of the water jet.) His mother smiled and very tenderly took him to her breast. "Congratulations," she told him. "You've become a man." At that his fears abated, and he felt a certain pride: he'd become a man. He remembered the event as though it had taken place the previous day, though in fact it had been when he was just under thirteen years old.

He had only ever lied to his mother once before, but that occasion ended in confession, a plea for forgiveness and a promise not to lie again. When he was in the fifth year of primary school, during break one day he saw that one of his classmates had a bird; he liked it and asked the boy if he could have it, but the boy wanted a quarter of a riyal for it: his whole day's pocket money. Hisham could not resist the sight of the frightened little bird, and gave over the money without hesitating, even though his mother had warned him only to spend it on food or drink. Carrying it home he began to fear the inevitable telling-off and the severe punishment his mother would mete out, which was normally matched only by her tenderness at the other extreme. As he entered the house he tried to think up a convincing story to explain why he had the bird with him; but the first thing he met was his mother's gaze, drilling into his skull to expose his 'crime'.

"Where did you get that bird from?" she said, her voice making him tremble all over.

"I caught it … I caught it, Mother."

"And how did you manage that?"

"I saw it sitting there on my way home from school and I picked up a stone and threw it at it and hit it."

"You hit it? First time? You certainly are a good shot. Let me have a look at it."

As his mother reached out and took the bird, Hisham felt scarcely able to stand up. She began turning the bird over in her hands. "That's funny," she said quietly, "I don't see any sign of an injury! Did you hit it with a stone made of cotton?"

He tried to say something, but could not. His mother threw aside the bird, which began audibly flapping around the room in joyous surprise, until it found a way out. An instant later Hisham felt his mother's palm hit his face with a slap that sent his whole body rocking. He burst into tears, but his mother paid no attention and instead took hold of his shoulders and squeezed them tight as she gave him a hard shake.

"Hisham," she said angrily, raising her voice, "tell me the truth. Where did you get that bird?"

He wished his father were there to protect him from his mother's tyranny, but he was still at work; so, in broken words between sobs he confessed that he had bought the bird with his whole day's pocket money, and solemnly swore he would never do it again. His mother calmed down, her anger dissipating just as suddenly as it had descended. "Is that the truth?" she began repeating over and over, still holding him by the shoulders, "Is that the truth?" He promised her again that it was really so, and she drew him near and began wiping away his tears. "I want you to be honest with me no matter what," she said, "no matter what. Understood?"

"All right, Mother, all right," he repeated, still sobbing. His mother told him to go and wash his face; when he got back she gave him another quarter of a riyal that instantly erased all trace of the slap. He went straight out and bought a copy of 'Magic Carpet'.

And here he was, lying once more with no idea how often he would need to do it again. But there was no little bird this time; it was a giant griffin. Yet what else could he tell her? That he was an activist in a clandestine organisation? At the thought of his mother and the organisation together his stomach tightened in the now familiar way, and at the same time he felt contempt for himself. But he soon regained some peace of mind: he hadn't lied. He hadn't done anything wrong. It was part of the struggle, and one day his mother would be proud of him ... Hisham got up and went to the bookcase on the other side of the room and rummaged through the books. He found what he was looking for and sat down near his desk on the floor. For the umpteenth time he began reading *Mother*, immersed before long in the sorrows of Pelageia Nilovna.

⇴ 27 ⇴

The weekly meetings of the comrades at Fahd's house continued. Nothing new transpired there, only discussions of the sensitive nature of the current historic turning point through which the Arab nation was passing, as well as readings of declarations and pamphlets. Whenever they had no particular subject to discuss, everyone would take part in a general political debate of current affairs. There was no shortage of topics, beginning with the War of Attrition fought by Egypt along the Suez Canal and its effects. They also discussed the commando operations of the *fedayeen* in Jordan, and the transition from conventional warfare to a popular, guerrilla war that had lifted the confrontation with imperialism and Zionism to new levels in the form of direct participation. Most of their debate, however, was taken up with al-Saiqa, the Palestinian guerrilla group established in Syria, how it alone brought hope for the future while neither Fatah, with its bourgeois colouring and its lack of ideological clarity, nor the Popular Front for the Liberation of Palestine, with its puerile left-wing posturing, were capable of leading the Arab nation. They argued that only al-Saiqa and the Baath Party, with its new principles, could assume this role.

Hisham began to get tired of these meetings with people with whom he had no emotional ties; he missed Adnan, Abd al-Karim and his other friends, Salim and Saud and Abd al-Aziz. He went back to joining them at their daily meetings at Abd al-Karim's house. Everyone made a great fuss of welcoming him back the first afternoon he turned up, but Adnan and Abd al-Karim were happiest, embracing him as though he had returned from a long voyage. The moment he sat down Abd al-Karim put himself next to him.

"Where have you been, man?" he whispered, offering Hisham a cup of tea. "Did you come across some buried treasure, or did Noura make you forget your friends?"

Abd al-Karim chuckled as Hisham looked at him without comment and smiled with genuine love. He was as fond of these friends as they were of him. Affection was forbidden in the organisation and friendship was non-existent; the bond between comrades was everything, but it was a cold, dry relationship with none of the warmth of life. Life was here where his friends were, and love was there where Noura was. He smiled as thoughts of Noura came to his mind, and felt a kind of gentle soothing inside every atom of his being.

Noura: a raindrop on parched earth, a cool breeze on a hot night. She had a bronze-coloured complexion and was about two years younger than Hisham. Her family was from Nejd and even though all they knew about Nejd was its name, they retained a strong Nejdi accent and kept up old customs of the region which even families who still lived there had abandoned. Noura's father was one of the leading dealers in building materials in the Eastern Province who did business with Aramco. He was as rich in values as wealth, nothing in his appearance or demeanour betraying his moneyed status. His house was much the same as that of any middle-class person; the family had only one car, similar to the Peugeot Hisham's father drove, and they had no servants even though they could have afforded many. Noura's appearance was utterly traditional: she wore a long, shapeless, full-length dress with long sleeves, her pitch-black hair hanging down her back in two long plaits half-way down her bottom, which was round and pert and full of the simmering heat of youth. She was rather short, but that only made her seem prettier; as for her face, its most distinctive features were her big black eyes. She had a fine nose and a small mouth with full, rather dark lips, and white teeth that were uneven, especially the upper ones; yet their unevenness made her mouth still more beautiful. Her chin seemed almost to slumber beneath it, so delicate and fine it made one afraid it might break if touched. Noura always wore a black veil over her head, its edges hanging down over her chest and making her face and the bare parts of her neck and upper chest – which had begun to develop when she first caught Hisham's eye – even more compelling.

She used to bring them milk every evening. Her family kept three cows on the grounds of their home, and Noura's mother would milk them, churn the milk and give whatever they did not need themselves to the neighbours, Hisham's family among them. One evening he was in his room, in the grip of Emile Zola's *Nana*, when he heard a knock on the front door. He did not so much as stir, knowing it was just 'the neighbours' daughter' as usual and that his mother would open the door for her like she always did. But the knocking continued without anyone opening the door, intruding more and more upon Hisham's absorption in the novel. He dragged himself to his feet, grumbling, "All right, all right," and quickly opened the front door with the intention of returning straight to the book. But when he set eyes on Noura he felt as though he were seeing her for the first time. He stood where he was, neither moving nor taking his eyes off her, as she lowered her gaze and shyly bowed her head.

"Is Auntie Umm Hisham there?" she stammered in a near-whisper. "I've brought the milk."

Hisham stepped aside from the open door, letting her pass. "Come in," he said, "she's inside."

He had no idea whether his mother was in or not, but he wanted Noura inside. She entered with her head still bowed and went past him, knowing her way perfectly well. He could not stop himself from watching her as she went, his attention fixed on her buttocks, which trembled with every movement, her tripping way of walking making them sway all the more. 'God, she's so fetching and so pretty! How could I not have noticed that before?' he marveled to himself as he followed her inside the house. When Noura got to the kitchen, Hisham's mother was just coming out of the bathroom, drops of water still sprinkled on her face and hands. She greeted Noura and took the pail of milk from her after glaring at Hisham, who quickly left the kitchen and headed off to the little garden of the house. He wanted to see Noura when she went out. A few minutes later he overheard his mother saying goodbye, telling her, "Give my regards to your mother," and then Noura appeared, making her way to the front door. Hisham leaped up to the door and quickly opened it before she got there.

"Thank you," he said and smiled gently as she passed through.

She looked at him. Their eyes met, and then she, too, smiled, cheeks burning, before abruptly looking away and scurrying outside. Hisham went out after her and watched her as she hurried nervously away, dropping the empty milk pail and rapidly picking it up again without looking round. When she got to the turning that led to her house, she looked back; once more their eyes met, and once more she swiftly turned her face away before disappearing around the corner, and as she did so it seemed to Hisham that she had smiled again, and he felt the burning heat of her cheeks.

He began to look forward to her visits impatiently; whenever the time approached, he would go out into the garden, making up some excuse or other if he happened to bump into his mother, as it was not something he usually did. As soon as he heard the knock on the door he would quickly open it and feast his eyes on Noura before she disappeared inside. She had become like the breath of life to him, and he had become addicted to her; he had to see her at the same time every day. It became so that the sound of the call to prayer at sunset had a particular effect on his feelings, because it was always after this that his beloved would come. Even his friends in the gang noticed how keen he was to leave before sunset with enough time to get back home before the call to prayer. All of them commented on it, but only Adnan and Abd al-Karim knew the reason for his behaviour. His mother had also noticed that he was always in the garden just before sunset; Hisham detected a certain suspicion in her eyes, but she said nothing; she still saw him as that little boy, far above doubt, whom she knew how to bring up, and not one of the 'rude' young people she had always warned him against mixing with.

Noura, of course, noticed his interest in her, and every day on her way out she would give him a fleeting smile. With each day her smile got wider and her gaze bolder. One day he plucked up courage and wrote the words 'I love you' in big letters on a small piece of paper, which he thrust into her hand as she scampered out of the house. She took the paper, quickly hid it in her hand and went out, almost stumbling on the way. His heart pounding, Hisham hastily shut the door behind her instead of going out to watch her vanish around the corner as he usually did. In a sea of mixed emotions and intense anxiety he waited for the next day to come. What did she think of him? Would she regard him as crude? Would she be angry and tell her father or mother? His heart raced at the thought. That would be a disaster; he wouldn't be able to deny a thing, as she had 'material evidence' in his own handwriting. Her parents would be furious and would tell his parents, and he would lose his father's trust and break his mother's heart … No, she wouldn't do that, he told himself. She used to smile at him herself and she had taken the piece of paper; she must feel the same way about him, or she wouldn't have taken it.

The next day came and the time of her usual visit approached. At sunset the muezzin made the call to prayer, but another half hour went by and still there was no knock at the door. Hisham was overcome by fear and worry. Perhaps she had told her parents after all, and they had forbidden her to come? His mother would not give him a hiding like she used to do, but he would lose her for good, and his father would be sure to give him a severe dressing-down and hold him in contempt ever after. And then suddenly, just as Hisham was sinking in anxiety, there was a knock on the door. He went and opened it quickly, and there she was before him in all her femininity. She flashed him a smile, then turned and went inside, leaving him leaning against the door in relief. She had come and she had smiled. He stayed put, waiting until she reappeared on her way out. When he opened the door for her she made her exit without looking at him. Once she was outside, she glanced at him and said quickly, her face ablaze, "I love you too."

He shut the door and leaned against it again, smiling and exulting like the master of Heaven and Earth together.

⇝ 28 ⇜

Hisham's relationship with Noura began to develop after that; he took to writing her florid love letters, which he would slip into her hand on her way out, or would wait for her outside and pass them to her there for fear that his mother might see him. Noura herself began doing the same thing. She would drop her replies on the floor as she left the house or slip them into his hand if she had a chance. Hisham preferred to receive her replies directly from her, because it allowed him to touch her soft hand. Her letters almost burned with love, even if he did find fault with their poor style and weak use of language; but none of that mattered when the words had been written by his beloved's own hand. He was too besotted to be able to hide his feelings, and wanted to be able to share the joy of this first love in his life with someone. He told Adnan, who warned him against the relationship and asked him to end it immediately, and Abd al-Karim, who got all excited and asked Hisham to tell him more details about his encounters with Noura.

To this day he could remember the taste and heat of his first kiss from her lips – the first kiss of his life. When Noura came to the house that day, his mother was out visiting one of the neighbours to congratulate her on the birth of her new baby. As always,

Hisham let Noura in and she headed to the kitchen with just her usual smile, neither of them saying anything to the other. Without her being aware of it Hisham followed her into the kitchen. She put down the pail of milk and turned around, calling, "Auntie Umm Hi –" but stopped the moment she saw him immediately behind her. Noura's face flamed crimson, and she dropped the letter she had been intending to slip him. He snatched it up and thrust it into his pocket as she left the kitchen. He swiftly caught up with her in the hall and took her hand. She tried to wriggle away, but he gripped her hand tighter until he could feel that fire erupting from her body. He pulled her to him as she whispered nervously, "No, it's wrong ... it's wrong, Hisham ..." But in the state he was in he was neither able nor willing to tell the difference between 'right' and 'wrong'. He felt her hand trembling violently in his own, like that bird he had bought for a quarter of a riyal, and with every shiver of her hand his heart pounded. He led her to his room and she followed, hesitating and stumbling as she went and still saying over and over, "It's wrong, it's wrong ... this isn't allowed," but he did not hear her. They went into his room and he locked the door behind them and took her to the bed. He sat her down on the edge of the bed and then sat down beside her, his hand still holding hers. Several times she tried to slip away from him, but he did not let her go and eventually she gave in and remained sitting there silently, her head bowed and blushing so deeply she looked as though the blood was ready to burst from her cheeks.

"I love you," he said passionately, gazing at her wide-eyed. "I love you, Noura."

She remained silent, her head lowered, but then in a barely audible whisper said, "I ... I love you too."

He released her hand, reached for her black veil and began pulling it off her head, but she held on to it. He took her hand again and started squeezing it gently, then brought his face close to hers and gave her a quick kiss on her still burning cheek. "It's wrong … wrong," she said, leaping up, but he drew near to her again, still holding her hand and pressing it softly. He reached for her veil with his other hand gradually lifting it without any serious resistance on her part. Her shiny, oiled, black hair appeared, cascading down either side of her face with a perfectly straight parting in the middle. Quite tenderly he began touching her hair, which was so soft and extravagantly anointed that he felt as though his hand were sliding through it. He came closer still and sensuously smelled her hair, then reached out and felt the softness of her cheeks. His hand slid down to her delicate chin and, cupping it in his palm, he raised her head to look at him. Noura's eyes were lowered, her lips trembling. Gently, he brought his face close to hers and touched his lips to her own. Instantly he felt as though he had been burnt by a red-hot coal. She jerked her face away, repeating, "It's wrong, this isn't allowed," but he took hold of her chin again and once more their lips drew near. He wanted a real kiss, a kiss like the ones the actor Kamal al-Shanawi gave the Egyptian film star Shadia in those films on television every night. He planted his lips on hers and felt her trembling, burning; reaching out, put his arm around her and began gently feeling her back. He pressed his mouth more firmly to hers until he felt their teeth bump together and the embers of her lips burn more fiercely. They remained like that for a while, though for how long he could not tell. Time stood still and they were immersed in total silence.

Suddenly he heard the front door open. His mother was back; it had to be her, his father never came home from seeing his friends earlier than an hour after supper. Their fevered lips parted as he quickly let go of Noura, his heart racing anew. Noura jumped from the bed, grabbed her veil and hurriedly covered her head while Hisham sat down at his desk, snatched a book and opened it at random.

"Quick, go into the kitchen," he told Noura, speaking quickly, nervously. "I'll tell my mother you just came a moment ago. Go on, hurry!"

Noura raced off to the kitchen, stumbling on her way. Hisham pretended to be reading, and after a short while he heard his mother seeing Noura off in her usual way:

"Goodbye, and my regards to your mother."

A few moments later his mother looked round his bedroom door. "How long was Noura here?" she said straight away.

"Good evening, Mother," he answered, looking up with feigned indifference and trying to make his reply sound as natural as possible. "I don't know. Less than a minute, maybe. I opened the door for her and then came straight back to my desk. Why?"

His mother did not utter a word, but stood there looking at him long and hard. Then at last she went away, muttering something he could not hear, and Hisham was left alone, steeped in the memory of the little firebrand who had been in his room.

✣ 29 ✣

Salim, Saud, Abd al-Aziz and Abd al-Karim were all playing Plot as Hisham and Adnan sat nearby in a corner of Abd al-Karim's sitting room talking about the last picture Adnan had painted, which he had called 'Freedom'. It was of a giant man bound in chains, raising his hands to the sky; one of the links had begun to break and around the man there were smaller faces of men and women with different expressions, looking at the giant and screaming, the men's clothes in shreds and the women's hair hanging dishevelled over their faces.

Adnan had been Hisham's best friend since they shared the same class in the first year of primary school. Their parents were friends from the same city; after years of travelling all over the region they had all come to Dammam in search of a living, and the friendship between them had been passed on to their sons.

Adnan was talking to him, but Hisham was thinking about something else and not taking anything in. Why didn't he invite Adnan to join the organisation? He was sure Adnan would accept, if not as a matter of principle then for the sake of his friend.

"Hisham … Hisham … Are you there? Lucky Noura!"

Hisham caught the teasing tone of Adnan's voice. "Look, Adnan," he said, as though waking from a dream, "I want to see you in private. I'll drop by your place tomorrow afternoon. It's of the utmost importance."

Adnan was taken aback, but agreed without hesitation. "All right," he said, "as you like. I'll be waiting for you."

They both fell silent, while the cries of their friends around them got louder and louder as the excitement of the game mounted. Eventually they finished playing and threw the cards aside as they got at each other for mistakes made during the game. Afterwards they all sat talking and joking with one another and drinking hot tea in a loud general hubbub. Then Abd al-Karim raised his voice, asking the others to be silent.

"Quiet, everyone. Quiet, please."

The talking stopped as everyone looked at Abd al-Karim, who put on a stern expression.

"You all know Nasser's going to give a speech tonight," he said. "What do you say we meet up and listen to it together?"

He looked at the others, expecting a response. Hisham and Adnan nodded in agreement without saying anything; Saud turned down the suggestion, saying he had some things of his own he had to see to; and Abd al-Aziz promised he would try to come if he managed to finish some chores. As for Salim, he said he was not very keen but would endeavour to be there for their sakes.

"At any rate, we'll be here, and everyone's welcome to come," said Abd al-Karim. "And our neighbour Ibrahim al-Shudaykhi will be here too," he went on after a short pause. "He's a passionate Nasserite and … an atheist."

Abd al-Karim fell silent again, smiling and looking round at the others as he tried to make out the effect of this last word on them. No one gave the slightest hint of any reaction except Salim, who said in astonishment, "An atheist! You mean he doesn't believe in God? God forgive me."

"Yes," said Abd al-Karim. "He doesn't believe in anything that can't be proven scientifically."

Everyone had been expecting this reaction from Salim, who was the most devout one among them and the most conscientious about performing all the religious obligations. Often when they were playing cards or chatting in the evening he would get up when the muezzin made the call to prayer, face towards Mecca and pray, then come back smiling and say, "So, have I missed anything?" and pick up where he had left off. Salim could imagine and accept anything except the idea that someone did not believe in God wholeheartedly.

"If God doesn't exist – Heaven forbid! – who created the universe? How did Heaven and Earth come about?" said Salim, narrowing his eyes and furrowing his brow.

"Just like that. By coincidence, evolution. Everything's based on Nature. It's creator and creation at the same time. That's what Ibrahim says," said Abd al-Karim in a calm, offhand manner, as he slurped his tea and looked Salim in the eyes.

"Rubbish, rubbish," repeated Salim. "Every creation must have a Creator, and the Creator can't have been created. Nature is a creation, so it must have a Creator; it can't be both Creator and creation simultaneously."

"So who created God?" asked Abd al-Karim, taking another sip of tea.

"I told you: the Creator wasn't created. You're trying to get us into which came first, the chicken or the egg. Anyway, what you're putting forward is an odious line of argument, in fact, one that was expressly forbidden by the Prophet, peace be upon Him, precisely because it leads nowhere. The Prophet told us to reflect on God's signs and His creations, not on God Himself. God simply exists. And He manifests Himself in His creations and through His messengers and His prophets." There was a moment's silence before Salim went on. "Does this friend of yours Ibrahim deny them, too?"

Abd al-Karim laughed. "He doesn't believe in the one who sent the prophets, so how do you expect him to believe in them themselves?"

"Almighty God, forgive me," said Salim, grimacing and shaking his head, "Almighty God, protect me. I was thinking of coming along tonight," he continued, jumping to his feet, "but if this infidel friend of yours is going to be here, I'd prefer to stay away and find something better to do. Plus I don't like your pal Nasser or his speeches. Wasn't the defeat enough, you idiots? I don't like that man! He's a communist," he added quickly, and headed to the front door.

"Where are you going?" Abd al-Karim shouted after him. "Are you angry?"

"Why should I be angry?" came the reply. "You've all got your religion and I've got mine. God didn't send Ibrahim and his sort to lord it over us, did he? Or you lot to lord it over all Muslims, for that matter." And with that the door slammed shut and all the others burst out laughing.

⇒ 30 ⇐

That night Hisham, Adnan, Abd al-Karim and Abd al-Aziz met up, joined by Ibrahim al-Shudaykhi. He was about thirty-five years old, short and thin, with long hair, grey sideburns and a huge, flowing beard from which a few white hairs shone. His face was faintly pockmarked and he had a slight squint in one eye, but overall he had an air of great dignity. Ibrahim was wearing a white robe and headdress without *iqal* cords, and gave off a scent of fine incense and sandalwood oil.

Abd al-Karim brought over a transistor radio and tuned in to 'Voice of the Arabs', on which the presenter was just announcing that President Nasser would soon give his speech. Abd al-Karim got up to look both ways down the alley, then shut the windows firmly and sat back down with the others, all of whom were silent. A few moments later the presenter announced that the president had arrived, and shortly afterwards Nasser's voice came floating over the airwaves, fine and delicate, belying the physical size of the man. (This was in contrast to King Hussein of Jordan, whose rich, deep voice gave the impression that he was of enormous stature when quite the opposite was true.)

"My brother citizens," Nasser began, before going on to speak about how the colonialist powers had set upon the Arab nation and its liberal forces. Then he discussed a new peace initiative and declared Egypt's willingness to accept any solution that would lead to a just peace. His speech ended amidst a storm of applause, followed by the Egyptian nationalist anthem 'A Long Time It's Been, O My Weapon,' from the days of the Suez crisis.

It was a strange business about this man, Hisham noted to himself. Since the Setback Nasser had offered nothing new, yet he was still worshipped by the masses. Even his speech that very night had nothing new in it; it was a retreat, in fact, from his ideas before the war, and even from the famous 'no's of the Arab summit in Khartoum afterwards: no peace with Israel, no recognition of Israel, no negotiation with Israel concerning any Palestinian territory. In this latest speech Nasser announced that he would even accept peace and reconciliation, yet his words still had that mysterious galvanizing effect. Hisham remembered the overwhelming impact of Nasser's pre-'67 speeches, which had the power to shake one physically. (The President's words from previous years still rang in his father's ears. To this day Hisham would hear him quote the speeches with a kind of wonder: "Lift up your head, brother ... The age of colonialism is over ..." His father used to say that "if there had been another prophet after Muhammad, it would have been Nasser.") Yes, despite the spectre of defeat Nasser was still defiant, and was loved. If one were to have gone out just then into any Arab street from the Atlantic to the Gulf, one would have found them empty: everyone was listening to Nasser, just as the first Thursday evening of every month was given over to the radio, in front of which everyone would sit and listen to the great Egyptian singer Umm Kulthumm, 'The Lady', give one of her shows. Nasser and Umm Kulthumm: they weren't merely two individuals; they embodied their times.

"What do you think of the speech?" said Abd al-Karim, trying to initiate a discussion after he had turned off the radio. There was a short silence during which they all looked at one another and then Ibrahim spoke up quietly, his face a picture of dignified gravity and wisdom.

"I trust Nasser. No doubt he only accepted the peace principle once he found it expedient to do so, during this current phase, at least."

It was plain from Ibrahim's last phrase that he was looking for some justification for the Leader's new position, which no one had been expecting after all the refusals and the War of Attrition and all that talk about colonialism and Zionism and the American conspiracy.

"That's odd coming from you, Ibrahim," said Abd al-Karim in amazement. "Weren't we talking about this the other day, when you said quite confidently that Nasser would never accept anything less than the total liberation of Palestine?"

"Yes," said Ibrahim, becoming a little agitated, "but we were analysing the situation based on speculation, not concrete facts. As for Nasser, he must make his decisions on the basis of detailed information, and he wouldn't make any decision unless he knew it was the most appropriate and the most advantageous for the Arab nation."

"Yes, like the decision to close the Straits of Tiran to Israeli shipping in 1967, eh, brother Ibrahim?" said Abd al-Aziz with overt scorn.

Ibrahim flew into a rage, losing all of his dignity in one fell swoop. "1967 was an obvious conspiracy," he said. "Yes, a conspiracy. Everyone took part, even the Soviet Union, which used to make itself out to be a friend of Nasser's. 'Don't attack first,' they said, and Nasser trusted them. It was a conspiracy stitched up from all sides."

"Conspiracy my foot," yelled Abd al-Aziz, gesticulating wildly. "Any half-wit knows that closing the Tiran Straits means strangling Israel, and that means war. So how come our revered Leader, if he wasn't ready for war, why did he provoke the other side into it? He's a joke of a leader, as the Egyptians say."

"He *was* ready for war," said Ibrahim, breathing hard, the eyes and the veins of his face bulging. "But there was treachery! The treachery of Field Marshal Abd al-Hakim Amer and his frantic retreat from the Sinai!"

"God, what did you want him to do?" Abd al-Aziz said caustically. "The air force had been destroyed and the army was left in the desert without cover. If he hadn't retreated, there would have been a complete and utter massacre. Treachery? Conspiracy? Look for another excuse to pin it on, brother."

Ibrahim looked furious. "He should have resisted to the last soldier," he replied. "He shouldn't have surrendered so easily!"

"To the last soldier for the sake of the immortal Leader, right?" said Abd al-Aziz, throwing back his head and laughing. "Sorry, Ibrahim. Can't you see that your love of Nasser has blinded you to the naked truth? Look at Syria. The Golan Heights only fell after the fall of Sinai and the collapse of the Egyptian army, the most powerful fighting force in the Middle East."

Hisham followed the conversation, caught up by what Abd al-Aziz had said. He'd make a good element in the organisation; perhaps he'd invite him to join one day.

"You're obviously a Baathist, brother Abd al-Aziz," Ibrahim said, giving him a filthy look. "The Baathists are the only ones who hate Nasser so vehemently."

Abd al-Aziz sat up straight. "It's not a question of love or hate," he said sharply. "It's about where the truth lies. Now that you've lost the argument, you're trying to change the subject." He leaned back again and caught his breath. "And supposing I am a Baathist," he went on, "what's wrong with that? Aren't you a Nasserite? With all due respect, Ibrahim, I'm sorry to say you're naive. Naive in your analysis of politics, and naive in your atheism. If you analyse religion like you do politics, Salim must be right."

Ibrahim went pale and gave Abd al-Karim a look of reproach for apparently having betrayed a confidence. For several moments he remained silent, his embarrassment plain to see on his face. Then he got up quickly and headed to the front door, waving abruptly. "Pleased to meet you all," he said, his voice trembling. "Goodbye." Abd al-Karim got up after him and the two of them remained standing by the front door, whispering something vague and incomprehensible. Then Abd al-Karim came back, glowering.

"You've insulted the man," he said to Abd al-Aziz, as he was about to sit down again. "You had no right to speak about religion. You've really embarrassed me."

Abd al-Aziz jumped up. "Don't embarrass me and I won't embarrass you! I was wrong to come here in the first place," he added as he took his leave. "Salim was right."

He had already got to the front door when Abd al-Karim stood up and went after him, but by the time he reached the door, Abd al-Aziz was already in the street and Abd al-Karim retraced his steps, repeating the traditional phrase, "There is no power and no strength save in God, there is no power and no strength save in God. Why are people like that?"

He sat down beside Hisham and Adnan and poured himself a cup of tea. Hisham said, "You were the one in the wrong, Abd al-Karim. We're a gang, and you brought along a stranger. He's older than us and wanted to look down on us and become our leader. That wasn't right of you. That wasn't right."

Abd al-Karim looked at him blankly as he sipped his tea, then looked at the teapot, repeating, "Whoever goes away always returns ... Whoever goes away always returns," while all the others remained silent.

31

The following afternoon, Hisham went to Adnan's house with one of the organisation's pamphlets about internal matters, which he folded carefully and hid under his vest. Adnan's little sister Samiya let him in, and he went to the sitting room he knew so well, where Adnan and his brother Majid were playing Kiram. Hisham was livid. Adnan had promised he would be alone yet here he was, casually playing cards with his brother. He took a seat between the two of them, pretending to be calm and follow the game which Majid seemed so keen on, but inside he was seething with rage, and all the more so when he saw how indifferent Adnan was.

Ibtihal, Adnan and Majid's half-sister by their father's Syrian wife, brought him some tea on a tray with various kinds of cakes and put it next to Hisham, giving him a quick smile and glancing at him with her honey-coloured eyes before leaving the room, her lovely, clear cheeks blushing. Hisham followed her with his gaze as she vanished beyond the door, unconsciously comparing her to Noura. Ibtihal might have been more beautiful, with those eyes and her pure white complexion, wavy, chestnut-brown hair and slender figure, but Noura was still the more attractive.

Hisham was woken from his reverie by the sound of Majid shouting for joy after throwing down an ace and following it up with the trump card, marking his victory. In the meantime Adnan was stacking the cards again in preparation for another round, trying to avoid Hisham's angry glances. While the two brothers were engrossed in the new game, Hisham poured himself another cup of hot tea and began sipping it and munching a cake with no real appetite as he slipped back into his daydream.

The game ended with another of Majid's cries; Adnan began stacking the cards for another round, but Majid stopped him, laughing sarcastically.

"No, I'm not playing with you. I need someone who can give me a real challenge," he said. "What do you know? You're better off sticking to painting." Majid poured himself a cup of tea and drank it down quickly, still laughing. "Are you any good," he asked Hisham, "or are you like your friend here? I'll bet you four fils you can't beat me, however many times we play."

Hisham forced a quick smile to his lips as he raised his thick eyebrows and shook his head. "No, man, don't bother with me. There's no beating you at this sort of thing."

Majid grinned with pride and poured himself another cup of tea, which he began drinking slowly, savouring it as he looked at his brother. "It looks like there's no one else on the battlefield, brother. Come on, stack the cards."

Without a moment's hesitation Adnan began doing so, still avoiding Hisham's gaze.

"Adnan," said Hisham, jumping in before a new round could begin, "have you forgotten our rendezvous with Abd al-Karim?"

Adnan glanced at him and then looked at the teapot. "No ... no," he said in a whisper, pouring himself some more tea, "I haven't forgotten. I'm ready to go when you are."

Hisham put his cup down on the tray still half full and stood. "Let's get moving, then. If you'll excuse us, Majid."

Hisham got up quickly and Adnan followed, but just before he stepped outside the house Majid called out from the sitting room, "You silly fools! Every day these stupid meetings of yours. Don't you get bored of them? They're such a waste of time."

Majid was the second son in the al-Ali family and Adnan's blood brother from their father's first wife; their father had a total of three wives, six sons and seven daughters, and they all lived in the same house. Majid was only a year younger than Adnan, but his complete opposite. Adnan was highly sensitive; he disliked confrontation to the point where he would be reluctant even to enter into a discussion or debate, and if he did so would always let the other party take the initiative and steer the conversation. His favourite moments were those he spent alone with his paintbrushes and pictures, or with Hisham, with whom he could speak freely and fluently about his impressions and art.

Majid, however, was pragmatic in the extreme and sociable, where social relationships could lead to direct personal benefit, that is. He used to criticise his brother for his preoccupation with 'nonsense', as he put it, his obsession with drawing and his relative insularity. "Money's what counts in this world," he would always say, "and the only thing worthwhile is making it and saving it." Majid worked as much of the time as possible in order to make money; when he finished school he would rush to do his homework and then look for a way to make money. Some days he would buy a bottle of concentrated mulberry juice, heavily dilute it and sell it to the children in the neighbourhood; other times he would sell sweets and dairy products on the black market. On Fridays he would buy vegetables, meat and fish for some of the neighbours in return for a small fee, or go to auctions of basic goods and resell them at a considerable profit. During the long summer holiday he would work in a shop for a monthly salary or spend his time at auctions if he was unable to come by any steady work. His greatest pleasure was rushing to the bank to pay whatever money he had made into a savings account, without spending a penny either on himself or anyone else in the house; on the contrary, he would still take pocket money from his father like any of his siblings, and even strive to save as much of this small amount as possible. The Eid festivals were paradise to Majid. He would get up early in the morning to wish his parents a happy Eid and receive his Eid present from them, before shooting off to see his friends and relations, his eye always on the presents he would get – and all this before midday. Then he would go to one of the traders he knew and buy a certain quantity of fireworks, which he would sell to the neighbourhood children. By the end of the Eid, Majid had always scraped together a small fortune, and he would never feel that it was truly Eid until he had deposited it safe and sound in the bank.

Adnan's father was full of admiration for his son Majid and would frequently take Adnan to task in front of his brother, also for his preoccupation with 'nonsense'. "Why can't you be like your brother?" he would say. "You're the older one. He makes the most of his time, while you just waste it on drawing and all that rubbish. Drawing! What kind of future is there in that?" And smacking his hands together dismissively he would leave, shaking his head and saying with pious resignation, "There is no power and no strength save in God". In the meantime Majid would burst with pride, while Adnan seethed and glared at his brother without saying anything, before going off to spend time with the gang or his paintbrushes.

The two friends went out into the street as Hisham quickly thought of a place where they could be alone together. He happened to set eyes on the mosque of Sheikh Mousa, an ascetic who had renounced worldly things after a lifetime spent drinking heavily. He had built this mosque and devoted himself exclusively to worshipping there and offering his services to anyone who needed them.

"The mosque's the best place to get some privacy at this time of day," Hisham said, now smiling at his friend. "It'll be completely empty. Let's go."

They set off towards the mosque as the sun was beginning to set. It really was empty when they entered, apart from an old man leaning against one of the walls and nodding his head as he recited from a small Qur'an that he held in his right hand. They both recognised him as Sheikh Mousa, from his thick, snow-white beard and the moustache twisted with an elegance only he could muster. The sheikh glanced at them when they entered and smiled with genuine affection, reciting and nodding his head before once again becoming completely immersed in his Qur'an. They made towards a corner far away from the sheikh, Adnan following Hisham's lead. They sat down, each of them leaning against one of the walls, and for a while they both remained silent, Adnan's eyes full of questioning about the 'important thing' his friend had spoken to him about.

Without a word, Hisham looked about, then slipped his hand under his vest and took out a carefully folded piece of paper which he quickly gave to Adnan. "Take this," he whispered, looking around again. "Read it quickly."

Adnan took the paper, spread it on his lap and began reading, his eyes growing larger the further he got. Hisham repeatedly urged him to finish, looking left and right and saying, "Quickly, quickly." By the time Adnan had finished reading his eyes were wide open and he was in a cold sweat, the drops of perspiration running down his forehead. His hands were shaking as he gave the pamphlet back to Hisham, who hastily folded it again and slipped it back under his vest.

"So? What do you think?" he said.

Adnan tried to speak, but his tongue would not obey him; his hands were visibly quivering. "Thi … thi … this is dangerous talk," he stammered, in a voice dry and faint. "The sort of talk that could land you in prison." He swallowed and wiped the sides of his nose with his palm. "Where did you get this paper from?" he asked. "And what is this National Union of Students of the Arabian Peninsula?"

"Save the questions till later," said Hisham, interrupting him curtly. "What do you think about what it says?"

"It's good," said Adnan, still agitated, "but it could lead to disaster. Where ..."

"I told you to forget about asking questions for now: you'll find out everything in due course. All I can tell you now is that it's from a clandestine organisation. An organisation of freedom fighters," he said, looking around again. "You believe in freedom, don't you?"

"Of course I do!" said Adnan, smiling for the first time. "Have you ever heard of an artist who didn't? You know that."

"In that case the organisation calls on you to fight for what we believe in, too."

"Yes, but ..."

"No buts. Belief on its own isn't enough; it has to be backed up by action. I'm inviting you," Hisham went on after a short pause, "to join the organisation."

There was another pause as Hisham looked at his friend, who had bowed his head and clasped his hands together in a futile attempt to stop them shaking.

"Anyway," said Hisham, breaking the silence, "there's no need for you to give an answer now. Think it over and tell me what you decide. We'll be late for the others," he said, preparing to stand up. "Let's go."

As Hisham got to his feet Adnan remained still for a few moments, before rising and catching up with him at the door of the mosque. The first person had arrived for the sunset prayers; Sheikh Mousa's rich, deep voice could be heard in the distance, reciting the

'Ta Ha' sura of the Qur'an: "We have not sent down the Qur'an to you that you should be distressed …"

❧ 32 ❧

Hisham was certain that his friend would consent to join the organisation. He understood Adnan better than anyone, and also knew just how fond of and dependent on him Adnan had always been, since they were at primary school together. Adnan always stood by him unequivocally; he would not hesitate to agree this time, either.

Meanwhile, fear, loyalty and pride churned volcanically within Adnan for three days after Hisham's invitation. Adnan was struggling with a mass of contradictions he had no idea how to reconcile. The thought of participating in any kind of subversive activity terrified him, especially given that one of his uncles had gone to prison after taking part in one of the marches during the famous strikes and demonstrations staged by the Aramco workers. When he was released several years later he was in a pitiful state; for a whole year afterwards, he still trembled with fear whenever night drew near, for some reason – he never told anyone why. Even now he would walk along talking to himself and laughing, and then suddenly revert to a state of supreme self-command. Adnan's uncle had since cut off all involvement with politics for good, to the point where he would leave a gathering of people if he detected so much as a whiff of politics. Adnan's maternal grandmother would ritually repeat her 'famous' saying in front of her grandsons as she observed her own son in this state: "This is the prison of the old; nothing left on the inside and like a baby on the outside." Then she would praise God all the same. Yet, though his grandmother's words still instilled fear in him, Adnan did not want to disappoint his friend's hopes in him. Hisham was the only friend of his who understood him, the only one who had any regard for his art, the only one he could talk to about his feelings; if he let him down now, he might lose him forever. Just thinking about losing him made Adnan panic. He loved Hisham so much he would feel jealous if he saw him so much as talking to another person affectionately or walking with someone new. Though it rarely happened, when it did Adnan's blood would boil and he would soon manage to get between Hisham and the new 'threat'.

At the same time Adnan felt proud that Hisham had invited him to join the organisation, rather than Majid or another member of the gang. It proved Hisham's trust in, and respect, for him. He wished he could shout at his brother and father and tell them, "Look! I'm the best of all. One day I'll liberate mankind! Majid can remain a slave of gold ..." But this feeling of pride suddenly evaporated when it occurred to him that Hisham might have already invited someone else in the gang to join, and his worst suspicions took hold. How did he know Hisham had only spoken to him on the subject? Wasn't he allowed to talk to Abd al-Karim or Saud or Abd al-Aziz first? But Adnan soon banished these doubts and his peace of mind returned. No, there was no one else; if Hisham had spoken to anyone other than his best friend, he would have said so. Adnan went back to his brushes, feeling overjoyed, and began to paint.

Hisham informed his cell commander Fahd of the nomination, though he did not mention his having already spoken to Adnan about it; doing so was against the organisation's security regulations. Fahd asked him to prepare a detailed report on Adnan, covering the reasons that had prompted Hisham to nominate him: Adnan's acquaintances; his family's social class and other information. Hisham was angered and humiliated by this sort of request. How could he write a report on his friend? He was quite aware that reports like these were only ever written for the notorious intelligence agencies, prepared by people for whom the general public had utter contempt mixed with deepest fear. Had he become one of those people? For a while he carried this hateful feeling inside him, before telling Fahd that he would not be preparing any such report. At first Fahd was angry; Hisham told him that he would never at any price turn into an informer, and at this Fahd gave one of his resounding laughs. Lighting and dragging on a cigarette, Fahd told Hisham that he was a freedom fighter, not an informer, and that it was for the sake of the struggle that everything had to be known about new candidates as they might be Secret Police infiltrators sent to expose the organisation. However, Hisham was not convinced. He insisted that because he knew Adnan intimately, there was no need for reports. But Fahd was unmoved, explaining that these were the rules of the organisation, to be obeyed without question, and that everyone else had done the same thing and had the same thing done to them. Finally, Hisham gave in and reluctantly wrote the report, mentally spitting on himself as he did so, in self-disgust. Whatever the justifications, he felt, there was now no difference between him and the perfidious eavesdroppers. He made up his mind never to nominate anyone else, to avoid having to repeat the experience.

In the report Hisham nominated Adnan to become a member of the Students' Union, not the party. When Fahd asked him why, he replied that Adnan was not yet ready to join the party and take part in its activities. Though he was a true patriot, Hisham said, ideas and ideology in general were alien to him and the party itself was based on an ideology that might put him off the work of the organisation altogether. Fahd accepted these explanations and delivered the report to the leadership, whose reply promptly came back agreeing to Adnan's joining the union and instructing Comrade Abu Huraira to carry out the necessary steps.

In actual fact, Hisham had not been entirely honest in his justification. It was true that Adnan was not on his intellectual level, but the party's ideas were not so complex as to require a high degree of intelligence to comprehend them; and in any case, once someone had agreed to take part in clandestine activity, there was no reason why they should not join the party from the outset and be schooled in its ideas later on. But Hisham's reason for excluding Adnan from the party lay in his desire to maintain a distinction between them. Hisham, as a member of the party which controlled the union, would therefore carry a higher rank. For all his affection, Hisham had never once considered Adnan his equal. He regarded him as a virtual possession that he did not want anyone else to usurp. Adnan must remain his follower, even within the context of a covert organisation. (Hisham, perhaps, could not admit to himself more plainly that only with Adnan did he feel important and influential.)

More than a week after Hisham had extended his invitation, the gang met as usual in Abd al-Karim's house. Abd al-Karim and Abd al-Aziz were talking about a new novel, a copy of which Abd al-Aziz had got hold of from a relative just back from Beirut. They spoke with obvious excitement – especially Abd al-Karim, who was fidgeting a great deal and squeezing his legs together. Abd al-Aziz was holding the novel and whispering sections of it to Abd al-Karim. It was one of Alberto Moravia's novels, *The Time of Indifference*; on the cover was a picture of a fair, blonde woman with dark red lips and large, green eyes, sitting back seductively with her white thighs completely exposed. She had her arm behind her head and was giving the reader a lustful, enticing look through half-closed eyes, while her open mouth revealed her brilliant white teeth. Hisham had not yet read the novel, but would come to do so several times, particularly the sections describing the character Carla's loss of her virginity on the night she slept with her mother's lover. For days after he first read this passage, the scene remained in his mind; time and again he would return to it in his imagination, alone on warm winter evenings and during quiet siestas on hot summer days …

Salim and Saud were playing Kiram in a corner while Hisham and Adnan sat next to each other in another corner, the ornate teapot in the centre. They were all listening intently to the words of Abd al-Aziz's reading and following Abd al-Karim's movements with mirth.

"Abd al-Karim, why don't you just go to the bathroom and get it over and done with?" said Saud.

"Now I know why there's so much soap in there," said Salim.

"I don't know about Abd al-Karim, but Abd al-Aziz has other ways, really creative ones," said Saud, and burst out laughing as he clapped his hands and nodded vigorously.

"You lot are awful! Don't embarrass them," said Hisham with mock seriousness, before laughing along with the others.

"God, there's no one like us," said Abd al-Karim. "Hisham's got glasses; Saud, you've got a face like a knobbly old root; and you, Salim, are always dribbling. What's the reason for all this?" By way of an answer he made an obscene gesture with his hand and wrist that sent them all into fits of laughter.

"Get away with you, Abd al-Karim!" Salim shouted. "You'd have people turning in their graves with the things you say. Your father's so devout, yet you're a complete good-for-nothing!"

The laughter continued as Salim and Saud went back to playing Kiram and Abd al-Aziz and Abd al-Karim to reading the novel. All the while Adnan had been quiet as usual, weighing in with a smile or chuckle without making any comment. Once the others had resumed what they had been doing, Adnan leaned towards Hisham and whispered in his ear, "All right." Hisham looked at his friend and flashed him a smile, then nodded and went back to drinking his tea calmly. Adnan drew back a little and leaned his elbow on one of the cushions, gazing inscrutably at the others.

✻ 33 ✻

Hisham informed Fahd of Adnan's agreement, and at the next meeting of the cell Fahd gave him a password to convey to Adnan: 'Hauran's a great place'. At the same time Fahd instructed Hisham to cut off all contact with Adnan. At this Hisham was taken aback. How could he do such a thing? This Fahd had no idea of the kind of relationship that bound him to Adnan, friend, comrade and faithful follower all in one; if it had not been for that relationship, Adnan would never have agreed to join. He had only invited Adnan to join the organisation because he was a friend, not for any other reason; would he really sacrifice Adnan for its sake? It was impossible, quite impossible.

Hisham discussed the matter with Fahd to no avail. Fahd insisted that the ties between comrades came above all others, that by comparison all other relationships and sacrifices paled in significance. When Hisham in turn resisted this argument, Fahd replied angrily that ending the friendship was a party order that Hisham had to execute to the letter, or else make himself liable to punishment by the organisation, which might be of the utmost severity.

On his way home after the meeting, Hisham turned those words over in his mind. 'Punishment! Orders! Are we really getting away from the authority of the government and our parents? are we rebelling against the punishments inflicted by the state and the people alike, only to fall into a web of new orders and other sorts of punishment? We've gone from the frying pan into the fire. At least obeying the government doesn't land you in prison, whereas obeying this lot ...! In the end it's just another kind of obedience, just another kind of submission.' He made up his mind to appear to give in, while disobeying them in practice, and the party and the organisation could go to hell.

Hisham told Adnan the password and explained that everything had been arranged, that all he had to do was wait. Deep down he wished Adnan would suddenly tell him he had second thoughts and no longer wanted to join the organisation, or instead that he himself could tell Adnan to forget it, that he had only been joking; then he could tell Fahd that Adnan had changed his mind. But Adnan did not change his mind, and neither did Hisham have the courage to tell him anything contrary to what he had said before.

Meanwhile Hisham took to observing Adnan closely at school. He wanted to know who the contact was – Goat-Face, or someone else? He did not let Adnan out of his sight for a moment, and Adnan himself was visibly pleased with the extra attention. One day during Mr Wasfi's physics class, Hisham noticed Mansur Abd al-Ghani, sitting at a desk directly behind Adnan, pass him a little piece of paper. So, that monkey was the contact! When Adnan read the note, his jaw dropped and he looked behind him, his eyes wide and his face breaking into a sweat. He remained like that until the teacher told him off. Hisham, seething, counted the seconds until break time. Adnan put the paper inside his physics book and looked at the blackboard, wiping his face from time to time.

At last the bell rang; Mansur got up quickly and whispered something in Adnan's ear, and the two of them went out together while Hisham stayed seated until the last pupil left the classroom. He raced over to Adnan's desk and opened the physics book: the note read, 'Hauran's a great place'. Hisham went outside quickly and caught sight of Adnan and Mansur whispering at the end of the corridor that led to the headmaster's office. He felt something like fire spreading through him, along with an urge to strangle Mansur; but he suppressed his emotions and, feigning indifference, began looking around the courtyard without really seeing anything. Mansur soon finished speaking to Adnan, then made his exit, passing Hisham on his way to the courtyard; their eyes met for a fleeting moment. Hisham turned to look at Adnan, who came to where he was standing. Adnan stood there, still perspiring, his hands trembling visibly. They were silent for a while, looking and not looking at the crowds of pupils in the courtyard. In the distance, Mansur appeared, having got to the courtyard himself and joined a group of boys sitting near the rear exit of the school.

"So? Everything all right? What did he want?" asked Hisham, nodding with open disgust towards the courtyard. But Adnan remained silent and wiped the side of his nose with one of his hands. "Did you agree on a meeting place?" Hisham went on, trying to push Adnan to speak by giving him the impression that he knew everything.

Adnan glanced at Hisham, wide-eyed. "How did you know it was him?" he asked, astonished. "He told me you knew nothing and that I shouldn't tell you anything, either."

Hisham smiled, full of pride, and raised his head a little. "God!" he said, looking his friend in the eyes. "Have you forgotten that I'm the one who invited you to join the project? There are lots of things I know that you don't." He half-smiled as he uttered the last sentence, as though to say, 'Nothing's changed, I'm still the same old friend you've always known'.

Adnan bowed his head and leaned against the wall. "We're meeting this afternoon in front of the municipal park," he said, in a barely audible voice.

"And then what?"

"I don't know. Mansur's arranged everything."

At that moment Mansur approached on his way back from break, and Hisham fell silent. Mansur smiled briefly at Hisham before entering the classroom. All the old loathing boiled up inside Hisham again. How he despised that arrogant monkey! When the bell rang at the end of the day, Hisham and Adnan left together as usual, and walked without speaking to Hisham's house.

"See you tomorrow," Hisham said.

"Bye," replied Adnan. Hisham knew he would not see his friend with the gang that day.

He went inside; the smell of fried fish filled the house. On Thursdays his mother usually made fried fish with white rice and a green salad for lunch. Other days, the main dish was normally meat stew or chicken, if his mother did not feel like making fried food with chilli and pickles. 'Syrian rubbish', his father used to call any dishes other than those his mother usually prepared on winter evenings: *kabsa* stew; *jarish*, crushed wheat cooked with meat and vegetables; *marquq*, a dish made of wheat dough cut into small pieces and cooked with meat, vegetables and tomatoes; *mataziz*, similar to *marquq* but made with thick, round pieces; and *qursan*, made of fine bread with meat and vegetable stock poured over it.

Hisham went into the kitchen and greeted his mother, who was busy with her preparations; his father was not back yet. Then he had a quick shower outside, after which he lay on his bed and flicked through the latest issue of 'Superman' until lunch was ready. Without realising it, he nodded off; he did not know how long he had been asleep when he heard his mother's voice in the distance as though in a dream, calling him to lunch. The table had been laid in the room with the air conditioner, and his father was sitting and rolling a lump of rice in his hand while his mother was still busy in the kitchen. Hisham greeted his father and took a seat.

"Where have you been? You've kept us waiting so long you've made us hungry!" his father teased, through a mouthful of rice and with a smile full of unadulterated affection that Hisham reciprocated even more warmly. As his parents ate they spoke about the same old things, none of which Hisham took in. He was eating mechanically, his mind on matters other than food. When he heard the muezzin calling from the nearby mosque he jumped up as though he had been stung by a scorpion, rice flying from his right hand as his mother and father looked at him in surprise.

"Are you all right?" his mother said, as his father glared at him. "What's the matter? Why are you in such a rush? You haven't finished eating!"

"Sorry Father, sorry Mother," said Hisham. "I just remembered that I've got a few books borrowed from the public library, and I've got to return them this afternoon or they'll cancel my membership. If you'll excuse me ..." He dashed off to the bathroom, his father now looking after him with pride.

"There's no one like our Hisham," he said, putting a piece of fried vermicelli in his mouth, "no one like him."

"There's only one God and only one Hisham. God has truly blessed us in him," his mother said, before adding, "God forgive me, God forgive me," in a customary expression of humility.

Hisham hastily washed his hands. Lying had become easy to him ever since he had joined the party; he did not feel as guilty as he used to do. In fact, he could now quickly make up excuses and justifications with enviably steady nerves, and if he still felt the prick of his conscience from time to time it quickly vanished without trace. Back in his room he hurriedly put on his robe, skullcap and headdress and rushed outside. He had hated wearing these clothes, much preferring a shirt and trousers, but his father had occasionally told him off for going to school or visiting family friends dressed like that and would force him to wear traditional clothes. The robe was bearable, but Hisham could not stand the skullcap and headdress, and after a battle of wills with his father it was settled that he would just wear a robe to school and the skullcap and headdress on special occasions and visits. At all other times he could have his own way and wear a shirt and trousers. The strange thing was, after that conclusion, Hisham began to prefer the robe, and wore one most of the time.

The streets around the small municipal park were almost empty but for a few labourers from Oman and Yemen who were lying down around the walls of the gardens. For some it was siesta time, while for others it was time for afternoon prayers. Hisham disappeared down one of the alleyways off the park and, from a distance, began watching the gate where Mansur stood. Mansur held his satchel and paced up and down, pausing occasionally to crack his fingers nervously before pacing again. He was an odd one, thought Hisham; they'd finished school early that day, so where had he spent the last few hours, given that he didn't live in Dammam? He must have been with some of the comrades, as he couldn't afford to eat in a restaurant and had no relatives here.

Hisham's thoughts were cut short by the appearance of Adnan in the distance, approaching from the direction of the fish and vegetable market in a grey robe and a red and white chequered headdress despite the extremely hot and humid weather. Hisham pulled his own headdress over his face, adjusted his glasses and began watching closely. Mansur met Adnan halfway and shook hands with him quickly; then they both set off towards the centre of town, Hisham following them with his gaze without their noticing him, despite the fact that Mansur kept looking round constantly. When they reached the car park they boarded a small bus which drove off, heading west along Baladiya Street. Hisham returned home, wondering where they could have gone; he had been determined to go and see the gang, but now he just wanted to be alone without having to speak to anyone.

❧ 34 ❧

During the fortnight before the start of the university term, Abd al-Rahman showed Hisham another Riyadh – a Riyadh that gave up its secrets only to those who sought them out, while jealously withholding them from either lifetime residents or those who were merely passing through. Or both: a person might live in a place from cradle to grave and still remain no more than a transient. This boy knew secrets about Riyadh of which even people born and bred there were ignorant.

What was left of the standards instilled in Hisham with his mother's milk fell away in Riyadh; he picked up new ideas and mannerisms completely unrelated to either her fierce virtue or the strict orders of the Baathists. In the party he had learned to lie easily and fluently, with no painful pricks of conscience, thus shattering the principal basis of virtue as taught him by his mother. Those kinds of lies might be entirely justifiable; in fact, seen from a certain angle they might not be lies at all, but rather a necessary part of the struggle required by clandestine activity, as Fahd once explained to him. By the tough standards of his mother, however, they were still lies, justifications be damned. To her the world was black and white, Heaven and Hell, with no grey areas and no halfway points. To not tell the truth, or to distort it, was to lie. But perhaps life did not obey his mother's criteria or, indeed, any ideal moral standards: life was not something abstract, and was not practised with unadulterated virtue. States lied both to one another and to their own people and called it politics. What was propaganda if not a kind of deceit? What was diplomacy if not an elegant, elaborate and most acceptable form of falsehood? The party did this, too. Was deception a vital part of any organisation? Or was everything relative, were there no absolutes in this life, so that what applied to one situation might not apply to another, and what held true of one thing might not be true of something else? Most of the time Hisham no longer had a satisfactory answer, and found he had lost the certainty he used to think he possessed.

In Riyadh he smoked his first cigarette and drank his first drop of alcohol. In Riyadh he discovered a taste of women far removed from the romantic notions that framed his relationship with Noura. In Riyadh he learned to flirt with women in the Suwaiqa market and al-Thumairi and al-Wazir Streets. He learned how and when to look for women who sold forbidden pleasure cheaply in the alleys of al-Shumaisi and the neighbourhoods of al-Daira. In all this his teacher was Abd al-Rahman, who showed him every inch of this new, exciting world. Hisham in turn embraced this thrilling universe, filled with desires the likes of which he had never known before and which had come upon him all at once. He could find no clear reason for it. Was it the result of deprivation, of urges pent up for years, which had exploded at the first opportunity? Or was it the sense of having escaped, like a genie from a bottle he had been forced into by his mother? Was it that now he was free to do whatever he wanted? Or was it fear that he was trying to escape, following the exposure of the organisation and others like it, and the subsequent mass arrests? He neither knew nor wanted to know; all he was sure of was this new world of pleasure and excitement, far from the severity of his mother and the harshness of the party.

Life in the party had been exciting too, but it was a terrible, frightening kind of excitement, whereas this was pure pleasure.

In Riyadh everything was forbidden, and everything permitted. Cinemas were non-existent, but he watched the latest films there that were not even screened in Beirut or Cairo. Around any sports club or the film rental shops in al-Murabba and al-Nasiriyya, one could watch or hire any film one wished. In Riyadh he saw the Egyptian film *My Father's Up The Tree*, with its scenes of passionate kissing and Nadia Lutfi, whose body oozed desire and sensuality. He watched *Gentlemen Prefer Blondes*, the first film of Marilyn Monroe's he had seen, and though he thought her not beautiful, he found her body bursting with the suggestion of pure physical pleasure. From watching these films Hisham developed a new philosophy about women, until now only ever seen in such an erotic light in his dreams since puberty. There were three types of women, he reckoned: the beautiful, the pretty and the sexy. A woman might be extremely beautiful, but lack either prettiness or sexiness or both; a woman who appeared pretty to the eye and pleasant company besides, might have no trace of beauty about her, and she might or might not be sexy; a woman neither beautiful nor pretty might however be desirable, arousing lust in every atom of one's body. The pinnacle was a woman who was beautiful, pretty and sexy at the same time, but where could one find a woman like that? Even if she did exist somewhere she might be brainless, and in that case she would lose all her appeal as soon as he had any contact with her.

In Riyadh he saw overtly pornographic films, but after the first few scenes they utterly sickened him. The strange thing about sex was that everyone thought about it and chased after it, but seeing the sexual act directly made one feel revolted at the sight of those forbidden zones that had nothing beautiful or erotic about them. It made him realise the sense behind concealing those body parts, even if only with a fig leaf. Despite the fact that everything revolved around them, that everything led to them, that life itself sprang from them, they were ugly. Beauty and erotic appeal did not lie in the body parts and orifices themselves, he was certain, but rather in covering them up, though they might be the ultimate goal.

One morning Abd al-Rahman came to see him in his room upstairs after everyone had gone to work. Hisham was staving off boredom by flicking through some magazines.

"Quick, get dressed," Abd al-Rahman said to him. "There's something urgent we've got to do."

Hisham got up hastily and dressed without uttering a word, then flew out of the house behind Abd al-Rahman. His cousin's old white Mercedes was parked by the front door with the engine running, Abd al-Rahman sat behind the wheel. Hisham got in next to him and the car shot off.

"You remember the girl I told you about who lives in the area?" Abd al-Rahman said as they drove down the dusty road that divided Old and New Shumaisi Streets. "I've arranged to meet her by the Umm Salim roundabout." He looked at Hisham, raising his eyebrows and smiling. "It's time you tasted some flesh."

Hisham said nothing as Abd al-Rahman chuckled and continued driving. His heart was beating violently. This would be the first time he had seen a naked woman's body in real life. He felt a heat spread through him and concentrate itself in that region where all paths met, a heat mixed with fear and apprehension. How often had his mother warned him about women since the day he had run to her in alarm over the white spurts in the shower? His old feelings of guilt were returning, but he pushed them aside and remembered that he had shattered the idol of his mother when he joined the party; whatever was left of it he would smash to pieces as well, come what may.

At the Umm Salim roundabout Abd al-Rahman turned down a dusty, narrow street. After he had driven no more than fifty metres a girl appeared, walking slowly and swathed in black from head to foot with only her fingertips showing. Abd al-Rahman drove alongside her and beeped his horn, then passed her, parked nearby and opened the back door. The girl slipped nimbly into the back seat with the utmost self-assurance, shutting the door behind her, and the car drove off in a dust cloud. For a while Abd al-Rahman drove aimlessly through the alleys of the adjacent neighbourhoods, then returned to New Shumaisi Street.

"What shall we do?" he asked, turning to Hisham. "Where shall we go?"

"How should I know!" replied Hisham naively. "This is your city."

"What do you think about going to your room? It's secluded and there's no one at home at the moment."

"Are you crazy?" said Hisham, his eyes bulging. "Moudhi and Said are in. And anyhow, it would be wrong."

"You're right," Abd al-Rahman said. "It was just an idea, anyway. But where shall we go?"

For a while there was silence, and then Abd al-Rahman cried out: "I know! The only place for poor wretches like us is the Kharid Road." Without waiting for a reply he turned east, crossing al-Batha, then University Street and Al-Ahsa Street. At the Air Academy at the end of al-Umran Street he headed eastwards along the Kharid Road, the desert spreading out on either side. A short way before reaching Khashm al-An he turned left into the red sands and drove on into the desert for about a kilometre until he reached low ground, and stopped the car.

"This is the best place," said Abd al-Rahman with a smile as he got out to open the boot and took out a small blue mat that normally never left the car. He spread it on the soft sands, then opened the back door and asked the girl to get out. She had been completely silent throughout, as though she were not even there. Hisham had practically forgotten about her, but became extremely anxious again.

"I'm afraid someone will see us," he said, looking left and right. "That would be a scandal."

"Don't worry," Abd al-Rahman replied, laughing confidently. "There aren't even any genies around here. The taste of flesh will make you forget everything , even your own mother and father." He carried on laughing as he went over to the girl, but Hisham was not calmed.

The girl had taken off her veil and wrap and thrown them inside the car, revealing her plump figure. She was of medium height and dressed in a long floral dress with an open neck that showed off her large breasts. She had skin the colour of coffee brought to boil over a low flame, and the smoothness of her complexion was apparent from her arms, which were bare almost to her shoulders. Her behind was large but not flabby, and as she walked over to the mat it wobbled with an even rhythm. She was not as pretty as Noura or Moudhi, nor as beautiful as Ibtihal, Adnan's sister, but she was attractive and sexy according to Hisham's lately defined standards; her full, parted lips, especially, seemed to offer 'an invitation to an inferno of kisses', in the words of Hisham's favourite singer Muhammad Abd al-Wahhab. Everything about her was large, but in wonderful proportion and in a way that awakened one's innermost desires.

The three of them sat down on the mat with the car screening them from the main road. "Really, Abd al-Rahman," the girl said coquettishly in her Riyadh accent, speaking for the first time and with a giggle, "is this the best place you could come up with?" She had a very delicate voice that lingered in the ear of the listener.

"Complain to God about it, not me," replied Abd al-Rahman. "There's nowhere else to go."

The girl was neither anxious nor afraid, and there was no sign of nervousness about her at all; she was confident and relaxed as though she were accustomed to escapades like this. Hisham's fear began to subside as he got used to the surroundings; that familiar internal heat had returned, sweeping over him and concentrating in his loins, in Rome ... where all roads lead.

Abd al-Rahman brought out a thermos full of tea from the car along with three cups, which he placed on the mat. This guy is a devil, Hisham thought. When had he made the tea? Hisham had not seen him doing it. He poured it out and the girl began sipping hers.

"Is that all you could get, tea?" she said. "Why didn't you bring some arrack?"

"Tea's my limit," said Abd al-Rahman, laughing in his usual way and gulping the tea down in one go. "If it's arrack you're after, you'll get that with my brother Hamad."

"I'd better get to know him, then," the girl said, sitting up and giving Abd al-Rahman a wink as she put her cup to her lips. Abd al-Rahman took out a packet of Marlboros gave one to the girl. He lit her cigarette and then his own with the same match. They smoked, savouring every drag. Yes, thought Hisham, this boy was full of surprises.

"I didn't think you smoked!" Hisham said to Abd al-Rahman.

"Sometimes, on special occasions," said Abd al-Rahman without looking at him, smoking away with relish. He looked at the girl with a smile.

"At last your friend speaks!" she remarked. Her glistening thighs showed themselves as she sat. "At long last we discover he's not mute!"

They both laughed cheerfully as Hisham's face turned into something resembling a squeezed tomato. He smiled, looking at the ground and toying with the sand between his fingers.

"This is my cousin Hisham," said Abd al-Rahman. "Don't worry about him being quiet; he's just shy. And he's also a beginner. This is Raqiyya," he said to Hisham, indicating the girl, "the most beautiful girl in our neighbourhood."

"You're such a hypocrite! But I like it," the girl said. "I mean, you were a beginner too once," she went on. "Do you remember that day?"

"Who told you that?" said Abd al-Rahman somewhat tersely. "I was just a bit tense that day. All your family were at home, and the room was dark. That's all there was to it."

"Are you cross, darling?" the girl said, laughing flirtatiously. "I'm sorry." She lay down on her right side, leaving her left leg and a large part of her thigh exposed, while her dress clung tightly to the rest of her body, showing off her left buttock in vivid detail. It was a sight that sent the heat soaring in Hisham.

At this point Abd al-Rahman got up and called Hisham over to the other side of the car. "So? Do you want to go first, or shall I?" he asked. "You know what," he went on, without waiting for an answer, "you go first. You are my guest, after all, and one should always defer to one's guests." He began laughing. "I'll go and walk around for a bit. Go on, do us proud." Abd al-Rahman lit another cigarette and went off into the surrounding desert, laughing and puffing smoke into the air.

Hisham was extremely nervous. He had no idea how or where to begin. He silently cursed his cousin for putting him in this embarrassing position. If this girl were Noura he would know what to do, a bit of kissing and hugging and talking. But for this girl, it went much further than that. He had no idea how long he remained in that state, unsure of what to do and unable to move, sweat pouring off him and the sun feeling even hotter than it was. His heart was pounding so hard he could feel it inside his head.

"You haven't gone and left me, have you?" the girl said distantly, impatient. "Where are you, Abd al-Rahman?" Apparently Abd al-Rahman heard her, because he back-tracked some distance and gestured at Hisham to go forward. Hisham dragged himself over to Raqiyya, feeling as though his pores would soon ooze blood, as if his heart somehow did not belong to him.

He found her lying on her back with her arms behind her head, her dress pulled right up over her thighs, which were glistening under the burning rays of the sun as though they had been basted with olive oil. Her middle was raised a little off the ground, creating a small gap between her upper buttocks and her lower back, and she was wearing short, blood-red drawers which displayed in graphic detail the place where all *her* roads met, standing out like a small mound in a valley surrounded by high mountains watered by recent winter rains, the tangled grasses of their slopes plain to see under the fabric of her drawers.

"Where have you been?" the girl yelled when she saw him. "Are you intending to spend all day here? I've got sunburned already."

Hisham sat down facing her, inhaling that distinctive smell of sweat mixed with the rose and lemon water that the girl had drenched herself in, which hardened his erection even further. He reached out with a trembling hand and began stroking her thigh, which lay seductively exposed before his eyes. He felt a softness and a moistness he had never felt before; even those rough parts his hand touched gave him a strange, pleasurable sensation. Heat coursed through him as he forgot all his fears. The only thing on his mind was that embodiment of pleasure lying there in front of him. The girl turned onto her right side, placing her left thigh on her right one after bending her leg so that her knee was pointing towards Hisham. He lay down facing her and continued touching her, then reached under her drawers and began feeling her soft, round behind. Over and over his hand moved down into the crack between her buttocks; he would keep it there for a while and then begin the journey all over again, as the girl lay with her eyes half closed and moaning faintly as if she were dying. The heat inside Hisham reached boiling point and he felt as though his groin were almost exploding. Suddenly the girl got up and took off her dress; she was bra-less, thus instantly revealing full, round breasts with nipples dark and erect like two dates in early June. Hisham took them in his hands and began to squeeze them until he felt them stiffen and become like two unripe grapes. He drew near to her and pressed his mouth to hers, and a moment later felt her sucking hard and painfully on his lips and forcing her rough tongue into his mouth. He felt a slight disgust at the wet sensation of her saliva in his mouth, but the pleasure swept away both his pain and disgust together. The girl removed her drawers and threw them aside, then pulled off his robe. Unconsciously he put his hands over his groin. "What a lovely beginner!" she said, laughing coquettishly. Hisham felt acutely embarrassed, but relaxed his will and followed her every lead. She lay on her back and parted her legs, which she kept straight, pulling him onto her chest by the hand and once again sucking greedily on his lips. His hand passed over every part of her body; when it reached her vulva he felt himself shudder as he touched that coarse hair, which had become hot and sticky like saliva, and he felt heat emanating from her.

The girl's moans had started getting louder when Hisham suddenly got up and began hurriedly putting his robe back on. "Where are you off to? What happened?" Raqiyya asked dreamily, as if semi-conscious, but Hisham took off without looking back. He had suddenly felt a sense of revulsion and painful contempt for himself when he saw her jet-black triangle with its ugly, dark red mouth. And at that moment, for some unknown reason, a vivid image of his mother had come to his mind; he felt as though a coldness had swept over him; the temperature in 'Rome' had dropped to zero and he had gone limp.

"Well, give us the good news," said Abd al-Rahman with intense curiosity, when Hisham went over to him. "Have you finished?"

"I couldn't," Hisham replied. "I was, I was –"

"Don't worry," said Abd al-Rahman, laughing. "The first time's always hard. You'll have better luck next time." He headed over towards the car, but before he got there Hisham called over to him and asked him for a cigarette. Abd al-Rahman gave him one without comment and then proceeded to Raqiyya while Hisham sat on the ground, lit the cigarette and cautiously took a drag. No sooner had the smoke reached his lungs than he began coughing violently. After his coughing fit subsided he took another drag; this time he choked less hard, and with the third drag his coughing stopped altogether. Halfway through the cigarette he felt deliciously giddy, his mouth watering and filling with saliva, his desire coursing back as 'Rome' recovered its energy, while in the distance he could hear the girl's ardent moaning. Hisham finished the cigarette and got up, swaying a little, then dropped the cigarette and trod on it as Abd al-Rahman looked up from behind the car. Hisham returned and found Abd al-Rahman getting his breath back as he buttoned up his robe and tried frantically to tidy his dishevelled hair. On the other side Raqiyya was attempting to squeeze her behind into her tight drawers, her breasts wobbling with every movement and her nipples like two desert plants that had just sprouted after rainfall.

Once again they were on the road to Riyadh, the sun midway through the blue dome of the sky that was clouded with dust, and all three of them quite silent as the voice of Talal Maddah on the radio sang, "How often have I recalled the hours of the late afternoon ..."

❧ 35 ❧

Abd al-Rahman dropped the girl off where he had collected her
after giving her ten whole riyals, which she slipped under her
clothes next to her chest without comment. The two men then
returned home and went to Hisham's room. Hisham lay down on
the bed while Abd al-Rahman sat and leaned against a nearby wall.
Hisham still felt slightly nauseated from the effect of the cigarette,
after the initial feelings of pleasure had worn off, and his eyes
gradually began to close. In the distance he heard Abd al-Rahman
leaving and saying, "You look sleepy. I'll see you at lunch," and
images once more began to gather in his mind …

❖ 36 ❖

The day after Mansur and Adnan met, Hisham went to school on his own. Adnan had not passed by his house in the morning to join him as usual. At school he noticed Adnan avoiding him. There was not even a 'Good morning' forthcoming after the register had been taken and they all went into the classroom, nor did Adnan rush over to talk to him once the first lesson was over. Instead of going with him in the break to have something to eat, Adnan begged off, saying he had some homework to finish. He stammered as he made his excuses, wringing his hands and looking out of the corner of his eye at Mansur, who was leaning against the wall of the corridor outside the classroom with his arms folded, watching them. Hisham realised that they had instructed Adnan to end the friendship, just as they had told him to do likewise, and he had no doubt that Mansur would report him to the party. That did not bother him; in fact, he felt rather glad. They might get so angry with him they would decide to expel him from the organisation, and then he would be free from this nightmare from which he did not know how to awaken.

That afternoon he went to Abd al-Karim's house early; the rest of the gang had not yet arrived. Abd al-Karim was relaxing with his legs stretched out in front of him, wearing only a pair of shorts and a short-sleeved vest. He was engrossed in Albert Camus's *The Outsider* and, as always, drinking tea. The door to the courtyard of the house was open as it usually was at that time of day, so Abd al-Karim did not realise that Hisham had come in and was standing in front of him until he said, "My, what lovely legs." Abd al-Karim put down the novel and greeted Hisham with a smile, then invited him to sit down while he stood and picked up the tea tray. "The tea will be ready in a minute," he said, as he scurried off to the main part of the house. A few minutes later he returned, wearing a white robe – or at least, it had once been white, but was now covered in brown and yellow stains.

"I don't understand," he said without any introduction, sitting down opposite Hisham. "Are there really people like the Outsider that Camus talks about? Or is it just the author's invention, an expression of his state of mind at a certain point? Someone like that …! He doesn't take any notice of his mother's death, and not even of his trial and his *own* death! I think it's all a bit over the top, don't you?"

Hisham stretched out one of his legs and, folding his arms behind his head, leaned back against the wall. "That kind of absurdity might seem exaggerated to us," he said, "but if we knew the circumstances that Camus was living through and the state of European society after the war, maybe we'd realise that absurdity is a part of life. Perhaps what we call fate is simply the absurd, and what they call the absurd is simply fate."

"I don't understand," said Abd al-Karim.

"The question is how we look at things, not the things themselves. There is no truth *per se*, the question lies in –" Hisham broke off as their other friends began arriving: Abd al-Aziz, then Saud and finally Salim. They all sat down and Saud began pouring out the tea, which Abd al-Karim's mother had pushed in to them from behind the door, saying in a low voice, "Abd al-Karim, the tea ... Good afternoon, boys."

"Good afternoon, Umm Hamad," they all chimed in. Hamad was Abd al-Karim's older brother, who worked for Aramco, and whom they only ever saw on special occasions as his work took up all of his time. There was also the fact that he was busy with his American wife and his three children, who could barely speak Arabic. They had been born in Houston, Texas, where Hamad had studied petroleum engineering on an Aramco scholarship. It was there that he had met his wife, Barbara, and they had had their sons Shadi and Fadi, and their daughter Sarah. Now they all lived in 'Senior Staff', the area for senior Aramco employees, and the children went to American schools in the neighbourhood.

The boys began drinking and talking about all sorts of subjects. Time went by, and still there was no sign of Adnan. Mixed feelings of worry and tension, jealousy and curiosity came over Hisham. Where could the fool be? Was he with that monkey Mansur? Or had he given in to the organisation's silly orders and cut off contact with him? What a coward he'd be to go and obey them, Hisham thought, paying no attention to what was going on around him. He only came to his senses when he heard the others giggling and saying, "Get away with you, Saud! What rubbish you come out with!" Saud had probably told them one of the dirty jokes he always had up his sleeve. They noticed that Hisham was not joining in and began to direct their comments at him. "Look, that's how people are when they're in love," "I spy someone suffering from unrequited love," "Ahem, ahem ... We're over here."

"What a lot of idiots you are," Hisham said with a smile, quickly changing the subject and trying to seem as natural as possible. "I was thinking about Adnan and wondering why he hadn't got here yet. But it looks like he's no friend of yours."

"You're the one who should know," said Saud. "Of all of us you're the one who's closest to him. Anyhow, don't worry, he'll turn up. If not today, tomorrow." Saud gave a brief laugh as he looked at the others and winked, and they looked at Hisham and began laughing themselves.

"You really are a lot of idiots," Hisham said, suddenly getting up. "I'm off, anyway."

"You're not angry, are you?" exclaimed Saud. "I was only joking."

Abd al-Karim got up after Hisham. "You know Saud and his smutty jokes," he said. "He didn't mean anything by it."

"Don't worry about it," said Hisham, and then added, addressing the others, "Whoever sits with idiots must be a idiot too, and idiots don't get angry with each other – right, idiot?" he said, looking at Saud and smiling.

"Right you are, you prize idiot," answered Saud with a smile, "so why don't you sit back down?"

"I've got a few things to do. I'll see you all tomorrow," Hisham said, and took off. As he left he could hear Salim calling out for the cards and challenging the others to a round of Plot and Saud humming, "Poor are those who fall in love …"

Saud's comment had annoyed him, and the moment he made it Hisham had felt an intense loathing towards him, but his curiosity to find out where Adnan was pushed every other thought out of his mind. The instant he was outside he forgot all about the gang, and unconsciously he hurried off to Adnan's house, his flip-flops slapping against the soles of his feet as he went. When he knocked on the door Majid opened it and greeted him quickly as he stepped outside.

"If you're looking for your friend, he's amusing himself in his hermit's cell," he said. "Sorry, but I can't stay; I've got a job at Abu Salih's shop and I don't want to be late. Goodbye."

As Majid raced off Hisham made his way to Adnan's studio in the room under the stairs leading up to the roof terrace. This room was extremely cramped, but Adnan's touch had transformed it into something magical with all the pictures and decorations with which he had covered the walls. He found Adnan sitting there, engrossed in painting a new picture and sweating from every part of his skinny body in the stifling heat that only Adnan could bear when he was painting. He was sitting cross-legged on the floor with his back to the door, and he had leaned the picture he was painting against the wall. He was wearing long white trousers and a white vest wet with sweat. Drops of perspiration glistened on his neck and ran down his back. He was completely absorbed in what he was doing, the air around him hot and humid and smelling of oil paint and fried food as well as a rotten odour from the drain of a nearby house.

Hisham knew Adnan always behaved this way when troubled. He went up to him quietly, undetected, and without greeting him placed his hand on a clammy shoulder.

"Is something the matter?" he asked. "We missed you today."

Adnan gave a start and looked behind him. "Hello, Hisham," he said in a near whisper before returning to his work, his hand trembling. "I had an urge to paint, that's all." Hisham remained standing as he tried to work out what his friend was painting, and Adnan avoided his gaze. There was a short silence before Adnan spoke again, without interrupting his painting this time. "Damn this place," he said, as though talking to himself, "it's so pokey. I'm going to build myself a nice big den on the roof where no one will disturb me."

Another silence. All the while Hisham had been pretending to be calm. Perhaps Adnan would bring up the subject himself without his having to ask. But he continued painting without uttering another word, and eventually Hisham lost patience. "Adnan," he said, "I want to talk to you, if you don't mind."

"Sorry," replied Adnan, without stopping what he was doing, "I really want to paint."

Hisham, at the end of his tether, laid his hand on his friend's shoulder. "I won't take up much of your time," he said, trying to control his voice so as not to betray anger at the insult. "No more than five minutes."

The two friends' eyes met; Adnan put down his brush, resigned. "Just a minute while I get dressed," he said.

"Fine, I'll wait for you outside." As Hisham went out Adnan headed into the main part of the house, shaking his head.

They set off for Sheikh Mousa's mosque, which was completely empty at this hour, immediately after the sunset prayers; even Sheikh Mousa himself, who usually spent this time of day in the hostel he had set up for wayfarers, was not to be found.

They sat down near the pulpit. "What did you two get up to yesterday?" Hisham asked without any introduction, his voice tense. "You and that ... Mansur?"

"How do you know we met? Were you spying on me?"

Hisham snorted. "Spying on you?" he said with heavy sarcasm, "Why would I spy on someone like you? You told me yourself. And anyway, I know lots of things you don't." With this last sentence Hisham looked at Adnan out of the corner of his eye, giving him an impression of importance and secrecy.

"We didn't get up to anything," said Adnan, bowing his head. "I met him by the municipal park in the afternoon, we talked for a bit and then went our separate ways."

'You've learned to lie quickly, Adnan,' Hisham said to himself. "That's not true," he said firmly. "You got on a bus. Where did you go?"

Adnan opened his eyes wide. "So you *were* spying on us!"

"That doesn't matter now," Hisham snapped, waving his hand in the air. "Where did you go?"

"We went to a house in the village," Adnan stammered. "There were two other people there. We talked for a while, and then he gave me a few books and I came back." Adnan paused for a moment before going on, "I shouldn't really be telling you any of this. That's what Comrade Ja'far – I mean, Mansur – gave me to understand."

So that was the monkey's movement name, Hisham said to himself. "The village?" he asked. "What village?"

"It's near Qatif. Mansur lives there."

"Never mind. The main thing is, why are you trying to avoid me? Aren't I your friend?"

"I'm not avoiding you. You're imagining things."

"Imagining things?" Hisham snorted. "You'll be telling me you think I'm crazy in a minute."

Adnan cleared his throat nervously. "The truth," he said, trembling, "the truth … the truth is that he told me to cut off all contact with you. There must be no friendship outside the work of the organisation. There would be security implications. That's what Mansur told me."

'To hell with you and Mansur *and* the organisation,' Hisham thought. "Sod you, Adnan," he said. "Do you obey everyone who tells you to do something? We've been friends since we were children! Would you sacrifice all that for anything?"

"I really don't know who to listen to and who not to," Adnan said, extremely agitated.

Hisham got up and laughed bitterly. "Do whatever you think best, Adnan," he said. "He asked me to do the same thing, but I put our relationship above all other considerations. But it looks like you're not worthy of it." He hurried out of the mosque. Adnan wanted to catch up with his friend but decided against it; he felt a strong impulse to chase after Hisham, but something held him back and he remained sitting where he was until people started to arrive at the mosque. At that point he returned to his house, the studio, his paintbrushes and his picture.

❧ 37 ❦

During the days that followed, Hisham kept out of Adnan's way completely; in fact, he ignored him as though Adnan did not exist. Hisham could tolerate anything except humiliation (real or imagined), and he felt he had been put in that position by someone he regarded as one of his 'possessions'. Hisham was trying to tell him, 'I'm the one cutting off contact with you of my own accord; I'm the one who makes the decisions, and we'll see who misses whom. We'll see who needs whom. I hope that arsehole Mansur does you good.'

After only a few days had passed, Adnan gradually began to approach him again. Sometimes he would greet him with a grin; other times he would sit next to him during break as they had always done. But Hisham was determined to avoid him. No sooner would Adnan sit next to him than he would get up and walk away, and he never returned any of Adnan's greetings. Even when Adnan came to the gang meetings Hisham would keep his distance, shunning him conspicuously to the point where the others noticed this unusual behaviour and tried to patch things up, insisting that whatever they had fallen out over should not be allowed to come in the way of a friendship like theirs. But Hisham tried to convince them that there had been no estrangement or disagreement and that he was simply tied up with other things that were on his mind; though he did begin treating Adnan more warmly in front of the gang while maintaining his distance at other times.

This was as much as Adnan could bear. Relationships with his comrades were no substitute for his friendship with Hisham. With them he could not discuss his worries and feelings, whereas in Hisham he used to find sanctuary, a refuge from the chronic tensions of a household shared with his father and brother. He missed Hisham's interest in his pictures and way of painting, and came to feel desperately lonely. He needed encouragement and praise, things he only ever got from Hisham.

One day, while Hisham was sitting in his usual place during the break, Adnan came up and sat down beside him. Hisham was about to get up, but Adnan pulled him by the elbow.

"Hisham, I'm sorry," he said. "I could bear losing anything except you. I'm sorry ..." And he began to cry.

Hisham looked at him, and all feelings of hatred vanished in an instant. "I knew our friendship came before everything else," he said with tremendous affection. He leaned towards his friend and they embraced.

"You know I only joined the organisation for you," Adnan said wretchedly after they had separated. With that they got up and headed to the classroom hand-in-hand, as the ringing bell marked the end of the break – and the end of their estrangement.

Adnan's apology restored Hisham's feelings of superiority and importance. He felt as though he had recovered something that had been stolen from him, and in his mind that represented a victory over Mansur and Fahd and the whole organisation: he was stronger than them all. He had defeated them in the end, and they and their orders could go to hell.

❧ 38 ❧

During the course of the next few days the region was rocked by a series of momentous events. In Libya a military coup deposed King Idris al-Sanusi, and a republic was proclaimed. It was apparent, through the slogans they used and the principles they declared, that those behind the coup were of Nasserite leaning; Egypt followed with swift recognition of the revolutionary regime. The identity of this 'Libyan Nasser' was not yet known, but there was no doubt that the conspirators were Nasserites.

The next session of the cell following these events was devoted to a discussion of them in order to define the party's position. Fahd went through the usual formalities and opened the session, saying:

"Comrades, we all know about the events that have occurred in Libya. The leadership wishes to ascertain your opinions so that the party may reach a clear position. What are your views?"

There was a short silence, before Comrade Hudaijan spoke up. "I'm wholeheartedly behind the revolution," he said. "It's a revolution against colonialism, imperialism and exploitation, and we must support it with all our might. The revolution will reinforce the progressive forces in the Arabian Peninsula and throughout the Arab nation. I'm with it unreservedly."

Comrade Hasan al-Sabah was next to speak. "But it's obvious that the people behind the revolution are Nasserites, and that will only lead to the strengthening of Nasser, especially given that Libya borders Egypt and has vast oil reserves."

"And what's so bad about that?" asked Comrade Hudaijan, excitedly.

"What's so bad about that," said Comrade Hasan al-Sabah with a flickering smile, "is that Nasser's strength means the party's weakness, because it won't have the resources that Nasser will."

"But the party has been in power in Iraq since the July Revolution; that's a rich country with unlimited resources –"

"I'd like to correct you on one point, Comrade Hudaijan," interrupted Fahd, sharply. "Those in power in Iraq are not the party. They're a pack of opportunists and reactionary traitors with no relation whatsoever to the great revolutionary party. As we already discussed last year, when the movement of reactionary traitors was formed in Iraq. But it appears you have a short memory, comrade, or else you haven't taken in the principles of the party."

Hudaijan lowered his gaze and bowed his head silently. Once Fahd was quite sure that the message had got through he calmed down. "Traitors to the party who nominally belong to it are more dangerous than those who are openly hostile to it," he said.

"You're right, comrade," said Hasan al-Sabah. "And anyway, I don't trust military adventurers and their coups … unless they belong to an organised party.".

"That's true," said Fahd, "but we mustn't forget that the only way revolution will ever come about in the Arab nation is through the army. There's no possibility of a popular revolution happening here as in France, Russia or China. The army is the vanguard and all our hopes are pinned on it, as long as it belongs to a genuinely progressive party; and the only one in the Arab nation is our party and our movement, the movement of the Arab awakening."

Hisham and Abu Dharr had been silently following these remarks, when suddenly Fahd turned to Hisham.

"Comrade Abu Huraira," he said, "we haven't heard your opinion yet."

Hisham nodded. "The truth is that any movement opposed to colonialism, imperialism and oppression is a genuine revolution we must support, regardless of whomever's behind it and their political leanings," he said. "And anyway, it's better to have Libya governed by Nasserites than for it to remain under the control of imperialists and their reactionary traitor henchmen."

"You're wrong, comrade," snapped Hasan al-Sabah, raising his voice a little. "That's a naive attitude. It's better for the party that colonialism and its agents *do* remain." He leaned forward, his prominent ears seeming to stick out even further and his eyes bulging as he pointed his finger at Hisham. "Colonialism and its servants are an overt enemy that the party can rally the revolutionary masses and their leadership against. But now! Now the enemy is a covert one, because the party cannot oppose a movement that claims to be revolutionary, progressive and pan-Arabist while in reality it's the opposite." Hasan al-Sabah fell silent and sat back with a faint smile on his lips.

Hisham was insulted by the description of his attitude as naive, but remained calm.

"And how do you know that the movement in Libya isn't genuinely revolutionary and progressive?" he asked.

"That's another naive point, comrade. It's perfectly clear. There's only one revolutionary party in the Arab nation and only one progressive movement: our own. Anything else is different, without question. Do you understand that, comrade?"

Hisham's face turned blood red; he felt the volcano erupting inside him and would have liked to slap this insolent wretch who was piling insult upon insult. But he kept his composure and was just about to reply when Abu Dharr broke in, saying,

"I agree with Comrade Abu Huraira. Every revolution against injustice and oppression is part of the Arab revolutionary movement, whoever's behind it."

"The party and the movement – our principles and ideals – are a means to an end, not the other way round," remarked Hudaijan. "If it can be shown that a certain movement really serves the things we believe in, why don't we support it, regardless of the name of the party behind it?" He smiled briefly at Hisham and Abu Dharr as he spoke, and Hisham reciprocated warmly. He had always liked Comrade Hudaijan, as much as he had loathed Hasan al-Sabah and Fahd since first setting eyes on them. Fahd, meanwhile, followed the exchanges with close attention.

"You must be aware, comrades," said Fahd, "that the party comes before everything."

"Even our principles?" asked Hudaijan.

"The party is our principles, comrade. Without it, there *are* no principles," came Fahd's stern reply, bringing the discussion to an end. The session continued for a while longer as Fahd read out some internal party directives. Then he asked the comrades to write an analysis of regional events for delivery to the provincial leadership, which would adopt a position accordingly and report in turn to the national leadership; thus would the party's position be defined at the level of the Arab nation as a whole. Comrade Fahd added that this was genuine democracy, and went on to attack "bourgeois democracy" as false class consciousness and an expression of bourgeois interests alone.

❧ 39 ❧

When Hisham left the session on that hot, humid September day, he considered going up to al-Hubb Street and hanging around there for a while before going home, as he had no desire to see the gang that day. He began wandering about in no particular direction, peeking at women's large behinds in the market as they swayed to and fro with the slightest movement, their erotic lines clear beneath the folds of wraps pulled tightly around their bodies. He looked at the shops selling fabric and women's items, especially underwear and nightdresses, until he ended up at a café near Thamantash Street. It was a small place where labourers, unemployed people and loafers were sitting and drinking tea with milk, eating sandwiches filled with egg, tomato and red pepper or cheese with watermelon jam.

The only times Hisham could remember having been to a café had been during the Eid festivals, when he and Adnan would go to al-Khobar and eat in a restaurant on Prince Khalid or al-Suwaiqat Streets, then sit in a café and have coffee with milk as part of their Eid celebrations. When he was in Syria or Jordan during the summer he would often sit with his father in the cafés in al-Midan and al-Marja in Damascus, and Ras al-Ayn, Misdar Hill and King

Talal Street in Amman. There his father would spend time with old *aqilat* friends, smoking hookah pipes and talking, while Hisham enjoyed a coconut milk drink and sometimes a plate of Nablus *kunafa* or *harisa* decorated with almonds. Apart from those occasions, his experience encompassed only school, the gang, his room and, now, the organisation.

Hisham was just about to turn into Thamantash Street on his way home when he happened to notice Hudaijan and Abu Dharr sitting in the café. They noticed him as well, and smiles were exchanged all round. Hisham continued on his way, but soon felt someone pulling him by the shoulder and saying, "Please join us, brother; you must have something to drink with us. If that's all right with you, that is." It was Hudaijan, who gave him no time to think about it, dragging him into the café by his arm and sitting him down in the chair where he had been sitting and then drawing up another one for himself.

"So," Hudaijan cried, clapping his hands, "what'll it be? A tea, or something cold?"

"Tea ... tea, please," Hisham stammered in reply. The word 'brother' that Hudaijan had used when calling out to him was still ringing in his ears; he had almost forgotten it of late, instead having got used to 'comrade', a word that had made him laugh when he first heard it but which had since come to repel and then finally frighten him. Hudaijan was wearing the same clothes as always: a black suit – this despite the heat and the humidity – with a white shirt and black sandals without socks. Abu Dharr was dressed like Hisham, in a white robe and plastic sandals. Hisham did not know how Hudaijan could bear such clothes in such suffocating weather: from late May to mid-October, the weather in Dammam was unbearable. The rest of the year it was lovely, except for a few days in January and February when the cold could be bitter.

The waiter brought tea in a glass with marks all over it just as Hisham was trying to swat away the flies buzzing incessantly around his face. The tea had been mixed with condensed milk and a lot of sugar that had settled at the bottom of the glass. Hisham preferred his tea with only a little sugar and no milk, but he began drinking it without objection while Hudaijan munched an egg sandwich and drank a Coca-Cola and Abu Dharr sipped a glass of 'Super' orange. They all simultaneously fought off the flies, so determined, it seemed, to irritate them as much as possible by stubbornly sticking to their clammy skin.

It was evident to Hisham that Hudaijan and Abu Dharr knew each other from outside the organisation, as they had been talking and laughing together in confidence when he first noticed them. Hudaijan swallowed the last bite of his sandwich and swigged a big gulp of Coke.

"Let me introduce myself," he said, trying to swallow at the same time. "I'm Marzuq Ibn Didani al-Mitrani. And this," he went on, nodding at Abu Dharr, "is my friend Zaki Baqir Abd al-Nabi."

He fell silent, looking at Hisham meaningfully and narrowing his small eyes as he finished his drink. Hisham realised that he was inviting him to identify himself in turn.

"I'm Hisham Ibrahim al-Abir," he said without hesitating. "I'm in secondary school."

"We work at the Dutch bank ABN in al-Khobar," said Hudaijan. "We come here afterwards, you know …" He broke off and looked around before continuing, "to pass the time while we're waiting for the minibus home."

Throughout all of this Abu Dharr was extremely tense, and the anger on his face was quite obvious as he looked at Hudaijan. But the latter paid no attention.

"I'm from the al-Artawiyya settlement; you must know of it if you've heard of Ibn Dawish. I'm sure you do," said Hudaijan, his eyes glowing with pride at the mention of the tribal leader and rebel against Ibn Saud, founder of the Saudi kingdom. "I was born there, but my father came to the Eastern Province when I was going on five years old to work for Aramco in oil drilling and exploration."

Hudaijan raised his empty glass to his lips, in search of any drop of Coke that might be left, then set the glass back down in the table, smacking his lips audibly.

"I left school after getting my middle school qualifications to work in the bank," he said. "But I go to evening classes. When I get my high school diploma I'm going to leave my job at the bank and go to military training college; I want to be an officer."

Hudaijan fell silent as Hisham watched him inquisitively and Abu Dharr looked on, still obviously angry. "Waiter, bring us another cold drink," Hudaijan called out, clapping his hands again. "Will you two have anything?" he asked, looking at the others. They both shook their heads. Abu Dharr frowned and leaned back, folding his hands over his chest.

"And what about you?" said Hudaijan, crossing his legs and sitting back with his hands behind his neck. "From your accent it sounds like you're from Qusaim."

"True," said Hisham. "My father's from Qusaim, but I was born and brought up here. So I'm really an Easterner," he added with a brief smile.

"But the way you talk makes you sound like you've just moved here from Qusaim. You don't use a single word of the Eastern Province dialect."

"Says you with your Dammam accent! The first time I heard you I thought you were fresh from the depths of the Empty Quarter." They both laughed, and a faint smile even tried to make its way even onto Abu Dharr's lips.

"They say people from Qusaim never change," said Hudaijan, grinning with his white teeth showing. "Wherever they are, their accent and their customs stay just the same. And as traders they're always moving from place to place, so much so that some people call them the Jews of Nejd," he added, laughing.

"Why not say the Jews of the Peninsula?" said Hisham, laughing along. But Hudaijan shook his finger.

"No, no; that title's reserved for Yemenis from Hadhramawt."

They all laughed again, including Abu Dharr this time, who got up when their laughter had died down. "I'll go on ahead to the bus stop," he said, looking at Hudaijan. "Don't be long." And he slipped out of the café and disappeared down al-Hubb Street.

The other two remained silent for a moment as they looked towards the door of the café, and then Hisham said, "What about your friend? He is your friend, isn't he?"

"Yes," said Hudaijan causally. "I met him at the bank. He's a good-natured guy and kind, too, but he's extremely suspicious and he won't trust anyone easily. Once he does come to trust someone, they'll find him the gentlest soul alive." Hudaijan paused to finish his Coke in one gulp. "He's from Safwa," he continued, burping. "His family lives in Rahima, and he comes to evening classes with me. He wants to get a degree in accounting and business administration. I mustn't be late or he'll get even angrier with me," he added quickly as he got up. "Waiter, the bill please," he called out. But Hisham refused to let him pay, and Hudaijan left hastily and vanished among the women and labourers on al-Hubb Street.

After that they saw one another again on a personal level, meeting up on the beach nearby after the cell sessions, not far from the Imara building. The beach was a peaceful place far away from the crowds and noise. At that time of year a foul smell rose from the sea where the water mixed with sewage and rubbish, but one got used to it and the sea was still beautiful despite everything. At first it was only Hisham and Marzuq who would meet, but later they were joined by Zaki, who really was quite different from Hisham's first impression in the café: he was mild-mannered and gentle, and altogether unlike the Abu Dharr Hisham saw in the cell. The three of them would meet on the beach after sunset, sit and stretch out, shoeless, facing the sea. Then they would begin to talk about anything and everything, albeit most of the time about politics. Hisham found out from Marzuq that Zaki had reproached him for the way he had behaved in the café that day, but Zaki was later to feel extremely glad about what he called the "happy coincidence" that had led him get to a new friend. Friendship was the highest form of relationship, as he later put it when speaking of the bond between them.

From his new friends Hisham also learned the real names of the other comrades in his cell: Fahd was Farid al-Madrasi, an employee of the National Commercial Bank in Dammam, and Hasan al-Sabah was Muwafiq al-Mijari, a secondary school pupil. Hisham was astonished that they knew their comrades' real names, but Zaki explained that he had known Farid before joining the party through his job at the bank and from the fact that he was always going to Dammam on business connected with the bank where Farid worked. It was Farid who had brought Zaki into the party, just as it was Zaki who had later introduced Marzuq to it. As for Muwafiq, he had discovered his name on a party day trip to a nearby farm, during which it was impossible to keep using everyone's movement names for the duration of the trip. Hisham was surprised that Zaki and Marzuq, who had been friends before joining the party, had been allowed to belong to the same cell, and for that matter Fahd, who had known Zaki beforehand; this was contrary to security regulations. They both laughed at Hisham's naivete. Zaki explained that things were not exactly as Hisham imagined. When he had brought Marzuq into the organisation it had been through the Union, and only later did Marzuq join the party at the rank of Auxiliary; it had been coincidence alone that had brought them together in the same cell.

The meetings of the three comrades on the beach were a source of renewed anxiety for Hisham. The information they gave revealed just how false were the impressions he had previously formed about the party. It was not as large as he had imagined if it was small enough for Zaki and Marzuq to meet in the same cell, and it was marked by sufficient laxity to organise a group trip for its members during which they all got to know each other, throwing security regulations out the window. What did that mean, if not foolishness and a disregard for the fate of people who had put their trust in the organisation and its principles – or even an actual lack of faith in those same principles, a recklessness which might bring untold consequences? This new worry was mixed with revulsion, and Hisham began to think seriously about leaving the organisation before certain disaster struck.

❧ 40 ❦

Hisham produced the report that was required of him about the situation in the Arab nation following the Libyan September movement. He tried to make it as scientific as possible, drawing heavily on Marxist-Leninist analysis. Notwithstanding the anxiety and disgust that had gripped him of late, he tried diligently to make his analysis unique, imagining at times that he would become an inspector for the party – a highly attractive idea to him despite everything. In reality, what he wrote was simply a reworking of views he had expressed before, supported by quotations from Marx – in particular his work *The Eighteenth Brumaire of Louis Bonaparte*; Engels's *Anti-Dühring*; Lenin's *Imperialism, the Highest Stage of Capitalism*; *Socialism and Man in Cuba* by Guevara; Regis Debray's *A Revolution in the Revolution*; Frantz Fanon's *The Wretched of the Earth*; plus various extracts from the *Quotations from Chairman Mao Tse-Tung* and the speeches of Ho Chi Minh and Castro. He was showing off the breadth of learning he was so proud of, and felt confident that the party would respect him for it and give him the position he deserved.

At the next meeting the comrades read out their reports, none of which were on the same level as Hisham's, who felt the utmost pride as he read out his own weighty, scientific analysis while Hudaijan and Abu Dharr looked on with admiration. Hasan al-Sabah stared and shook his head in disagreement from time to time, while Fahd watched and listened without making any movement other than to drag on his cigarette and drink his lukewarm tea impassively. When Hisham finished reading out his report he folded it and handed it to Fahd, looking round at the faces of his comrades with pride in his eyes.

Fahd took the report and put it to one side. "We, Comrade Abu Huraira, do believe in Marxist philosophy, but we are not Communists. I think you've read the Theoretical Principles of the Sixth National Conference and understand the difference between believing in Marxist philosophy and being a Communist, and believing in it and being a Baathist Arab nationalist." Fahd paused to light another cigarette and take another sip of tea before going on, briefly suppressing a cough. "No one who read your report would have the slightest doubt that you were a Communist. Where are the writings of Ali Salih al-Saadi or Elias Farah in your analysis? First and foremost you are a Baathist, and you must always have the Baath in sight." As Fahd stopped speaking, Hasan al-Sabah's eyes were shining with a message Hisham could not fail to understand. Fahd then continued with the rest of the session, but Hisham was oblivious. He was filled with utmost frustration, anger and hatred for the party and everyone else present, even Hudaijan and Abu Dharr.

❧ 41 ❧

Fahd brought two pamphlets to the next weekly meeting of the cell; both dealt with the events in Libya and the party's position regarding them, but one was intended for circulation within the organisation and the other for public distribution. The content of the first document went no further than the view already put forth by Hasan al-Sabah and was signed in the name of the party. The second one was signed in the name of the Students' Union; its content was the same as the opinion expressed by Hisham, Hudaijan and Abu Dharr, minus Hisham's Marxist analysis. Fahd read out both pamphlets and informed them that the first was secret and for internal consumption only, while the second would be handed out to the people.

"But Comrade Fahd," said Hudaijan, unable to hold back, "which of the two expresses our position? They're almost contradictory; the first says we should deal cautiously with the Libyan revolution and the extension of Nasser's influence, and the second offers unlimited support to the revolution. What's our real position, comrade?"

Fahd laughed, exhaling cigarette smoke through the gaps between his teeth. "You're not practised in the ways of the struggle yet, comrade," he said. "Not all positions are stated openly and broadcast far and wide. Our genuine position is the one laid out in the party's pamphlet; the union's pamphlet is for the masses."

Fahd fell silent after taking a greedy drag on his cigarette and looked at Hudaijan through half-closed eyes. Hisham was overcome with tension. He had learned the art of deceit and how to lie quite coolly and innocently, and that had become part of the struggle and covert activity; but what about hypocrisy? If this practice was not implicit hypocrisy, what was it? Even though lately he had come to care little about what was said or discussed in the cell, he could not contain himself. As he spoke he tried to keep his voice calm, but he did not succeed and his anger was audible. "Why don't we tell the masses our real position, comrade? I can't defend two contradictory positions. For that matter, I can't even take in two contradictory positions."

Fahd laughed again. "You're still new to the struggle, comrade," he said. "And anyway, isn't contradiction the essence of the Marxism you believe in?" He laughed again. Hasan al-Sabah broke in, saying, "Comrade Abu Huraira, the question is –"

"Sorry, comrade," Hisham said, interrupting him sharply, "but there's someone sitting here who's responsible and he's the one I'm talking to and the one I want an answer from."

Hasan al-Sabah shrank back into his corner, looking round at Fahd and the other comrades.

"Generally speaking what you say is correct, comrade," said Fahd. "But there are special circumstances to the struggle. The masses sympathise with Nasser and support whatever he does; they have a false consciousness and all we can do is to go along with them in order to lead and direct them, until the opportunity arises when we can express our genuine position which is in the interests of the masses, even if they are unaware of their own interests themselves. You know enough about Marxist philosophy to understand the difference between true and false consciousness."

"So this is hypocrisy!" This last remark escaped from Hudaijan, and Fahd smiled ironically.

"Call it what you like," he said, "but such moral standards don't apply to the work of the struggle or political activity in general. Even states don't do as they say, or say as they do."

"But we're not a state," said Hisham tersely, working up to a fervent pitch, "we're people with principles, and the masses should know that. That's when they'll respect us, with a respect based on morals, and not on evasion."

"No, comrade, we're not a state," Fahd replied severely, "but we will be." He paused before continuing. "And in order to achieve that we have to do things you don't like, and leave morals to prophets and philosophers. Read Lenin's *What Is to Be Done?* to learn about struggle."

"You mean politics."

"There's no difference. They amount to the same thing. Read the book and you'll discover the difference between the struggle and utopian dreams," Fahd said, trying to bring the discussion to an end by shuffling the papers in front of him. But Hisham was not pacified.

"I've read Lenin and others, but what you're saying is straight out of Machiavelli, not Lenin. If we become a state like that, what will be the difference between us and any other state we disagree with?"

Fahd exhaled smoke with exasperation. "We have different aims and principles that we want to apply, aims for the Arab nation and the masses. That's the difference, comrade."

"And is it for the good of the nation that we lie to it from the outset?"

"It's not like that. When we have a state things will change."

"If that's what we do when we're freedom fighters, how will it be when we're politicians?"

"This is the problem with intellectuals," Fahd groaned loudly to the other comrades, "they're not suited to the struggle." Levelling his bloodshot eyes at Hisham, he went on angrily, "A lot of discussion and arguing is no good in the work of the organisation."

Hisham was about to retort, but Fahd stopped him with an abrupt wave of his hand. "You should be aware, comrade, that you are not in a debating society," he said quickly, practically spitting as he spoke. "The important thing in the organisation is putting things into practice, not discussing them. We've talked about everything before, and now it's time for implementation." He took a long drag on his cigarette. "And in order to demonstrate your commitment to the party and its decisions, it will be you who distributes the union's pamphlet at the school."

Hisham took this in with a shudder and felt a sharp cramp in his stomach. He was unable to speak as Fahd stared at him intently. Hasan al-Sabah was smiling ambiguously and Hudaijan and Abu Dharr looked at him blankly without comment.

"Tomorrow," Fahd said, "Comrade Khalid will call you and give you an envelope with the pamphlets in it, and you must distribute them in the pupils' desks. This is an order from the organisation, understood?"

Hisham, gripped by fear, gave no reply. He had not imagined that he would ever have to distribute pamphlets himself. As far as he was concerned, the organisation was simply a matter of turning up at the sessions and discussing things, but as for distributing pamphlets … The session ended without Hisham's taking in another word.

When he met Marzuq and Zaki on the beach his fear was quite apparent. They assured him that the matter could not be simpler, that there was no need to be so anxious, but he kept repeating, "I didn't join the organisation to distribute pamphlets that I don't even believe in."

These words touched something inside the other two. Marzuq's thoughts drifted off as he watched the reflection of the great red disc of the sun in its descent towards the waters of the Gulf. "We all feel like that, my friend … We all feel like that," he murmured, as though to himself. After a short silence he continued, "I hate the Americans. I learned to hate them from my father, who was treated badly by Aramco; that's why I joined the organisation. I love Nasser," he added, laughing bitterly, "and my father does, too. Have I ended up fighting him?" He began to laugh harder; Zaki looked at him wretchedly and said in a faint voice, "I was always against the class system, ever since I first became aware of it in our village. My father was a *nakhlawi*; he'd get up at dawn and go to work on the farm till dusk, and then when the dates were ripe he'd take most of them to his master, and all that was left for us was what the master didn't want. The best dates and almonds and spring onions and other vegetables always went to him. I don't care about the Baath or Nasser or Libya," he said with a wry smile. "What I care about is justice; that's why I joined the organisation. And it looks like I took the wrong way." All three of them fell silent, watching the sun go down towards the sea and turning blood red for a few minutes before the armies of darkness began their advance.

❧ 42 ❧

"The ionic bond between two particles is formed as a result of one of the particles losing one or more of its electrons and the other particle gaining one or more electrons …" Mr Wasfi was giving a chemistry lesson when the classroom door suddenly opened and Rashid Abd al-Jabbar put his head round, with his wide, exaggerated grin and his big moustache, asking the teacher's permission to call out one of the pupils. The teacher paused reluctantly and looked at his watch. there were only about ten minutes of the lesson to go. Hisham realised he was the one concerned and once again felt the old pain in his stomach.

"Hisham Ibrahim al-Abir, wanted in the headmaster's office," Rashid called out, looking at the class. Hisham heaved himself to his feet and made his way past the teacher, asking if he could leave.

"What is it with you and the headmaster, Hisham?" Mr Wasfi asked in astonishment, but Hisham simply waved his hand, tightening his lip and raising his eyebrows without saying a word or stopping in his tracks.

Outside in the empty corridor Rashid took out a large school envelope and quickly shoved it at Hisham, saying hurriedly, "Distribute them during the break, one in every desk," before dashing off back to the office. As Hisham took the envelope he felt a shiver pass through his entire body; he slipped it under his vest next to his skin and retraced his steps to the classroom, feeling dizzy and breaking into a sweat.

When he opened the classroom door the bell was ringing, marking the end of the lesson and the beginning of the break. Mr Wasfi was gathering up his papers and stuffing them into his case, while the pupils were noisily crowding around the doorway. Hisham remained outside without moving until most of the pupils had left; then Mr Wasfi passed him and gave him a genuine smile; Hisham tried to return it, but could only force a feeble expression to his lips similar to a smile and yet manifestly not one. Mansur came out after the teacher, also smiling, but Hisham looked at him indifferently as a wave of nausea swept over him. As he entered the classroom he almost bumped into Adnan, the last person to leave. He told Adnan he was sorry but he could not go with him to have something to eat, saying that he had a headache and would rather rest for a while in the classroom before the next lesson began. Adnan tried to find out from him why the headmaster had summoned him, but Hisham managed to brush him off, saying he could not speak because of his headache and promising to meet him in their usual place once he had had a chance to relax for a bit.

At last the classrooms were completely empty of pupils. Hisham's heart raced. He was almost paralysed with terror, about to do something that could land him in prison.

Finally he removed the envelope from under his vest and opened it with a trembling hand. It contained a collection of fine, translucent pieces of paper printed in poor blue ink. Hisham put a pamphlet in his own desk first of all, then Adnan's and Mansur's, then the rest. He moved on to the other classrooms, casting glances sharply in all directions, his nausea almost overwhelming. He opened the first desk in the classroom next to his and deposited a pamphlet, then the next, and so on until he completed that room.

But when he got to the next classroom he suddenly lost his nerve and could no longer control himself; his hands shook violently, the perspiration flowed and the dizziness accelerated so that he felt about to faint. Then his body went strangely cold. Hisham grabbed a handful of pamphlets and threw them up in the air, scattering them in all directions. He did the same thing in the remaining classrooms, and when he had got rid of the last bunch he felt an enormous sense of relief. He threw the envelope in the nearest bin he could find and shot off down the staircase to the courtyard.

As Hisham trotted down the first steps he looked back impulsively and got a terrible fright: someone was coming out of the lavatory at the end of the corridor, near the headmaster's office. The terror returned in an instant. Someone had seen him, he knew; someone must have been spying on him. The image of his mother appeared before his eyes, weeping from beyond some rusty steel bars, and he nearly collapsed. He managed to regain composure and hurried down to hide under the stairs: he had to know who the spy was. In fact, he did not have to wait long, as the sound of flip-flops slapping against the soles of someone's feet came nearer. Hisham shrunk back, trying to conceal himself completely, and then his 'shadow' appeared, looking nervously in every direction before hastily making his way out into the courtyard. Fury and disgust quickly took the place of fear as he made out the features Comrade Hasan Al-Sabah, aka Muwafiq al-Mijari, spy.

By the time Hisham reached Adnan he had calmed down a little. Adnan had finished his own food and put his friend's and a glass of Coke to one side. Hisham began chewing his sandwich mechanically, staring into the distance at Muwafiq, who was laughing with one of the other pupils and looking at Hisham in what seemed a peculiar way.

❧ 43 ❧

The pupils' discovery of the pamphlets did not provoke any unusual reactions; pamphlets were an ordinary occurrence those days, like the numerous organisations to be found everywhere. Before joining the party Hisham himself had read pamphlets from the 'National Liberation Front', the 'Arabian Peninsula People's Union' and the 'Democratic Front', whose pamphlets he had been accused of distributing by the headmaster. The strongest reaction this time came from the headmaster's office, which found itself in an unenviable position particularly, as Rashid told Hisham ecstatically a while later, since the Secret Police had become involved in the matter and had reprimanded the headmaster for his inability to control the school in an official letter couched in the severest terms.

The headmaster began summoning many of the pupils to his office, particularly those who had been active in the bulletins and extra-curricular societies, but spared Hisham. He had stopped contributing to the papers some time ago and took part in the history society solely out of loyalty to the memory of his departed teacher. He was afraid of being summoned, however, as this time he was guilty, and did not know how he would be able to face the headmaster; his nerve might fail him and expose his involvement in the affair. But time went by and still he was not summoned. With each passing day he felt an ever greater sense of relief, dogged by anxiety though he was, especially after Rashid told him they had recruited a number of spies among the pupils at the school. It was then that Hisham stopped going even to the history society gatherings.

At the first meeting of the cell after the pamphlets had been distributed, Fahd reproached Hisham for his panicked method of pamphlet distribution. Hisham was not surprised, having caught Hasan al-Sabah spying on him, but he tried to defend himself nonetheless.

"What difference does it make whether they were put in the desks or thrown in the air?" he said. "Isn't the important thing that they got into the hands of the people to tell them the truth?" As he uttered the last word, Hisham could not disguise the ring of sarcasm in his voice.

"You were ordered to do a specific thing in a specific way and you should have carried out that order as it was given, not as you saw fit," Fahd said, angrily. "I'm warning you for the last time against arguing about what you're instructed to do. On this occasion you have been let off, as it is the first time you have distributed pamphlets, but if it happens again you will be exposing yourself to punishment by the organisation."

Fahd shook his finger vigorously as he spoke, visibly agitated. Hisham felt a stab of genuine fear. For the first time he realised that all this went beyond debating principles and readings. But despite Fahd's threat, he managed to pluck up his courage and say,

"But Comrade Fahd, how do you know how I distributed the pamphlets?"

For the first time since the beginning of the session Fahd smiled, slyly. "We have our spies," he said. "Or did you think it would escape our notice?"

Hisham was silent. 'You have spies and they have spies,' he thought. 'It's all spies, spies and more spies.' He half-smiled at Hasan al-Sabah, who had bowed his head and was pretending to watch an ant struggling across the worn-out carpet with a grain of sugar.

❧ 44 ❧

When Hisham met Marzuq and Zaki on the beach that day he could not hold back his emotions, which burst out recklessly and unchecked. He erupted, voicing everything that had been pent up inside him, with no regard for caution. He told them about Hasan al-Sabah's spying, and how he had come to hate the organisation, which was no different from any government with all its security apparatus, the very things they said they were fighting against. He told them he was sick of the 'Act first, talk later' routine.

"What's the use in talking once something's been done?" he exploded. "What's the use in prevention once a disease has become incurable? Even after acting there's no discussion! It's more like 'Act first, then act again'. We're just a bunch of tools, no more and no less.

"What are we fighting for? I used to think the struggle was for principles and exalted aims, but day by day I discover that all we're fighting for is to replace one lot of people with another. What's the difference? Why don't the same people stay put, if it's all the same anyway? We're afraid of the Secret Police, but we don't realise that we've ended up working for another kind of Secret Police ourselves!"

Marzuq and Zaki listened quietly without comment. "I've become a professional liar and a hypocrite in the name of the struggle," Hisham burst out again after a short silence. "If this is the struggle, I want nothing of it, nothing." He began wiping his glasses with the corner of his robe; he was trembling violently and his broad forehead was glistening with sweat mingled with the damp sea air in the last rays of the sun.

Hisham felt a huge sense of relief after expressing the emotions that had been raging inside him. He filled his lungs with the sea air, tainted with the smell of dead fish and rubbish and yet somehow re-invigorating despite everything. Then he began to worry about the remarks he had come out with. He had only known these two for a short while, and who could tell what they might do? The organisation had changed the character of his friend Adnan, it had turned Hasan al-Sabah into a wretched spy and it had made even him write reports on other people, so what might it have done to these two comrades?

"I'm sorry," he said, trying to find a way out for himself, "I had to say something to get it all off my chest, and you two are the only ones I can do it with."

They both smiled. "Don't worry about it," said Marzuq, waving his hand. "I've got a lot of bitterness inside as well. Don't worry."

"So why don't we leave the organisation?" Hisham said, regretting his words as soon as they escaped him. "I mean, why don't we try to find a solution, any solution," he added, trying to mitigate the effect of his previous remark. "We can't keep going with things as they are."

There were still seeds of doubt in his mind. The organisation had taught him the 'virtue' of suspicion, though previously he had always assumed everyone to have good intentions. He had not once in his life experienced anything to make him change this belief, which he took for granted and by which he had always lived until he became a freedom fighter. It was then that many things had changed in his life, mostly unconsciously. Yet, he had never felt any affection towards Fahd or Hasan al-Sabah, from the first. Were relationships between people formed like those between chemical and physical elements as Mr Wasfi taught? Some elements attracted and others repelled one another, and there were some that were capable of joining to form molecules and others that were not. If people behaved likewise, that might also explain the notion of love at first sight that he had seen in films and read about in the novels of the Egyptian writers Ihsan Abd al-Quddus and Yousef al-Sibai.

"That wouldn't be a wise decision," said Zaki, commenting on Hisham's suggestion. "You don't know what they might do to you if you left the organisation. Do you really think they'd let you go just like that, with everything you know about them and their secrets? We've got to go on, until whatever God has decreed comes to pass."

Strange, noted Hisham, this was the first time he had heard God mentioned since joining the party. He often heard the word used everywhere else, except therein. Zaki's comment, though, struck a terrible fear into him. What could they really do if he decided to leave? But he did not want to think about it any more, and after the sun died down in the waters of the Gulf he got up and said goodbye to his comrades. All the way home, the phrase repeated itself over and over inside him, involuntarily: "Until whatever God has decreed comes to pass ... until whatever God has decreed comes to pass."

❧ 45 ❦

The organisation became just another part of Hisham's routine. He attended the meetings of the cell with no enthusiasm, staying out of the discussions and repeating the slogans robotically at the beginning and end of the sessions without any emotion or conviction. Lately they had let him off the hook a great deal, requiring nothing of him, whether writing reports or distributing pamphlets; Hasan al-Sabah had become the one they counted on for all that, in accordance with a decision taken by the leadership.

Soon even Hasan al-Sabah no longer came to the sessions, having been transferred to a different cell in another city, as Comrade Fahd gave them to understand. But in fact that was untrue: Muwafiq was still a pupil at the school, where occasionally Hisham saw him in the courtyard. Hisham surmised that Hasan al-Sabah must have been promoted in the organisational hierarchy for his loyalty and conviction. He was replaced by a new comrade, whose arrival was quite a surprise to Hisham: it was none other than his friend Adnan, known as 'Comrade Renoir'. Hisham had no idea when or how Adnan had become a party member, despite the fact that they saw one another every day, and so he was all the more jolted when he entered Fahd's house one day and found

Adnan sitting there. When Fahd introduced them to their new comrade he looked at Hisham with the trace of a smile on his lips, with a meaning Hisham thought he understood. Hisham kept his feelings to himself, but at that moment he hated Adnan and felt as though something had broken inside him that he could not quite identify.

Hisham's relationship with Marzuq and Zaki grew stronger as the days went by; they would visit each other in al-Khobar or Dammam, and spend time on the beach or sitting in one of the cafés on al-Hubb Street or the alleyways off Prince Khalid Street in al-Khobar. Once he invited them to Abd al-Karim's house and introduced them to his friends, including Adnan, and they all had a fun time. His friends had liked them and Abd al-Karim invited them to come again. They promised they would, but only did so on one other occasion, and that was the last his friends saw of them. (By that time things had happened to make Marzuq and Zaki decide against visiting again, and to make Hisham despise the organisation in general and Adnan in particular to the point of utter contempt.) At first his friends asked after them, but in time they were forgotten and the gang returned to the way it had always been, its harmony undisturbed.

It was during this period that two things happened which had a most profound effect on Hisham and caused him to loathe the organisation to the point of seriously considering resignation, come what may. Things couldn't get worse than they were already, he used to tell himself. One day he was standing in the corridor overlooking the school courtyard during break watching the other pupils come and go. He did not feel like eating or being with Adnan or anyone else; these days he found himself wanting to be alone more than ever before. Suddenly, while deep in thought, he felt someone pat him on the shoulder and a familiar voice say,

"What's up? Did the kids go without their supper last night?"

Hisham looked round and saw Mansur standing behind him with a smirk on his face as usual. "No," he said, smiling back. "I'm just a bit uptight, what with the exams around the corner, you know."

Mansur nodded. "I hope I'm not disturbing you?" he asked.

"Not at all, not at all," said Hisham. "What −" he hesitated, looking at Mansur directly. He was about to say 'What a pleasant surprise', but said instead, "What brings you here? Aren't we supposed not to meet?"

"True," said Mansur, "but I couldn't resist the urge to talk to you, especially when I saw you on your own and the place empty like this. Believe me, Hisham, I have a great deal of affection for you," he said, looking straight into Hisham's eyes, the emotion visible on his stern face.

"And I have a lot of respect for you, too," said Hisham, somewhat taken aback and saying to himself, 'No I don't; I detest you. What do you want? And what's this yarn you're spinning me about affection?' He felt a creeping suspicion about Mansur's intentions as he recalled his mother's advice against going around with people older than himself and his father's advice to steer clear of Shi'ites because they weren't trustworthy in their dealings with Sunnis. But he pushed these involuntary thoughts out of his mind, regarding them as prejudices unworthy of a young intellectual like himself. After all, he knew and liked Zaki and knew he was a Shi'ite, but there was a world of difference between him and this monkey Mansur.

"Have you started revising yet?" Hisham asked. "There are less than two months to go between now and the exams." It was just a question to put those black thoughts out of his head.

Mansur had leaned against the wall of the corridor and was looking into the distance with his hands tightly clasped. "Exams!" he said. "We've got a test of fate ahead that'll be much harder than any of that: the test of the revolution that's sure to come now, a test in which some people will be honoured and others humiliated ... Tomorrow," he continued after a pause, "tomorrow gallows will stretch from Jeddah to Dammam, from coast to coast." As he uttered these words he waved his fist in the air, and the expression on his face became even fiercer.

Hisham shuddered and looked around, afraid that someone might be eavesdropping. "Gallows!" he exclaimed. "Why?"

Mansur continued looking into the horizon. "For the enemies of the Arab nation, the Islamic people and mankind."

"Are there really that many of them, then?"

"The Islamic people will only become powerful and strong again when half of them are exterminated and the other half remain, the good half. They're rotten to the core. The bad limbs must be amputated if the body is to recover its health and well-being."

With this Mansur struck the wall as Hisham looked on in alarm, with a mixture of confusion, embarrassment and fear. "These are serious things you're saying, Mansur," he said. "Gallows! Blood! What kind of revolution is this you're talking about?"

Mansur looked at him with a faint smile. "The revolution of the enraged masses," he said. "There can be no revolution without blood. Lots of it."

"That's revenge, not revolution."

"Call it what you like, but it's what's got to happen. And it's what's going to happen, too."

Hisham was about to say something, but Mansur looked at him once more and said, "Your problem, Hisham, is that you're an idealist, a utopian. A sentimental intellectual. We need freedom fighters who aren't prisoners of their own emotions."

Hisham couldn't help smiling bitterly when he heard the words 'freedom fighter'.

"What would be left of life if we stripped it of all feeling and emotion?" he asked. "All its warmth, all its charm would be lost; life itself would be lost. There's nothing in the world worth all this violence and blood you're talking about," he said, catching his breath in the intensity of the moment. "You'd exterminate one half of the people for the sake of the other half! And how would you know that the half you'd finished off was the corrupt half? By what right would you make yourself judge and executioner? You might discover that half of the half that was left was also corrupt, and then you'd kill them, too, until not one member of your masses was left. Is this the revolution you're talking about? This isn't revolution, it's madness."

Mansur laughed with glee as he listened to Hisham. "What a pity, Hisham! What a pity." He wiped a tear from his eye once he had stopped laughing. "Didn't I say you were a utopian, whatever your claims to be a Marxist and a scientific socialist? Everything has a price, comrade, and the price of revolution is blood. Haven't you read Voltaire, where he says, 'The world will not be saved until the last bourgeois has been hanged with the guts of the last priest'? That's revolution, my dreamer friend."

Hisham smiled wanly. "Voltaire was a satirical philosopher. He intended those words as an ironic criticism, he didn't mean them literally."

"Life is a struggle, the class struggle. Or don't you believe that, for all your Marxist convictions?"

"The class struggle, yes. Class blood, no. I think you're the one who hasn't understood Marx."

"Not understood Marx!" said Mansur angrily, riled at Hisham's assumed superiority. "I've read all the writings of Lenin and Stalin."

"That's the problem."

"What?"

"Nothing. Nothing."

At that moment the bell rang and the first pupils began to appear at the top of the stairs on their way back from the courtyard. Mansur moved off, waving to Hisham and saying hurriedly,

"That day will come, you'll see. And I'll remind you of that."

"If you're in the good half, that is," replied Hisham once Mansur was out of earshot, and headed off to his classroom as Mansur went downstairs: it looked as though he was not going to the next lesson. Mr Naji had already entered the room and begun the Arabic lesson for the day by the time Hisham got there and asked his permission to come in.

Hisham felt a growing sense of dread following the conversation with Mansur, along with an aversion to everything connected with the organisation and its ideology. His close identification with Marxism remained, but to his mind there was a vast difference between the Marxism as found in *The Poverty of Philosophy*, *A Contribution to the Critique of Political Economy* and *The German Ideology*, and that espoused by the party's deeds and thoughts. But his repugnance towards the party grew with the unfolding of another event, which would remain long engraved on his heart before he was able to forget it; perhaps in reality he never did forget it, and it stayed tucked away in some unknown corner of his soul.

One day he was revising with Adnan, as they did every year before the exams. Hisham would snatch a few moments here and there to read Naguib Mahfouz's new novel, *Children of the Alley*, moments that were full of excitement and pleasure in the imaginary company of the book's characters. During one tea break, Hisham was immersed in the novel while Adnan rummaged through the books in his little bookcase. As he took one out, a thin piece of paper that had been folded up slipped out from between its pages. Adnan began reading it. When he finished he turned to Hisham, who was sitting on the floor, and held out the paper, saying, "Hisham, what's this?"

"Everything all right?" said Hisham blandly, slowly looking up from his book with an irritated expression. He recognised the paper as one of the party's pamphlets and went back to his novel, saying casually, "You know what it is."

Adnan refolded it and placed it on top of the desk. "But you know the orders," he said, still standing opposite Hisham. "We mustn't keep these sorts of things."

Hisham closed his book nervously. "God, are the party orders as sacred as the Ten Commandments or the Law of Muhammad?!" he lashed out. "And what right have you got to call me to account, anyway? You mind your own business! You can see I've got enough to worry about as it is!"

"We're friends," stammered Adnan, "and comrades. I just wanted to warn you, that's all."

Hisham jumped up, went to the desk and picked up his geology textbook. "You and the party and its orders can all go to hell," he barked, raising his voice. "Get out of my sight." He opened the book, but then began glancing at the door; he went over and opened it, peering into the main part of the house. Once he had checked that his mother was still in the other room in front of the television, which he could hear from where he was standing, he sat back down, reassured that no one could have overheard them. Adnan seemed deep in revision, having slunk into the chair opposite him and opened his biology textbook; red-faced, he stared at the book, clearly not reading. Hisham watched Adnan, who knew Hisham was looking at him but he pretended to be engrossed in revision. At that moment Hisham felt genuine contempt for Adnan, who he felt was weaker than he had imagined. While to a certain extent that satisfied him, it enraged him more.

Hisham's nerves calmed a little and he picked up the pamphlet, tore it up into little pieces and threw them into the wastepaper basket beside him. "There we are. That's got rid of the thing that was worrying you," he said quietly, trying to smile. "Are there any *other* orders?" He poured himself a cup of tea from the thermos next to him.

"You should have burned it," said Adnan without taking his eyes off his book, his voice somewhat agitated. "That's what the orders say."

Hisham got up again, spilling some tea on his robe before putting his cup down on the table. "Go to hell, Adnan," he said, shaking with anger. "What are you, some kind of sheep? How come all these years I never really knew you?"

Without saying anything Adnan gathered his books together and left the room on his way out of the house. Hisham did not bother to run after him; in fact, he felt glad Adnan had gone and he returned to his book.

At the next meeting of the cell, near the end of the session Fahd looked at Hisham calmly and said, "Comrade Abu Huraira, the leadership has learned of your recklessness and negligence, how you disobeyed orders and left a pamphlet in your house. We have every confidence in our comrades, which is why we entrust them with the pamphlets, which should either be distributed or burned."

For a while there was silence as Fahd lit a cigarette and gulped down a cup of tea, the others looking on in silence. Then Fahd continued impassively, "The leadership has decided to keep you in the rank of Auxiliary until you have demonstrated some self-discipline."

Hisham smiled involuntarily, and then quickly resumed a sullen expression, glancing at Comrade Renoir and sinking into silence until everyone began to leave one by one, Hisham last of all.

That day he did not go to the beach where Marzuq and Zaki were waiting, but straight home, his thoughts distracted all the way. He could not come to terms with the shock; his friend Adnan, betray him? He could never have imagined such a thing; he was unable to take in what had happened. That someone like Hasan al-Sabah would spy on him was understandable; there was nothing between them other than the comradeship of which he had grown so weary, but as for Adnan ... He felt a terrible pain in his throat and the urge to weep, but found he could not; the ache just stayed there. When he got home he went to his room and locked the door without greeting his mother and father, who were sitting in the television room. (They did not attempt to disturb him, having got used to such odd behaviour, attributing it to the ups and downs of youth.) Hisham picked up a novel by Balzac and tried to lose himself in the plot, but the image of Adnan would not leave him. He remained sitting on the floor staring at the first page, reading nothing, for a long time.

✤ 46 ✤

At Abd al-Karim's house the next day Hisham left immediately after Adnan arrived, as the rest of the gang looked on in surprise; but Hisham did not even bother to justify his departure. He could not bear Adnan's presence. He went into the street and began wandering in no particular direction; he had no desire to go home, but did not know where else to go. He thought of Noura; how he wished she were in his arms now, but how? He would have loved to be able to go to her house, knock on the door and say to her mother, "I need Noura, I want to see her," but that was obviously out of the question. Lately, during her milk deliveries, all he could get from her was a fleeting glance or a quick smile at the door from a distance, circumstances permitting; his mother now used to meet Noura and say goodbye to her at the door, since the day she had been surprised by their joint presence in the house upon her return from visiting the neighbours.

Hisham's mother trusted him implicitly, but that did not stop her watching over him to make sure that all doors through which the wind might blow were kept tightly shut. After he joined the party he began to imagine his mother as a member; she would be sure to succeed with her qualifications, perhaps rising to the leadership, even becoming its General Secretary. He would find these fantasies hugely amusing, but the image of his mother as she always was would return to his mind, pure love and severity rolled into one. The only way out left to him was to write Noura letters expressing his need for her. An idea occurred to him: he would write her a note arranging to meet her far from his mother's vigilance. Overjoyed at the thought, he ran home and began writing straight away.

That evening Hisham waited for her by the front door; when he saw her coming, he dropped his letter on the ground in front of the door and quickly returned to his room. He listened for his mother's usual goodbye – "Give my regards to your mother" – and realised that Noura now had his letter tucked away happily next to her breast. Hisham was ecstatic; he forgot all about Adnan and the party and Fahd and everything else, all that was left was Noura. His joy was was almost too much for his pounding heart to bear. He rifled through the books in his bookcase, took out *There's a Man in Our House* by Ihsan Abd al-Quddus and began re-reading it perhaps for the tenth time; but on this occasion Hisham transposed himself in the place of the hero Ibrahim and Noura as the heroine Nawal: different names, he thought, but the same love.

The next day he waited by the front door. As Noura approached, she dropped a piece of paper, which Hisham snatched up and waited until she had gone inside, then a little longer before quickly returning to his room, where he began reading breathlessly.

"Dear Hisham, I long for you. I wish I could spend my whole life before you, gazing at your face and rubbing against your chest. I, too, long to meet you, but you know I can't go out without permission or to any place my mother doesn't know. But I've got an idea: today, after my father gets back from evening prayers, he'll sit in front of the television for a while waiting for his supper and my mother will be in the kitchen. I'll leave the door to the

courtyard open and I'll be there waiting for you. Forever your darling, Noura."

Hisham lifted the letter to his nose and sniffed it eagerly, as though it were Noura herself; he was filled with joy, albeit a joy tinged with some anxiety at the adventure he was to embark on that night. For the first time in his life he was to enter a house without the knowledge of the family who lived there. The thought disturbed him, as well as the fearsome prospect of being found out; the ensuing scandal would be too much for his mother, he knew. But the prize for which he was risking all was great: it was Noura herself, and that was enough to overcome any doubts. The excitement, that pleasure mingled with fear and anxiety, was like a dish of *saliq* grain mixed with hot peppers: pleasure and pain together, the thrill of the combination.

Later that day, completely against habit, he attended evening prayers at the mosque near Noura's house where her father normally prayed. The mosque was hardly full, with only a few people there from the houses round about, so he was easily able to pick out Noura's father in the front row directly behind the imam. Hisham sat down to his right after scrupulously prostrating himself twice in deference to the mosque itself, then picked up a copy of the Qur'an and began reading a sura at random as he waited for the prayers to begin. Noura's father was reciting prayers and praising God in a murmur that was not quite audible. When prayers were over and most of those present had departed, Noura's father stayed behind for a while, performing the two final customary prostrations slowly and deliberately; Hisham did likewise. When Noura's father got up to leave, Hisham went up to him with a smile.

"Good evening, Abu Muhammad," he said. "May God hear your prayers."

Noura's father looked at him and smiled back. "Our prayers and yours, God willing," he replied. "How are you, my son?"

"I'm well, thank you." Hisham realised the man did not know who he was. "Do you not recognise me, Uncle? I'm Hisham, Ibrahim al-Abir's son. We're your neighbours."

"Yes, of course!" the man cried. "How's your father? Well, I hope? I haven't seen him for a long time."

"He is well, thanks be to God. Everyone has so much to do, Uncle. That's why no one ever gets to see anyone else."

"You're right, son. May God bring us all to a good end."

Walking along as they talked, they had drawn near Noura's house. Her father invited Hisham to join him for supper, but Hisham politely declined, explaining that he had to revise for his exams. Noura's father wished him success and guidance from God for every Muslim, before disappearing behind the iron gate of his house. Hisham continued walking a short distance until he was certain Noura's father had gone inside, then quietly retraced his steps. He was extremely hesitant, putting one foot forward, then one back; he was weighed down with guilt. This good man had prayed for him, little knowing that soon Hisham would be with his own daughter. Hisham almost returned home, but then Noura's image appeared in his mind; he felt as though he could inhale her, and when he looked at the house he saw that there was only that damned wall between them. His heart began thumping and his breathing surged, but all he could think about was Noura.

He found the door slightly ajar and pushed it open with a tremulous hand. He almost took to his heels when the door creaked: the sound was faint, but it seemed to him as though the whole neighbourhood must have heard it. However, he managed to get a grip on himself and push the door further still, until he could see the little garden sunk in darkness. In the distance he heard the muffled sound of the family's conversation and the noise of the television. Advancing a little, he closed the door behind him quietly, and all of a sudden felt a strong hand pulling him by his own. The fright was such that he almost passed out, sure that he had been exposed. All at once he pictured his mother lying shrouded on a white bed, her eyes filled with tears, but came to his senses when he heard Noura's voice whisper, "Over here, come with me." He was surprised by the strength of her grip, but followed her as she led him by the hand to a far corner of the garden, screened from the rest of the house by a short palm tree laden with clusters of dates. She sat down on the ground and drew him to her side, and their trembling hands joined in a sweaty, erotic stickiness. Hisham was still frightened, but she was strangely, almost suspiciously, calm.

"Are you sure we're safe?" he asked.

"Don't worry, darling," she replied confidently, in a gentle whisper like a northerly breeze. "They're all watching television and my mother's in the kitchen."

Hisham relaxed a little and reached his hand out to her face, touching her soft cheek, then removed her veil and drew her head towards him and inhaled the scent of musk in her hair. She laid her head on his chest, her fevered breathing lighting a fire inside him. He gently lifted her head and pressed his lips to hers, and at that moment they became oblivious to everything around them. Then suddenly he parted his mouth from her tender lips and began looking at her; her eyes were closed.

"Noura," he said.

"Sweetheart," she replied with her eyes still shut, resting her head on his chest again.

"Am I the first one ever to come here? I mean –"

Noura quickly removed her head from his chest, her eyes wide with hurt and anger. "I was wrong to love you," she said forcefully. Wrapping her veil around her head, she was about to get up when Hisham caught her by the hand.

"I'm sorry, Noura," he said wretchedly. "I'm sorry. I don't know what made me say it. Please forgive me." He gazed at her with wide-open eyes, and with only a moment's hesitation Noura threw herself back into his arms, sending his glasses tumbling to the ground; once again they were whirled away into oblivion. Deliriously he reached out and began stroking the light down on her leg, and then his hand started to move up under her dress, but Noura took her lips off his and said,

"No. No, Hisham. That isn't right."

He obeyed her wishes and they embraced again, each of them gently and pleasurably breathing in the scent of the other with their eyes closed. How long they remained like that neither of them knew, but when a voice in the distance called out, "Noura ... Noura!" she gave a start.

"It's my mother, it's my mother," she said nervously, getting up hastily to throw her veil back on and adjust her dress before darting off. Then she dashed back, planted a fleeting kiss on Hisham's lips and ran into the house again. Hisham could hear the mumbling sound of her speaking to her mother, and then there was quiet. Cautiously he made his way towards the door, and no sooner found himself outside than he took off home and went straight to his room and bed, his heart still pounding. Safe at last. His mother called him to have supper, which they had put off for his sake, but he claimed he had already eaten an egg sandwich while out with the gang.

"I'm amazed at the way you've been this last couple of days," his mother said, looking at him suspiciously. "Anyhow, it's up to you." She closed the door behind her. Oh, if only his mother knew where he had come from and what he had been doing ... But he put his mother out of his mind, replacing her with Noura and her scent, filling his entire being.

❧ 47 ❧

Hisham decided to leave the organisation regardless of the consequences. He could not bear it any more; it was not a life for him. What drove him this time was not just fear, even if that was ever-present, but his lack of conviction in the life of the organisation and all that went on in it. He decided to inform Fahd of his decision at the next meeting of the cell and made up his mind not to go back on it, whatever the circumstances.

He was determined to hand in his 'resignation' when the cell met on Thursday at the usual time, but the news Fahd brought to that session made him forget all about it and revived his terror more vividly than ever. Fahd looked unusually solemn from the moment the others came in, and remained so during the repetition of the party slogan. He was chain-smoking more than ever, his unshaven face pale and yellow like an overripe lemon. The others exchanged curious glances, and then Fahd said in a dry, agitated voice,

"I've got bad news, comrades."

He fell silent again and lit a cigarette from the end of another he had not yet put out, while the others looked at him, transfixed and tense.

"Some of our comrades have been arrested. The organisation has been discovered."

He stubbed out his old cigarette on the tea tray in front of him. Alarmed, the others began to speak up, their voices quiet at first but gradually getting louder. Fahd just watched them like an imbecile.

"How did it happen?"

"Who exposed it?"

"Where?"

"Why?"

Finally Hudaijan turned squarely to Fahd and looked at him. "How did it happen?" he asked. "What's the story? We want to know everything."

Fahd took another cigarette straight from the pack with his mouth, lit it and dropped the match on the floor, where it remained burning on the threadbare carpet for a while before Hudaijan picked it up and put it out on the tray. Fahd blew the smoke up to the ceiling with a sigh.

"It's a long story," he said, watching the smoke diffuse into the air. "Treachery, conspiracy. A former comrade in the leadership betrayed us. He had been expelled from the organisation for his opportunism and misconduct. Abd al-Qadir Sulayhaf. That filth Abd al-Qadir contacted Comrade Yaqoub Sheikhoun – they'd been friends from the same party cell – and said he was sorry for the way he'd behaved and asked to be forgiven and allowed to rejoin the party." Fahd smiled ironically. "Perhaps you find it strange that I mention the comrades' real names. Well, don't. They've all been arrested and now the Secret Police know all our names anyway. There's nothing left to hide." He paused for a moment, looked up at the ceiling and then at the comrades. "The main thing is that Sulayhaf wasn't accepted back into the party. And one evening he invited Comrade Sheikhoun to supper at his house, where he offered him some Sadiqi arrack and began asking him about the latest news of the organisation; Sheikhoun told him everything, the names of the new party leadership, the new comrades, everything. And the wretch had hidden a tape recorder behind one of the cushions. He recorded every word Comrade Sheikhoun said and then took the recording to the Secret Police, who arrested all the members of the leadership. Comrade Said al-Qammar, Hussein Musaydis, Abd al-Amir al-Nakhlawi and Yaqoub Sheikhoun himself, of course. Sulayhaf, what scum."

Fahd stopped to catch his breath as the others sat gripped by fear, the flies buzzing their heads and adding to their torment.

"So we're done for, all for the sake of a drink of arrack?" said Abu Dharr caustically, though unable to disguise the fear in his voice. After this there was uproar, throughout which Fahd continued chain-smoking.

"Why did Sheikhoun stay in touch with Sulayhaf when they all knew he was an opportunist?"

"How can anyone keep a secret when they're drinking arrack? And what about the organisation's orders and regulations? Or are they just for the likes of us?"

"So things were lax all along and we never knew! 'Act first, talk later!' 'Commitment to the organisation!' 'Accuracy and secrecy!' All this, and all along you lot were drinking arrack and toying with our fates!"

At last Hudaijan's voice drowned out those of the others.

"Listen, brother Farid. You've all deceived us and led us into a disaster. We thought we were freedom fighters, and now we find ourselves in front of a group of reckless idiots. You're all scum, not just Suhayhaf!"

Fahd was speechless at Hudaijan's tone and his audacity, his calling him by his real name, without even addressing him as 'Comrade'.

"Watch your step, comrade," Fahd said, visibly angry. "We're in a crisis. The party in this country is at a crossroads. We've got to think about how to handle the crisis and save the party. And how dare you address me as 'brother'? I'm Comrade Fahd to you, or have you forgotten the party traditions?"

Hudaijan laughed sarcastically. " 'Comrade' my foot! Mr Farid, we all know your real name; did you think it was top secret? No doubt the Secret Police know it too, now. You were having a laugh at us all along. The struggle, principles ..." Hudaijan began to laugh madly and then suddenly got up, saying, "In the end it's all a load of rubbish. Here's to your organisation and your party. With a little whisky this time," he added with a laugh. "Don't overdo the arrack! Come on guys," he said, looking at Hisham and Abu Dharr, but neither of them moved and he left on his own, muttering something incomprehensibly and waving his hands about.

Of those still sitting there, Adnan appeared easily the most terrified; he was in a corner, withdrawn into himself, his hands trembling noticeably. Throughout he had been staring at Hisham, who was silent, his face pale and his fringe wet with ceaseless perspiration. Abu Dharr was the most composed, although he kept biting his fingernails. There was a long silence after Hudaijan had left, following which Fahd got up and ended the session without repeating the party slogan this time.

When they left, one by one as usual, Hisham found Adnan waiting for him at the end of the alley leading on to al-Hubb Street, but ignored him and headed for the beach without looking back. Marzuq and Zaki were sitting there facing the sea, Marzuq still livid. He felt he had been made the 'laughing-stock' of people who were neither responsible nor honest – "just a bunch of clowns," as he put it. Hisham and Zaki listened as he put into words the bitterness they all felt, the humiliation of one who discovers at last that he has been the naive victim of people who failed to realise they were toying with the convictions and passions of others, while neither meaning what they said nor behaving in accordance with rules they themselves had laid out. It was about more than what had happened with Sulayhaf and Sheikhoun, it was about recklessness and indifference and what for some had become no more than an exciting adventure. It had all been exposed as a game, and a very silly game at that. There they had been, distributing pamphlets and recruiting supporters, while the others were off drinking arrack, giving orders and thinking themselves men of principle ... Marzuq laughed, his eyes strangely dark, and the Gulf returned the echo of his laughter.

When the three comrades parted that day, they agreed to meet again whenever the opportunity arose. Hisham later saw Zaki in Jeddah, but Marzuq he never set eyes on again.

❧ 48 ❧

Hisham went to the next meeting dying of curiosity, though at the same time he was wildly apprehensive. There was no other way to obtain more information than to keep going, as he reasoned that cutting his ties with the organisation would make no difference to the situation he now found himself in. The organisation had begun to collapse: arrests were coming thick and fast, and if his name had reached the Secret Police he too would be arrested in any case, while if it had not there was no reason to be afraid.

When he reached Fahd's house Hisham walked up and down the narrow alley until he was sure there were no passers-by in sight, then knocked on the door, still nervously glancing in all directions. Fahd opened the door and bade him come in quickly, then closed the door again after glancing out into the alleyway. When Hisham went into the sitting room he found four other people there, none whom was familiar to him; they were all about thirty to thirty-five years old, with large moustaches and rough, unkempt beards. The whole place smelled of sweat and the air was thick with cigarette smoke. None of the former comrades were there apart from Fahd. When Hisham entered the other four stood up, and they all shook hands and sat back down around the tea tray, which was full of cigarette butts. The others were evidently surprised that Hisham was there and looked inquisitively at Fahd.

"I didn't expect you to come, comrade," he said, addressing Hisham. "In fact, I didn't really expect anyone to come. Anyway, it's a good thing that you have," he went on, casting his eyes quickly over the others before looking at Hisham again. "We were talking about what's been happening and what can be done. Let me introduce you to the comrades," he went on, gesturing towards them. "Comrade Ahm –"

"Please, com – Please don't," said Hisham, interrupting. "Please don't. If they already know about me that's enough, but for my part I don't want to know their names."

Fahd nodded, exhaling smoke from the corner of his mouth and looking at Hisham listlessly. "The organisation has collapsed, comrades," he said, addressing them all. "The party has collapsed. No one's left except us. Everyone else has either been arrested or fled or abandoned the organisation in its crisis."

As Fahd fell silent one of the others burst out, "Our task is to save the organisation from total disintegration!" The speaker had the strong and unmistakable accent of the al-Ahsa oasis area and was smoking a strange kind of cigarette that came in an odd packet and had a foul smell. Hisham was surprised by this declaration. Everything was over, and yet here this man was, talking about the organisation as though it still existed. He was about to make a comment when one of the others got in first.

"We've received news that Comrade Said al-Qammar has died."

They were all quiet for a moment before Fahd said, "Let's stand for a minute's silence in memory of our heroic comrade." They all duly stood for a minute, which seemed like an age, then sat back down.

"It's our duty to rebuild the party," said one of the others. "We're here today to elect a new General Secretary and a new leadership to reconstruct –"

"You lot are strange," said Hisham, unable to hold back. "Everything's collapsed, there are arrests going on everywhere, and yet here you are, talking about continuing. This is madness."

"But resistance is imperative, comrade," said the fourth person, who had been silent until now.

"This isn't resistance, it's insanity," said Hisham, "yes, insanity. The only imperative is for everything to end, and the reality is that it already has."

"What our comrade says is fair," said the man with the al-Ahsa accent after a short silence. "But it's hard for us to abandon the organisation after we've spent all these years building it up. Perhaps we might freeze all activity indefinitely."

Hisham smiled despite himself: what was the difference between freezing the organisation and dissolving it? The end result was the same, but this person did not want to face the truth of the matter; he had to dress it up in some form he could accept. "Let's do that, then," Hisham said, "if you're all agreed."

Hisham moved to stand up; he could not believe that everything was over, that he had at last come to the end of the labyrinth. Now he could return to the real world that he had neglected for more than two and a half years, to his books and his mother and father and the gang and Noura ... At last the nightmare had ended. But perhaps the real nightmare was only just beginning? He felt his stomach contract at the thought of prison. Terror swept over him again.

"One minute, comrade. There's one last thing we've got to do." This from the man with the al-Ahsa accent again. Hisham sat back down, anxious. exasperated and curious all at once. The man removed a plastic envelope from a paper bag and opened it to reveal a bundle of new one-hundred riyal notes. It was plainly a large sum of money. The man threw the wad into the middle of the circle.

"There's seven thousand, five hundred riyals," he said. "It's the organisation's entire funds. What are we going to do with it?"

They all looked at one another in silence. It was a vast amount; Hisham was quite dazzled.

"Why don't you keep it till after the crisis is over, Comrade Abu Said?" someone said, addressing the Ahsai. "After all, we've frozen the organisation, not dissolved it."

"I don't think that's a good idea," he replied. "I might be arrested at any moment."

"Then let's put it in the bank until things are clearer," said one of the others.

"In whose name?" came the immediate reply. "That's not a practical idea, comrade! Whoever's account it was would be asked where he'd got such a large amount of money from, and we're all just ordinary officials."

"So what shall we do, then? Give it to the poor, or throw it into the street, or give it to charity?"

They all laughed briefly. "Why?" one of them commented with strange mirth. "The poor should rely on God."

There was another pause as they each bowed their heads and began smoking with the exception of Hisham, who was looking at the empty teapot in front of him.

Fahd spoke up. "Comrade Abu Huraira should look after the money. He's the youngest among us and the least likely to get arrested. No one knows him."

The proposal met with unanimous approval as the others quickly expressed their agreement, but Hisham protested.

"No, I can't. Where could I put a huge sum like that, when I'm still a student and live with my mother and father? It's too much of a responsibility for someone in my position. No. No, I can't."

He was not being completely honest in his excuse, but he wanted to be rid of anything that could tie him to the organisation – he, who could not believe that everything had ended as well as he had wished, especially now that he had confirmation that none of those arrested had known him. This instantly gave him greater peace of mind and enabled him to relax for the first time since the previous session, when Fahd had announced the discovery of the organisation. Fahd put the money back in the envelope and shoved it at Hisham.

"The decision has been taken, and all that's left is for you to carry it out, comrade," he said firmly. "You're the best choice." Before Hisham could say anything, Fahd stood, the others rising with him.

"So this is goodbye …"

They all shook hands and slipped out one by one, after hastily repeating the party slogan for the last time.

❧ 49 ❧

Hisham mulled over the strange game fate was playing with him. He wanted to be free of every tie to the party, but he was destined to be bound to them one way or another. Here he was, carrying a sum of money so large he could feel it weighing down on his chest where he had concealed it, with no idea what to do with it or where to hide it. He reached his house in a state of acute agitation, and went to his room and locked the door. He took the money out from under his vest and put it in the lower drawer of his desk, covering it up with some textbooks, then threw himself on his bed. What could he do about this disaster now confronting him? Why not give the money to his father to do whatever he liked with it? Hisham laughed at this foolish idea: if his parents had called him to account over a bird he had bought for a quarter of a riyal, what would they do if he came with a fortune of unknown origin? In any case, the money was not his, so how could he possibly spend it? Yes, he used to pay a contribution of five riyals every month to the organisation, but that did not give him the right to seize the lot; as salaried officials, for instance, Zaki and Marzuq used to pay a monthly contribution of ten riyals each, so from that point of view they had more of a right to it than he did: why not give the money to them?

But he quickly dismissed the idea. The money had been entrusted to him, and he had to look after it as it was until someone from the party came to collect it on its behalf. It could remain in his safekeeping until whenever. But where should he hide it in the meantime?

He got up and fetched some cellophane and tinfoil from the kitchen. Back in his room he wrapped the money in the cellophane and put it back first inside the plastic envelope, then the paper bag, before wrapping the whole lot in tin foil followed by the rag and putting it in a small empty 'Nido' milk carton. Next, Hisham checked that his parents were in the television room before slipping out into the back yard. Shrouded by the dark, he began burrowing with his bare hands into the soft, damp sand in a corner near the door to the women's quarters. His heart was racing; from time to time he would go over to the window of the television room and listen to make sure his parents were still there, then return to dig, until he had reached a depth he was satisfied with. He placed the carton in the hole and piled the sand on top until he had buried it completely. Having finished the job, he took a deep breath, relieved. After a quick shower outside, he returned to his room and gave in to his need for a short nap, waking later to his mother calling him to supper.

❧ 50 ❦

The next few days were a time of fear and anxiety. Exams had started and the arrests continued relentlessly, following the discovery of yet another organisation. Many of the people Hisham knew and who knew him had been taken into custody, and everywhere there was a feeling of panic. Rashid told him that Fahd and Mansur had both been arrested and that he himself had decided to flee to Bahrain, where he would decide where to go after that, and he advised Hisham to do the same. But he could not: exams had already begun, and he had no wish to force a burden on his parents that neither would be able to bear. That he would abandon his exams without getting his diploma and shock them with the story of the clandestine organisation and the possibility that he might be arrested and sent to prison, after they had placed all their hopes and trust in him, was something they would not be able to cope with. Instead he decided to leave his destiny to that joker, fate.

He grew more anxious each time he found out that another comrade had disappeared, or when people failed to turn up for school during the exam period. Even Hasan al-Sabah had vanished. Hisham tried to reassure himself that Fahd and Mansur would never confess and betray him. The days went by and still he had not been summoned, which enabled him to relax more and more as time passed. These days the headmaster's office was a hive of activity. Apart from the exams and all that went with them, unidentified men were coming to the school every day to meet with the headmaster in private, departing later accompanied by one or more pupils. The headmaster's office had become a veritable operational headquarters. Hisham tried to dispel his anxiety by concentrating on revising, as well as meeting Noura whenever the opportunity arose, but worry and fear still imposed themselves all the same. Even Noura's kiss no longer had any flavour for him, it was just the meeting of lips with no sensation as his mind was distracted by thoughts of the exams and prison alike.

Adnan's terror was alarmingly apparent on his face. He came to see Hisham once, after the end of the French exam. Adnan was a spectre, his face was wizened and dry from fearful insomnia. He was studying hard without achieving the results he had hoped for.

Hisham remembered their shared revisions in carefree, happier times. "It's not fair," Adnan once shouted straight out. "I revise all the time while you spend your time day-dreaming about Lolita and her exploits, and still you get better results than me. It's not fair. The earrings always go to the one who hasn't any ears, as the Egyptians say." Both friends had roared with innocent laughter. Adnan was no fool, but he was incapable of concentrating; furthermore his father had forced him to take science subjects – he, who was mad for the arts and could not bear the dryness of the pure sciences. Even Hisham had been obliged to take sciences, as his father wanted him to become a doctor or an engineer, but he was better able to concentrate even on subjects he disliked. His heart had been set on studying economics, but he took sciences to please his father; after that he was determined to do what he wanted to. Usually he and Adnan would revise in the street under the lampposts, to get away from the stifling heat indoors and the watchful eye of their parents, who gave them no room to talk freely.

As Hisham took his break on the little balcony overlooking the courtyard, Adnan approached him shyly and stood next to him for a little while. Hisham made to move away, but Adnan stopped him.

"Hisham, are you still angry with me?" he asked in an almost inaudible voice.

Hisham stopped and looked at him closely, noticing that Adnan's face had lately also broken out in spots. "Not exactly," he said, looking away quickly. "You don't matter enough to me for me to be angry with you or otherwise."

"So you are still angry with me," Adnan said, with deadened eyes. Hisham was hesitant; he stayed where he was, which encouraged Adnan to keep talking. "I haven't seen Mansur any more," he said, with fear in his voice, "and I don't go to the group, either. Do you think he's been arrested? When I last saw him he was scared. Do you think he's been arrested?"

"Mansur *has* been arrested," Hisham said quietly, looking at the courtyard. "Fahd, too. What are you going to do?"

"I've no idea. My father's got to know about it all. I'll think about telling him after the exams, God willing."

Hisham smiled despite himself: God's popularity was on the rise these days. If Marx himself were in their position he might be mentioning God a lot as well …

"Don't be afraid. I think we're in the clear. None of the people who know us will make a confession betraying us, and there aren't many of them, anyway. And everything's finished; I don't think they want to arrest any more people, as long as they've achieved their aim," Hisham said, trying to reassure himself more than Adnan. There was a silence.

"Hisham," said Adnan, turning to look squarely at him. Hisham remained impassive. "Hisham, please forgive me. Everything's over. I want us to be like we were before."

Hisham looked into Adnan's lifeless eyes, which somehow seemed smaller to him than they used to. "Do you listen to Umm Kulthumm, Adnan?"

"Of course. Is there anyone who doesn't?"

"So you'll have heard the song where she sings, 'He wanted us to be the way we were before … Tell Time "Turn back, O Time, turn back for us once more"' …"

At that moment the bell rang. Hisham went off to his classroom while Adnan stayed put for a while; when he entered the classroom his face was like an ancient Egyptian mummy that had just been discovered. Before taking his seat he glanced at Hisham, who could see that all the emotions in this world were rolling inside his former friend.

⇾ 51 ⇽

The exams came to an end without anything happening to either Hisham or Adnan. Hisham did not see Rashid at school any more, just as Muwafiq had also disappeared. He was still visited by an insistent anxiety, but as days passed without anyone asking about him he felt a little safer and more confident that no one had mentioned his name ... yet.

He celebrated the end of the exams with a trip to his favourite bookshop to buy all the magazines he could find: 'al-Hawadith'; 'Arab Week'; 'The New Public'; 'al-Jadid'; 'al-Arabi'; 'Superman'; 'Magic Carpet', even 'al-Yamama' and the papers that had nothing but local news in them. He spent that afternoon flicking through the magazines, and following the latest adventures of Superman and Tintin. His mother had prepared a small feast in his honour, making all the fried food and pies and chilli he liked and paying no attention to his father's objections to those 'silly Syrian dishes', though they were said with a smile on this occasion.

Afterwards Hisham raced off to see the gang for the usual rounds of Kiram and Plot. He laughed a lot and chatted happily with all of them, even Adnan. Everything that day seemed positive; he had a huge sense of well-being that he wanted nothing to spoil.

In the evening he met Noura and made up for all the distance and apathy that had marred their last tryst, surprising her with all the warmth and emotion he displayed. She told him then how impressed her father had been with him when speaking to her mother over their afternoon tea, noting Hisham's piety and scrupulousness in praying with the congregation at the mosque. Hisham simply gave her a smile in reply, followed by a dreamy look at her face and finally a long kiss. He knew what she was getting at, but marriage was hardly on his mind, though his parents would be thrilled if he brought the subject up with them, regardless of his youth; he was their only son and their financial position was comfortable.

His joy at the conclusion of the exam period had worn off, to be replaced with a new kind of anxiety, that of awaiting results. The fear of being arrested had not altogether dissipated, but it had greatly diminished. It looked as though Mansur and Fahd were standing up well and that neither had mentioned names to the authorities, and for the first time Hisham came to appreciate them.

The family was not planning to travel to Jordan or Syria that year, as Hisham's results and the preparations for his departure to university made such a trip difficult. Instead, his father decided to take a short holiday to Qusaim for a visit to his parents and his sister, none of whom they had seen since the last trip there three years earlier. Hisham thought it would be a wonderful idea to escape temporarily from the haunted atmosphere in Dammam. He would see his grandparents and his aunt, whom he adored. He was not so fond of Qusaim itself, which lacked both friends and seashore for comfort; he would, moreover, be inescapably obliged to perform the dawn prayers with his grandfather in the mosque. But, his aunt foremost in mind, he began to look forward to the trip despite everything.

Over the next few days his father let his facial hair grow in preparation for the journey, sporting a small, crescent-shaped beard separate from his moustache. (It was considered shameful in Qusaim for a member of a distinguished family to be seen clean-shaven, especially in his family's city, Buraida. People might forgive someone's missing the dawn prayers for one reason or another – they counted those present in the congregation – but they could not pardon his lack of a beard, especially once past youth.) Hisham occupied himself with gathering together a few books he had been putting off reading, as a hedge against the long and dreary Qusaim days. He chose Tolstoy's *War and Peace*, which he was forever becoming bored with after only a few pages. He also chose *The Iron Heel* by Jack London and *The Story of Philosophy* by Will Durant, to read again; *The Principles of Philosophy* by the Egyptian writer Ahmad Amin; and Jean-Paul Sartre's *Existentialism and Humanism*, as well as a study he had got hold of from Zaki a while ago called 'What Is A Leftist?' by a French writer, published in the French journal 'Les Temps Modernes' and translated by a member of the Communist Action Organisation in Beirut.

On the afternoon of a burning hot day in June the family got into their little 1967 Peugeot and set off first for Dhahran, then to Riyadh via Bufaiq. It was the first time they had used their own car for the journey to Qusaim; usually they travelled by train or taxi to Riyadh, then took one of the vehicles known as 'boxes' that ferried passengers in wooden compartments between Riyadh and Qusaim. They reached Riyadh shortly before midnight and went straight to the house of Hisham's uncle, Abd al-Aziz al-Mubaraki; he was still awake, reading the Qur'an, the rest of the family asleep. He received them and woke his eldest daughter Munira, who welcomed them while Hisham's uncle went back to the Qur'an. Munira made them a light supper of fried eggs with some yellow cheese and tea with milk, laying everything out for them on one of the empty roof terraces before returning to bed with an apology, saying she had been tired all day. Later, as they all went to sleep they could hear the heart-rending sound of Hisham's uncle sobbing in his room as he recited from the Qur'an.

The next morning, at the dawn call to prayer, Abd al-Aziz woke them up to come and pray, but Hisham's father asked to take leave instead in order to make the most of the time before the sun became too hot. After insisting for a while that they stay, Abd al-Aziz gave in and they sped off, his heartfelt prayers for their safety lingering in their thoughts.

As they descended the Dairab Heights on the Hijaz Road, the sun was timidly beginning to rise; by the time they got to Marrat it had entered its insolent phase, sending terrible, fiery rays down on them though it was still early in the day. Hisham's father stopped at one of the cafés in Marrat, where they had a quick breakfast of hot brown bread and white tea. Afterwards his father filled up their thermoses with tea and bitter coffee and topped up their flasks with cold water. They reached Shaqra shortly before midday, by which time the sun had become an inferno. A short way past Shaqra, Hisham's father turned off the asphalted Hijaz Road and drove into a sea of sand marked only by a few scattered lines running in all directions from cars that had left their tracks and then vanished. By now the sun had begun to sink towards the western horizon, still impudent. After a few kilometres the asphalt road disappeared from sight altogether and the family was left at the mercy of the boundless red sand dunes stretching out around them.

"God help us get through you, Jayb Ghurab," Hisham's father would say every now and then, using the name of the barren, sandy wastes between Riyadh and Qusaim. Everything had become limitless, dimensionless; there was nothing but sun, sand and the horizon, which never came any nearer. The sense of place itself was banished, and time seemed somehow to be suspended from the disc of the sun, which eventually took on a bashful aspect, clothed in red and threatening the very end of time itself as it was devoured by the horizon.

Darkness spread its cloak, and it seemed as though Ahriman, Zoroastrian spirit of evil and lord of the Earth, were astride the chest of Ahura Mazda, benevolent god of light and the celestial bodies, in another phase of their eternal struggle of alternating victories: this time the west, domain of Ahriman, was inevitably winning. The stars emitted silver rays, a worthless glimmer in this infinity of sand. The only sign of life was the sound of the Peugeot and the few words exchanged by Hisham's parents, perhaps simply to make their presence felt or to dispel their misgivings. Hisham knew they were surrounded by sand on all sides, but he could see nothing, only a few shadowy shapes hovering in the distance like the ghouls that haunted Sinbad on his voyages. Everything had stopped while only they moved on, like the Israelites through the wilderness.

Suddenly Hisham's father turned off the sandy track he had been following and stopped the car. "We can't go on in this pitch darkness," he said. "We'll spend the night here and keep going at dawn."

They all got out of the car and sat down on a nearby sand dune until their eyes got used to the dark, enough to be able to see by the diffident light of the stars. Then Hisham's father asked him to get out the tea-making things while he went to look for firewood. "This is my mistake," he said. "We should have travelled during the white nights, when the moon is full. But whatever fate God chooses for us is best."

"God's power is great, and only good things await us," said Hisham's mother as she took the tea-making implements out of a plastic bag. "So what's the hurry?"

Despite the heat, Hisham's father lit a fire that illuminated the area around them, lending a sense of calm to the moment. He filled the teapot and placed it beside the fire. Hisham watched his father with a smile: the man never changed. They had plenty of tea and coffee in the thermoses, but tea and coffee made over a fire in the desert had a different taste for his father; it made no difference to Hisham, but he was happy if his parents were happy – and they were, sitting around the fire with a strange contented gleam in their eyes. Once his father had finished making the tea he poured out the tea left over from Marrat, though they had only drunk a little of it, and filled the thermos with the freshly-made tea. Then he filled the pot with water again, this time for coffee. They all drank their tea with a few bites of brown bread, sitting in a ring around the fire in the still roasting heat, while around them an atmosphere of tranquillity enveloped everything.

After supper Hisham's father told stories of the *aqilat* traders at the end of their era, of their journeys to Syria, Egypt and Iraq, and the tale of his first voyage with them when he was not yet fourteen years old. At that time his wage was no more than his board, which itself was only a few small dates or some '*aqil* patties', cakes of wheat, sugar and fat. (If he was lucky, he might receive some 'fire patties', large loaves of bread baked in the hot sand under a fire.) He would work all day long in the service of the riders, walking on foot most of the time. Hisham and his mother had heard these stories on numerous occasions, especially on picnics in the countryside. They knew that these adventures contained a certain amount of exaggeration, but they happily condoned it. Ibrahim al-Abir had suffered much in his life, and had every right to be happy.

Hisham moved a little way off from his parents and sat on the soft, cool, previously untouched sand. He began running it though his fingers, content, and looked up at the distant stars in the dome of the infinite. The voices of his mother and father seemed to reach him from the ends of the earth, though he was only a few steps away. He realised why it was that only in this tranquillity and this infiniteness was God's message ever revealed to his prophets, where nothing was to be found but the secret of existence itself, which one could perceive but not see, feeling it deep inside without being able to define it.

Hisham heard his mother calling him to come and sleep in the car with her; he moved over to where his parents were and sat down facing his father by the fireside.

"I'm going to stay here for a bit, Mother," he said. "Goodnight."

"Fine," she said, giving in and going to the car alone. "But watch out for the animals."

"The animals!" his father said, laughing, "The only things that live around here are genies!"

Hisham could hear his mother murmuring in the distance, praying to God to protect them from His harmful creatures. "Don't forget to recite the Sura of the Seat of God and the Two Pleas for Divine Refuge," she said, referring to the Sura of Daybreak and the Sura of Mankind, used to invoke God's protection from evil. "And you, Hisham, don't fall asleep outside. There's room inside for everyone." And with that he heard the car door slam shut.

❖ 52 ❖

Hisham was woken by the sound of his father moving about as he lit a fire, though where and when he had got the wood Hisham had no idea. The sun had not yet risen, bathing everything in daylight; instead, there was only a distant glow in the east mingled with the last shadows of night before daybreak. It was clear that Ahura Mazda was advancing towards another victory, that the east was going to burst forth once again. Hisham vaguely remembered lying back with his arms behind his head and watching the stars, when sleep must have caught him. The air was utterly magical, though the faint sting of dawn prompted him to draw a blanket over himself. (He did not know where the blanket had come from, but his mother, he was certain, would have been unable to close her eyes knowing that he was asleep in the open air.)

Only once his father had finished making the tea and coffee did Hisham stir, and at the same time his mother came over from the car, eyes red and smiling as she looked at him. They all gathered around the fire, warming themselves and sipping tea with condensed milk accompanied by mouthfuls of the brown bread. There was nothing lovelier than the desert at first light, stretching away into the distance, with a fire lit and a nip in the air, or at daybreak when the sun rose over the boundless horizon, the dewy morning breeze caressing one's face with the allure of a virgin new to love.

The car moved off as the sun was about to erupt over the horizon, which was already ablaze with light; a few minutes later and the landscape resumed its appearance of a painting by the Artist of all Creation. Beneath the light of the sun the sand dunes resembled mythical creatures, their danger concealed within. For untold hours the car continued on its way. Once more the sun began to rage, and soon once again began its descent towards the west, as Ahriman honed his spear and whetted his arrows.

A troubled look appeared on Hisham's father's face. The water and fuel they had brought with them had almost run out. "We should be near Unayzah by now," he said, the acute anxiety in his voice betraying itself to Hisham and his mother, who stared ahead with frightened expressions. But the road would not end, and the horizon stretched on without any sign of life. As the sun began to set again, concern turned into terror. No water, no fuel and no food; the sand dunes would swallow them up, only to resume their appearance of beauty in the morning, as if by nature and intention they were good. But the desert, like fate, or like some kind of bashful sadist, would crush you, stifling you until you thought all hope had gone, and then suddenly release you, showing you all that was loveliest of itself.

Just as they had all reached the brink of despair, Hisham's father suddenly let out a cry like a small boy who has managed to find his parents in a crowd.

"Unayzah! it's Unayzah!"

Hisham and his mother craned their necks. "Where? Where?" they asked over and over, gazing at the horizon with eager eyes but seeing nothing.

"Over there," Hisham's father said with calm self-assurance, his smile and confidence restored. "Can't you see that black dot on the horizon?" he said, pointing into the distance. "It's the Unayzah water tower. Praise be to God, we're safe and sound." Hisham and his mother could not see anything where his father had pointed, but they took his word for it, and joyous expressions returned to their faces where only moments earlier there had been the expectation of certain death.

The sun had become blood-red when the Unayzah water tower became clearly visible, with a jumble of tightly-packed mud-brick houses beyond it.

"Unayzah," Hisham's father said happily as he saw it, "this is Unayzah." And at that moment it was the most beautiful city any of them had ever seen.

They stopped at a petrol station by the road with the city on their left and filled up with fuel and water, quickly washing their faces before heading north. As the sun sank completely into the sea of eternity, its blood spreading over the face of the sky, Hisham's father pointed at a spot no different from any other in that ocean of sand.

"There's Khashm Ali," he said. "After that comes Buraida." Sure enough, less than an hour later they were within sight of Buraida, with its rows of mud-brick houses and its cramped, dusty streets, the pale lights of lanterns hung from the buildings peeping out bashfully from those narrow openings. They went down al-Khabib Street, which was almost empty, and then, after crossing al-Jarda, turned off into a narrow street scarcely wide enough to let the car pass. The smell of *marquq* stock was everywhere. Hisham's father parked the car in front of a mud-brick house with a huge wooden door, like any other in the street. "Thanks be to God for bringing us here safely," he said. "We're here at last."

They knocked hard on the door for a while before they heard a feeble, quavering woman's voice saying, "Who is it? Who's there?" It was Hisham's grandmother, Umm Ibrahim.

"It's me," Hisham's father called out loudly, "It's me, Ibrahim, Mother."

Hisham heard the sound of the wooden bolt being slid back. Then the door opened and his grandmother's face peered round, her mouth and nose covered with her veil and only her tiny eyes visible, weepy as always from chronic trachoma. Her legs were no longer strong enough to hold her up unaided, and her hands trembled as she saw her son standing before her, her son whom she had not seen for three years. (The only news she would receive of him came through infrequent letters and 'blessings' or gifts of money that he would send her when circumstances allowed.) They all went inside, and then came warm embraces between Ibrahim and his mother, and between Hisham and his grandmother, along with a few tears.

Hisham's mother kissed her mother-in-law's forehead. "How are you, Aunt?" she asked mechanically, using the conventional term of address.

"Well, my daughter, well," replied Umm Ibrahim equally perfunctorily, and the conversation was over.

Hisham's grandmother was about sixty-five, but looked much older, having been ravaged by one disease after another. She was able to move only with the greatest effort. Yet she was on the plump side, and her face still bore the traces of an old beauty: her fair complexion was eye-catching and she had a little mouth and wide eyes, or so they had been before the trachoma had ruined them. Her nose was curved 'like the blade of a sword', as they used to describe it in days gone by, when her beauty had been proverbial. She was from an old family, and Hisham's grandfather had only been able to marry her after countless difficulties; his own family, the al-Abirs, were neither as ancient nor as wealthy as the al-Thabiti clan to which his intended belonged. In the end, the only things that had acted in his favour were that the two families were already distantly related and that Hisham's grandfather had accompanied his grandmother's father on his journeys with the *aqilat* to Syria and Egypt.

Hisham's grandmother led them into the house, although they all knew the way well and nothing had changed since the last visit. They passed through the courtyard, in the middle of which stood a palm tree with clusters of dates hanging down like the flowing locks of a Jerusalem beauty sung of in psalms and in *The Song of Solomon*; in a corner on the right was the *burj*, or lavatory, and in the opposite corner a small pen containing a cow and some goats with their young nearby. The courtyard ended in the entrance to the main part of the house, which was not large. It comprised two floors, the first consisting of the *qahwa*, or coffee room, the largest room in the house and its principal sitting room, with a small room next to it used as a larder and beside that another, slightly more spacious, multi-purpose room. It was a kitchen, a sitting room for the women and a guest room when necessary. The second floor consisted of two small separate rooms and another, slightly larger one overlooking the *qahwa* that was used as a bedroom in winter; in summer, the roof terrace was the preferred place to sleep.

Umm Ibrahim went first into the *qahwa*, calling out: "Abu Ibrahim, Abu Ibrahim, look who's here." Hisham's grandfather was sitting behind a small stove used for making tea and coffee, holding an elaborate fan made of palm leaves in his lap. He had nodded off with his head propped up on a cushion. Hisham's grandfather was in his early eighties, having married late in life as a result of his travels in search of a living. He was of medium height and slim, bald on top with thick hair around the sides of his head; he wore a long white beard and carefully twisted moustache. His face was the image of Hisham's father's own: round and pock-marked, with small eyes and a rather snub nose, little mouth, wheat-coloured complexion and thick, white eyebrows.

"Your son, your son! Is everything all right?" asked Hisham's grandfather, opening his eyes wearily and beginning to wave his fan rhythmically. Then, through half-closed eyes he looked at the others as they came forward. "Ibrahim! Is that you?" he said in a faint voice swinging between doubt and certainty. "Welcome, welcome." He tried to get up, but Hisham's father bent over him and kissed him on the head. Next came Hisham's turn to be wrapped in his grandfather's warm embrace, which exuded his distinctive scent of sandalwood and smoke. Last of all came Hisham's mother, who kissed her father-in-law on the head and then withdrew, while Hisham and his father sat down beside the old man around the stove.

Hisham's grandfather lit the stove and opened the high window, using a rope beside him like a pulley. Thick smoke filled the room for several minutes before the wood began to burn properly. After placing a tea kettle and a coffee pot on either side of the stove he began asking his son how things were and scolding him for visiting so little, Hisham's father giving various excuses in reply. Meanwhile Hisham's mother and grandmother were sitting in silence not far from the men.

Suddenly Hisham's grandfather looked at his grandmother and said, excitedly, "Umm Ibrahim, have you sent anyone to tell Sharifa that her brother's here?"

"No, I'll go myself," replied his grandmother with the same enthusiasm, getting up. Hisham's aunt's house was only two or three houses away. A few minutes later Hisham heard her delicate voice preceding her through the doorway of the *qahwa* that led into the rest of the house, as she called out, "Where's Hisham? Hisham …" And then her gentle face appeared. She had already removed her wrap, which she threw aside atop the first cushion she came across before going straight over to Hisham, who had risen to his feet to greet her with a beaming smile on his face. For several minutes Sharifa stood there, embracing Hisham and planting kisses on him, before kissing her brother on the head, embracing his wife, then greeting her father.

"You've grown, Hisham," she said, sitting down beside him and looking him over. "You've turned into a handsome young man. Oh, if only I weren't your aunt!" She laughed gleefully. "We must get you married off so you can fill the house with children to bear the family name." Still laughing, she gave him another kiss on the cheek. At that last sentence, Hisham's grandmother glanced at his mother and gave a half-suppressed sigh, before busying herself with her cup of coffee. Hisham's mother, embarrassed by her mother-in-law's sidelong looks, did likewise.

The relationship between the two women was strained, the former having wanted her son to marry another woman when it became clear that Hisham's mother was unable to have any more children. His grandmother's insistence on this point had greatly increased after her youngest daughter Hayla died of tuberculosis before her sixteenth birthday. Hisham's grandmother had also suffered the loss of a son before the age of one. Whenever she saw Ibrahim she would urge him to remarry, saying, "You've only got one son, and may God grant him a long life; but what would you do if, God forbid, anything happened to him? Would you stay like that without an heir to keep the family name going after you? The law allows you four wives, and there's nothing wrong with God's law." These conversations caused Hisham's mother to suffer feelings of inadequacy as well as hatred towards his grandmother, but she never diminished her outward respect for Umm Ibrahim. Hisham's father would listen to his mother's advice, considering it well-meaning, and say, "You only think of what's best." In truth he was quite satisfied with life with his wife and son, even if occasionally he did wish that a miracle would grant Hisham a brother. Whenever Sharifa saw that their mother had been alone with her brother she would go up to him and say, "Don't pay any attention to what Mother says. She's just a silly old woman. Just let it go in here and out here," she would say, pointing first at one ear and then the other. "Hisham's worth ten children," she would go on, "and may God grant him a long and healthy life." Hisham's mother sometimes overheard Sharifa's remarks, which engendered great affection for the younger woman, and whenever she saw Hisham's fondness for her and noticed the striking resemblance between them, the fonder she felt of Sharifa.

Sharifa was, in fact, almost the original model for Hisham: they had the same straight, pitch-black hair, eyes, nose and mouth; the same pointed, triangular face. The only real difference between them was Sharifa's darker complexion. Hisham remembered how, on visits to the family in Qusaim when he was little, he had liked only to sleep in the arms of his aunt Sharifa, who was not then married; he could not relax beside his aunt Hayla (which used to infuriate her). Only when he smelled Sharifa's scent and the musk she put in her hair would he close his eyes, nuzzling her breast and going to sleep. When she married their cousin, Suleiman al-Abir, he felt a sense of loathing towards the young man, despite the fact that Suleiman was extremely kind to him; Hisham had been seven years old at the time, and to this day he still felt little affection for Suleiman. He recalled how, on their wedding night, he had thrown stones at the door of the new couple's upstairs room; his punishment had been a beating from his father so painful he had never forgotten it. For a while afterwards he had remained angry with his aunt, but in the end she won him round with reassurance of her affections supplemented with bribes of sweets and nuts.

❧ 53 ❧

Hisham's father always enthused about Sharifa's incomparable *mataziz*, and on the evening of their arrival he had been looking forward to a supper of either that or *marquq*; but there was not enough time to cook either dish, so Sharifa made do with preparing a large bowl of *qursan* bread with meat stock, beans and big pieces of cured meat.

When the men returned from the mosque after evening prayers, the bowl of food had been placed on the table in the middle of the *qahwa*, filling the place with its delicious smell. Suleiman, Sharifa's husband, joined them for supper, having come to welcome them and then accompany the men to the mosque. He was a conspicuously tall man with a dark complexion, curly hair and heavy limbs, although the features of his face were extremely delicate; his right hand in particular was covered with the marks of burns inflicted in the traditional belief that they had a strengthening effect. All the men devoured their food by the pale light of a lantern, while the women sat in a room downstairs. The most delicious part of the bowl of *qursan* was the dried meat and green beans threaded together, as well as the fresh cow's milk that had been churned only that morning. By the time the men had finished eating there was little left, particularly of the meat, but it was enough for the women.

After supper they all gathered in the *qahwa* to have tea and coffee. Hisham's mother was the only one to cover her face; she did not actually cover it completely, but simply raised the scarf she wore draped over her head and shoulders as a kind of barrier between herself and Suleiman, who was sitting with the other men around the stove while the women sat near the entrance to the men's front door. Before taking his leave, Suleiman invited them to supper the next day, promising them some of Sharifa's *mataziz*; meanwhile Sharifa herself asked her brother and Hisham's mother to let him spend the night at her house, and to Hisham's absolute delight they agreed without hesitation. Off he dashed with his favourite aunt, forgetting about exams and the arrests; he exulted at being in a place where no one knew anything about him and where no one could reach him. Here there was no anxiety, no tension, no fear that could get through to him, and as he lay down on his perfumed mattress on the roof terrace, his aunt's kiss on his forehead was the last thing he was aware of in the waking world.

≫ 54 ≪

When Hisham awoke the next morning, Suleiman had already departed for his shop in al-Jarda and his aunt had prepared a sumptuous breakfast of fried eggs, hot fresh milk with lots of sugar, grilled pieces of *masabib* dough accompanied by fresh, white butter and tea. She sat next to him, urging him to eat without having anything herself and swatting away the flies that stuck to everything.

Hisham loved his aunt and pitied her at the same time: for all the long years she had been married, God had never given her a child to bring her joy and comfort her in her solitude. She had been pregnant and given birth several times, but for some unknown reason none of her children had survived. She had even gone to some folk healers, who tried all sorts of charms and herbs on her, but to no avail. Eventually, faced with no other alternative, she had left the matter to fate; in fact, she had gone so far as to ask Suleiman to marry another woman if he wanted children, even expressing a willingness to look for a prospective wife for him herself, but he had refused. From that moment on she had devoted her time to bringing joy and happiness into her husband's life and serving him to the best of her ability.

In cases like these Suleiman's behaviour was unusual, but he was, like his cousin Hisham's father, unwilling to take another wife. Children were not always a source of happiness, he would say, and it did not matter to him whether or not anyone carried his name on after him. Everyone else disapproved of this sort of view, but no one could force Suleiman to do anything. His father had died a few months after he was born; 1929 was the 'Year of Sibila', the battle at which Ibn Saud crushed the Bedouin troops who had helped him unite the Arabian Peninsula and then rebelled against him. Suleiman's mother died a few years later, and he had been brought up by one of his uncles who already had numerous children.

Hisham felt boredom setting in after he had finished his breakfast. Sharifa had gone to knead the dough for the *mataziz*, bake the *qursan*, milk the cow and churn the milk, then clean the house before Suleiman returned in the afternoon with a lamb to slaughter for the evening meal. Hisham considered going for a walk around the city, but where would he go? There was nothing to see, no one he knew; there was no better option than to read. He went back to his grandparents' house; his grandfather had gone out to sit and talk with his friends in the sun and then have a stroll in al-Jarda; his father was still asleep and his mother was cleaning the house while his grandmother churned the milk. Hisham took out *War and Peace* from his suitcase, but soon cast it aside and took up *The Iron Heel* instead and, going upstairs, lost himself among the labourers in the alleys of Chicago.

55

Suleiman had invited all of Hisham's father's peers and the childhood friends he would often speak about, some of whose names Hisham knew. A number of them had come accompanied by their sons, and there were four boys present of a similar age to Hisham. While the men spread out in the *qahwa*, Hisham's father and grandfather sat in the *mahkama*, the place at the head of the room reserved for elders and guests of honour. Suleiman was nearby, sitting directly behind the stove making the tea and coffee. The five boys were sitting near the door at the other end of the room; it was clear to Hisham that the other four already knew one another, as they were talking about picnics and the al-Nafud desert and al-Daghmaniyyat and Ain Wahtan; and since these were places Hisham did not know, he kept quiet throughout the conversation, looking at them and smiling without being able to join in. It was a kind of ordeal for him; at that moment he wished he were among his own friends in Dammam.

Sitting next to Hisham was a boy of a similar build, if a little shorter. The sun had left its mark on his face, which was dark brown, although his legs, one of which was almost half exposed, were paler. He was extremely handsome despite his very broad features. When this boy noticed that Hisham was not taking part in their discussions he looked at him with a smile.

"Don't you go picnicking in the Eastern Province?" he asked. "Or have you become too Americanised?"

"On the contrary," said Hisham, "we don't even set eyes on the Americans. They don't live where we do, and they've got their own 'camp'. But I don't know anyone here, and I don't know what you're all talking about, that's all."

Hisham felt cheered up to have someone talk to him. The good-looking boy smiled again. "In that case I'll show you Qusaim," he said. "You'll find it's more beautiful than you'd imagined when you get to know it and delve into all its hidden nooks and crannies. And I'll introduce you to our friends, as well. You'll see for yourself, they're some of the best young people around. My name's Muhaysin, by the way," he went on after a pause, reaching out and shaking Hisham's hand in a strange way that seemed inappropriate. "Well, my real name's Abd al-Muhsin, but they call me Muhaysin for short. Abd al-Muhsin al-Taghiri. I'm in secondary school."

"I'm Hisham, Hisham al-Abir. I was in secondary school. I mean —"

"So you've taken your diploma? Me too. What a coincidence! We're all going on a picnic in al-Rashidiyya tomorrow," Muhaysin went on. "You'll come with us, of course."

"Of course," replied Hisham.

"We'll pass by to collect you in the morning; make sure you're ready."

Hisham nodded, though he had no idea what this 'al-Rashidiyya' was. At that moment Suleiman brought in the tablecloth and spread it out in the middle of the sitting room, and at a wave from his father Hisham went to help his cousin bring in the food. Together they carried in the main dish, a large plate full of rice with a whole lamb on top, its head resting in the middle and scattered all around it the liver, stomach and intestines wrapped up together as well as some fried eggs. All that was decorated with raisins and pine nuts. Then came the big bowls of *jarish*, *qursan*, *maruq* and *mataziz*, with large pieces of cured meat on top, followed by fresh milk with plates of small dates and two large dishes of fruit. Muhaysin and the other boys helped to lay the table. Once Suleiman had made sure everything was as it should be he called everyone to the table; first Hisham's grandfather stepped forward, followed by his father, then one by one the others, each of them urging the rest to go first.

"Do start, do start," said Suleiman when they had all gathered around the table, standing at its head alongside Hisham. "Every year we have two feasts," he said, referring to Eid al-Fitr at the end of Ramadan and Eid al-Adha, the Feast of the Sacrifice. "This is the third. God bless Abu Hisham, who's the reason we've all gathered here together." With that he invited them to sit, and as he and Hisham took their seats a mass of hands reached out and began to tear apart everything in front of them.

❈ 56 ❈

The next morning Hisham sat in the *qahwa* beside his father and grandfather as they had a breakfast of dates and bitter coffee, while his mother sat behind the stove making tea. His grandmother sat on the other side of the stove, quietly enjoying a cup of coffee. Hisham was waiting for Muhaysin to turn up as promised. Suddenly he heard a knock at the men's front door and the sound of a car horn beeping intermittently; Hisham said goodbye to everyone, and as he left he could hear his grandparents' prayers for him and his father urging him not to come back too late; his mother murmured something inaudibly, but he knew she was reciting the Sura of the Seat of God and the Two Pleas for Divine Refuge.

Outside the front door, Hisham found an old red Chevrolet waiting for him. Muhaysin was behind the steering wheel, beside him a dark young man with fine but somehow quite un-handsome features, but a face that immediately put one at ease. He had curly hair and wore dark sunglasses and a small skullcap that barely covered half his head. All the picnic supplies were in the back of the van, together with four other young men who had pulled their headdresses over their faces like veils. There was nothing especially eye-catching about them except for one exceedingly tall person, thin almost to the point of emaciation with strangely pale skin and long brown hair that reached down to his shoulders. He had an elongated face, straight nose and a very broad forehead that neither his headdress nor his skullcap quite fit.

This young man got out and invited Hisham to take his place, but Hisham declined and went round to the back of the van. "There's room for everyone here," insisted the man, catching hold of him, and Hisham got in after all, this tall individual following. The van drove off, making a great noise and filling the narrow alleyway with exhaust.

"Slow down, Muhaysin!" cried the four in the back, their shouts mixed with laughter. "Take it easy, man, take it easy! We're not cattle, you know!"

When the van got to al-Khabib Street, Muhaysin pointed to the third person sitting in the front. "Let me introduce you to one of my dearest friends," he said, "Muhammad al-Ghubayra. And this," he went on, looking at Muhammad and laughing, "is Hisham, an expatriate Qusaimi." All three of them laughed. "He's going to become a friend of ours, too," Muhaysin added, looking at Hisham with a genuine smile.

Hisham had no idea how long they spent going up and down the soft sand dunes under the burning sun, everything around them arid and apparently bare of all forms of life but for a few small palms here and there: how these trees managed to grow in such conditions seemed a mystery. Just before midday they came within sight of a wide patch of green, full of trees of many varieties and surrounded by sprinklers spraying water everywhere. Hisham had no frame of reference for such a sight. Everyone in the back of the van began to whoop, and Muhaysin smiled as he said enthusiastically, "Behold, al-Rashidiyya."

Muhaysin parked in a remote spot in the orchard, surrounded by pomegranate and citrus trees. Everyone in the back leaped out with great shouts of excitement. Muhammad, Hisham and Muhaysin got out too, and as they did Muhaysin took Hisham by his fingertips, saying,

"Come on, I'll introduce you. Guys, guys," he said loudly, escorting Hisham to where the four boys were standing around the van and dusting off their clothes. He put his arm around Hisham's shoulders. "This is Hisham al-Abir," he said, "from the Eastern Province. He's a bumpkin from the oases really," he continued, laughing, "but he lives back east."

"A bumpkin and a *Rafidhi*," said one of the boys, using the familiar derogatory word for Shi'ite, "what is the world coming to? God rest the soul of Ibn Abd al-Wahhab," he added, referring to the founder of the strict Sunni sect associated with the unification of the Arabian Peninsula under Ibn Saud.

The others burst out laughing. "What rubbish, Salim," they said. "Don't claim to be progressive; God Almighty, you'd rather turn the clock *back*!" This brought more guffaws.

When the laughter had abated, Muhaysin pointed to the tall young man. "This is Dais al-Dais," he said. "Don't let his nickname 'Mr Awkward' deceive you, as he's one of the cleverest guys you'll ever meet. And this," he went on, "is Salim al-Sannour, Salih al-Tarthuth and Muhanna al-Tairi."

They all shook hands and began unloading the food, cooking pots and tea and coffee-making equipment from the van while Muhaysin and Muhammad collected firewood. Then they sat down on a threadbare old rug they had brought with them and spread out in the shade of the citrus trees. Muhammad al-Ghubayra started a fire at a distance and made the tea, while Salih al-Tarthuth cut the onions and tomatoes for the *kabsa* stew. It was a wonderful spot, infused with a refreshing atmosphere from the shade and the delightful moisture in the air given off by the sprinklers. As Muhammad began handing round cups of tea Dais spoke up.

"I finished reading *Les Misérables* yesterday," he said in a nasal twang, slurping his tea. "What a novel. Can you believe I actually cried when Jean Valjean died?"

Muhanna al-Tairi laughed. "You're weird, Dais," he said, "like your name." He laughed again and looked round at the others, but when he found that no one else was laughing he stopped. "You are strange, Dais," he repeated. "All that culture and intelligence, yet when you read a novel you cry like a girl in her boudoir!"

"What's so strange about that?" said Dais coldly. "Sensitivity is the essence of intelligence. But what would you know about it?" he went on, drinking the last drop of tea in his cup. "There's a world of difference between being sensitive and being a dope-fiend who smokes himself sense*less*."

The others roared with laughter to Muhanna's obvious embarrassment, although he too briefly joined in. Muhaysin laughed hardest, wiping tears from his eyes with the corner of his headdress, which had been lying beside him.

"Haven't you heard the news?" said Salih al-Tarthuth in the distance once the noise had died down. "They say Nasser has accepted the Rogers peace initiative."

"There must be some compelling reason why," said Muhammad.

"Or else it's a ploy to gain time," said Muhaysin.

"Abu Khalid definitely knows what he's doing," said Muhanna al-Tairi, using Nasser's nickname and calmly drinking his tea with a know-all look on his face. "There must be things he knows that we don't. You can trust him to know what's in our interests even if we're not aware of it ourselves." The others all nodded silently in agreement with Muhanna's remarks. Hisham remembered the time the gang in Dammam had met with Ibrahim al-Shudaykhi; this lot were all as mad about Nasser as Ibrahim had been.

"They say that Nasser's ill, and that he made his last trip to the Soviet Union to get treatment," said Salim al-Sannour after a short pause. "God forbid that anything should happen to you, Sheikh," he said, looking despondently at the ground. "God grant him a long life."

"If anything happened to him the Arabs would be lost," said Muhammad al-Ghubayra.

"You're right," said Muhanna al-Tairi, "but it's not illness I'm worried about for his sake, it's conspiracies. There's no way America and its secret services are going to leave a man like him alone."

"They know he's the Arab nation itself," said Dais with uncharacteristic fervour. "If he dies or he's killed, the whole Arab nation dies."

The others all nodded again in agreement and then fell silent, enjoying a sudden dewy breeze. Hisham had been quiet throughout, listening and smiling without comment. The breeze dropped just as suddenly as it had blown up. Muhaysin looked at Hisham and said, "We haven't heard anything from you yet, Hisham – or don't people talk politics in the Eastern Province? Perhaps the Americans keep you quiet?"

The others laughed and looked at one another, while Hisham himself continued smiling as the ghosts of old comrades passed through his mind.

"Seriously," said Salim, "what do you think, brother Hisham?"

"Please, brother Salim, there's no need for formalities."

"Fine. Then what do you think, Hisham?"

"About what?"

"Do you think the Americans will leave Nasser alone?"

Hisham looked at the others as they all turned their gaze on him. These lads were all infatuated with Nasser; he himself had many contradictory feelings towards the leader that he was unable to reconcile: he loved him and, like any lover with his beloved, would try to find justifications, whatever they might be, for his policies, for the bitter defeat the Arabs had suffered in June, for his recent acceptance of the principle of peace and his abandonment of 1948 Palestine. Yet, Hisham had been a member of a party that saw in Nasser a threat to both its ideology and its very existence. Though he had left the party and had come to loathe it, he could not forget its criticism of Nasser's agenda. Hisham had come to adopt a Marxist view that did not endorse the notion of 'the hero' in history. In this light Nasser was no more than an individual who gave voice to a class movement, and there was nothing extraordinary about that.

"I don't know," Hisham said. "But whether he dies or gets killed, he's not immortal, anyway. He's going to die one day, isn't he?" No one said anything, and he continued, "And when he does, will the Arab nation really die, too?"

"God forbid anything should happen to him," said Muhanna. "I can't imagine life without him."

"But the main thing is, will our lives come to an end when Nasser's does?" Hisham went on, as Muhanna gave him a look full of suspicion.

"What do you mean, Hisham?"

"What I mean is that we mustn't tie our own fate to that of one man. However important he is, he's still just a man in the end, and men die. Are we going to die with them?"

There was a general silence. Muhanna's tension was plain to see in his movements. Now and then he would shift his position, and he was drinking his tea astonishingly quickly. It was then that Hisham put his cards on the table.

"What we need is an ideology that's capable of lighting the way ahead, whether or not we have a great leader. It's ideology that makes men, and not vice versa."

"But Nasser isn't just a man," said Muhammad al-Ghubayra passionately, "he's an ideology himself as well. When he dies, God forbid, he'll still live on in his ideas."

"Well said, well said," said Muhanna, nodding, a smile on his face.

"All Nasser comes out with are slogans," said Hisham, repeating something he had read in the party literature, "general aims, not ideas."

"Good God!" said Muhanna, "Everything advanced by the July Revolution and the land reform and socialist laws, mere slogans? You're not being fair, brother Hisham."

"That's what they are," Hisham replied nervously, "all words and nothing more. 'Lift up your head, brother', 'Freedom, Socialism, Unity', 'Freedom of speech is the introduction to democracy'. It's all talk without application, slogans with no coherent thought behind them. Is this ideology or an agenda?" As Hisham spoke he looked at Muhanna, who was about to explode.

"What is ideology if not that?" burst out Muhanna. "He defined our goals and the way to realise them. Freedom of expression is the way to democracy, and freedom, unity and socialism are well-known objectives that don't need a commentary and a synopsis. There's 'The Philosophy of the Revolution' and 'The Covenant' and the 'Declaration of 30th March', as well as Anwar Sadat's writings about Nasser and the Revolution; aren't these ideas? What more do you want?"

Muhanna paused to catch his breath. The others, who were in a fever of excitement and anticipation, looked at him admiringly. Hisham felt embarrassed in this atmosphere of ardent Nasserism, the likes of which he had never come across in Dammam. Everyone loved Nasser, both here and in Dammam, but there it was not with the same infatuation he was encountering just then. It seemed to him that the Qusaimis were extreme in all things. For them everything was a matter of love or hate with nothing in between; either they were believers or they weren't, with no middle ground between Heaven and Hell. He was afraid that if he prolonged the discussion Muhanna in particular might go beyond mere words, a prospect that by nature Hisham both feared and hated. He preferred to keep quiet and let Muhanna enjoy his victory.

Just as everyone was stirred up and glancing at one another, Salih spoke up. "We'd better start getting the stew ready," he said, "if you lot want any lunch, that is!" He went over to the fire and Salim followed him to help. Salih put the meat, tomatoes, fat, onions and salt all together in a pot and added water, then put the pot on the fire.

"That's not how you make *kabsa*," said Muhaysin in surprise, after watching him do all this. "You should fry the meat and the onions in the fat first, then add the tomatoes and the water and salt later."

Salih laughed. "That's the old, traditional, tiring way," he said. "This way's quicker and easier."

"God cover up our shortcomings," said Muhaysin resignedly. "The main thing is not to let the rice get stodgy," he warned.

"Don't worry, your brother's a good cook," replied Salih with a laugh. He put the lid on the pot and left it on the fire and then, after pouring himself a cup of tea, went for a walk around the orchard, sipping his tea as he went. Meanwhile Muhanna was still caught up in his debating victory, and intoxicated with the admiration from the other members of his gang; what he wanted now was to deliver the *coup de grâce* to his victim.

"Well, you haven't said anything, brother Hisham," he said, looking askance at him. "Or are you convinced?"

He wanted a frank admission of defeat from Hisham in front of all the others. Silence was not enough for him. Hisham sensed the desire for humiliation in Muhanna's question and felt his blood boil. He tried to stay as calm as possible as he replied,

"You haven't said anything to convince me, brother Muhanna." Muhanna's face and movements tensed up again and the others listened as Hisham went on, full of unease inside but trying to retain his composure. "When you talk about freedom, socialism and unity you're speaking about concepts and things that are unclear even to Nasser himself. You certainly can't have read the minutes of the discussions of unification between the Baathists and Nasser, or between Aflaq and Nasser to be precise," he said, referring to the coming together of Egypt and Syria in 1958 to form the United Arab Republic. "Because if you had it would be clear to you that their differences were about exactly these concepts, even if they did reach agreement on them in the end, albeit with a different arrangement. And as for the books and sources you mentioned, they're full of general talk that's of no use to anyone; it means everything and anything and nothing, whereas what we need now is a comprehensive ideology that can take in the past and the present and light the way to the future."

Hisham finished talking. He had been trying to bring the discussion to an end and had spoken with all the frankness and clarity he could muster. But Muhanna would not leave it at that.

"Fine, brother Hisham," he said, smirking. "If you're not a fan of Nasser and his ideas, what in your opinion is the ideology that can save us?" He spoke with a sarcastic ring in his voice. "And please don't talk to me about the Baathists or the Arab nationalists, or even the whirling dervishes of the Muslim Brotherhood," he said, butting in just as Hisham had been about to answer. "They're all naive fools and phoneys. If it's that kind of ideology you're talking about, then I'm sorry to say you're just as naive and clueless yourself."

Muhanna thought he had cut off every possible way out available to Hisham, who felt he had no choice but to play his last card. "No, he said, "no, it's nothing like that. It's ... *Marxism*."

Everyone leaned forward, peering incredulously at Hisham, who felt a sudden sense of joy at becoming the object of interest. "Yes, Marxism," he repeated, with unfeigned calm and confidence this time. "Marxism is the complete, scientific way of thought that can give us the keys to history, society and politics; whoever holds these keys will have nothing to fear and nothing to regret."

"You mean Communism?" said Muhanna slyly.

"Are you a Communist, Hisham?" asked Muhaysin, aghast.

"Communism?" said Salih in astonishment. "That means not believing in God."

"It means the non-existence of freedom," said Said censoriously.

"Communists, Baathists and the Muslim Brotherhood are all the enemies of Nasser," said Muhammad, looking at Hisham with repugnance. "I detest the lot of them."

"I like the Soviets," said Salim, "but I don't trust Arab Communists. They're the enemies of Arab nationalism."

Hisham waited until all the comments had died down, as inside he felt an overpowering haplessness. "Marxism as a philosophy," he said, plucking up all his courage. "I'm not a Communist, nor do I support any of the Arab Communist parties."

"Oh, please," said Muhanna scornfully, "is there any difference between Marxism and Communism, esteemed comrade?"

"Yes," Hisham snapped, finally losing his cool, "yes there is, you half-witted sheep, chasing after big men and taken in by honeyed words."

"Me, a half-wit, you unbeliever, you atheist, you and your kind who screw around however you like?"

The atmosphere between them froze, and Hisham shrunk back silently as Muhanna got up, pointing at him and saying angrily, "It's not this one's fault, it's Muhaysin's fault for inviting him in the first place!" With that he stormed off towards the orchard, where he walked down the first path he came to.

"That's enough, everyone," said Muhammad, breaking the anxious silence that had followed Muhanna's exit. "What do you say we have a game of Plot?" Without waiting for an answer he went to the van, fetched a deck of cards and got together with all the others except Hisham and Dais, who stood up and went for a walk in the orchard in the opposite direction from Muhanna. "The stew will be ready in half an hour," they could hear Salih calling out to them. "Don't be long …"

❧ 57 ❧

The days in Qusaim passed by smoothly and happily, contrary to Hisham's expectations, once he had got to know his new friends and despite the shock of the Marxist convictions he had announced at the picnic in al-Rashidiyya. His friendship with Dais, Muhaysin and Muhammad grew stronger, but as for Muhanna, the picnic was the beginning and the end as far as their relationship was concerned. Hisham would see him from time to time at the Plot evenings with the rest of the group, but they would not say anything to one another beyond the conventional civilities. Muhanna did try to begin political conversations centred on Nasser, but Hisham kept quiet, playing Plot without uttering a single comment.

He went on many other picnics to the farms in Unayzah and al-Daghmaniyyat, which was a veritable paradise, as well as hot springs and numerous other places the names of which he could not remember. Best of all were the picnics to the al-Nafud desert on white nights, when the moon was full; they would spend the evening on soft, cold sand dunes where there was nothing but the moonlight and the sound of the fire crackling as it devoured the wood in the otherwise complete silence and tranquillity, as though the doors of Heaven had opened on an eternal night like that on which the Qur'an was revealed. Sometimes they would sleep there, awakening with the first drops of dew before sunrise when the sand was as cold as the silence itself; then the sun would send down its golden rays tenderly before becoming brutal. After Hisham returned to Dammam, memories of the trip to Qusaim remained with him and he set his heart on going back one day; by the time he did so, long afterwards, everything had lost its innocent delight.

The return journey to Dammam was not as difficult as that to Qusaim: Hisham's father had learned a lesson he would never forget. He had agreed with the driver of one of the 'boxes', a professional who knew the desert like his own name, to pass by the house in the morning so they could follow it through the wastes of Jayb Ghurab. Hisham longed to see the gang in Dammam as well as Noura, but his anxiety about the exam results and the arrests clouded his anticipation.

The day of their departure was truly painful, when his grandfather and grandmother and his aunt gathered to bid them a final farewell. Tears streamed from his aunt's eyes, his grandfather was fighting back tears and his grandmother was unable to speak. His aunt had made lots of *kalija* cakes with lemon and cardamom and *aqil* patties, which she brought that morning, emphasising that they were for Hisham. At the moment of parting she gave him a long embrace and tried to force a smile to her little lips, but could not hold back her tears. As they got into the car and drove off, Hisham gave one last look at the wooden door where his grandfather, grandmother, his aunt and Suleiman were standing, not knowing that that would be the last time he ever saw them. His aunt developed a strange illness and died soon afterwards, followed first by his grandfather and then by his grandmother. The news of their deaths reached Hisham in Jeddah, and he wished then that he could turn back the clock to plant one final kiss on his aunt's cheek and her forehead, and to smell for one last time his grandfather's scent.

❯ 58 ❮

They did not stop at Hisham's uncle's house in Riyadh on the way back but kept on to Dammam, which they reached at dawn on the second day after their departure from Qusaim. Instead of sleeping that day Hisham went to the school, where he learned that he had got his diploma. Finding that out made him feel important and capable; his results were not outstanding or even mediocre, but he had passed and that was the main thing. He went home and gave the good news to his mother, who gave him a big hug, crying and smiling at the same time before waking his father, who congratulated him soberly while containing his feelings of joy.

In the early afternoon Hisham took off to Abd al-Karim's house, taking some of the *kalija* cakes and *aqil* patties with him, but first he stopped by Noura's house and knocked on the door.

"It's Hisham al-Abir," he said, when he heard Noura's mother asking who was at the door. "My mother sends her regards and wanted me to let you know we're back."

His mother had not asked him to do any such thing and he was taking a risk by claiming that she had, but having passed his exams had lent Hisham a certain audacity. He wanted the message to reach Noura; surely it would, and that was what mattered, whatever else happened.

When he got to Abd al-Karim's house the rest of the gang was not yet there, and he and Abd al-Karim sat drinking tea, talking and eating the cakes. Then their friends began to arrive, Abd al-Aziz, Saud and Salim together and finally Adnan. Apart from his eyes, which were brighter, Adnan looked like a mummy drained of all its vital juices; his face was now scarred from acne. They all embraced and then sat down, gobbling up the *kalija* cakes and *aqil* patties that Hisham had brought with him so fast and with such relish that after a few minutes there was nothing left. Over tea they began discussing their future plans. Hisham and Adnan had got their secondary school diplomas and the others had all moved up into the sixth form; only one more year to go and they would all be university students. Hisham had already announced that he wanted to study economics and politics. He wished he could get a scholarship to study in America or Britain, but with his grades he was ineligible, and his father did not have the sort of contacts that would have enabled him to travel on a scholarship despite them. Even if he had, his father would not have been keen; he wanted Hisham to study medicine or engineering, and all his life he had wanted to see his son become a doctor of something. Hisham would have loved to fulfill his father's wish, but he could not bear either of these subjects; only in things related to ideas and culture and the conflict of political movements did he feel at home.

Adnan was full of uncertainty; he had also passed with a low average score and had no hope of getting a scholarship. He dreamed of going to Rome to study fine art, but he could not hope to. Even if he had been able to, his father was putting pressure on him to study 'something useful' instead of all that 'child's play' he was so taken up with. Adnan's indecision was such that he was even thinking of dropping his studies altogether and looking for work with his secondary school qualifications alone. One day he might be able to scrape together enough money to be able to get to Rome.

Hisham looked at his friends with affection now unadulterated in the slightest by political affiliations. Even the wrongs that Adnan had done him were now merely the scars of old wounds that no longer gave him any pain, even if their traces remained in memory. He thanked God then that he had not invited Abd al-Aziz to join the party after his angry clash with Ibrahim al-Shudaykhi following Nasser's speech that day; that day, which now seemed like ancient history. He felt wrung with pain inside as his glance fell on Adnan who seemed, however bright his eyes were, to be somehow shrouded as though dead. Hisham felt responsible for Adnan's state. The party and the organisation had spoiled their long and innocent friendship, and in the end he was to blame, from his need to prove to himself and to the party that he was not just any ordinary comrade, but capable of recruiting new supporters.

Shortly before sunset they dispersed, agreeing to meet earlier than usual the next day in order to plan a trip to 'Half Moon Bay' or Aziziya to celebrate their success and reunion.

☞ 59 ☜

Hisham had only got a short distance from Abd al-Karim's house when the muezzin began the sunset call to prayer; several people were heading to the mosque already, water from their ritual ablutions still dripping from their faces as they hurried along to get there before prayers began, even though the mosque was nearby and there was plenty of time. Hisham himself was in a rush, as he wanted to get home before Noura arrived with the milk. But before he reached the turn into the main street he heard Adnan's voice, and looked around to see him running along and almost tripping on his robe. Hisham waited for him with acute irritation, afraid that he would miss Noura. As Adnan reached him he was panting, even though he had not had far to run, and he paused for a few minutes to catch his breath.

"You've been gone a long time," he said eventually, still breathing fast and his face glistening with sweat. "I was worried about you." Adnan gave him a look that expressed all the emotions churning inside him.

"Don't worry," said Hisham, smiling and placing a hand on Adnan's shoulder. "Everything's fine." He wanted to get rid of

Adnan in any way he could: Noura would be on her way to his house by now.

Adnan gave him a feeble smile. "I was worried and I had no one to talk to. I'm scared, Hisham. There's no one left except us."

Hisham felt a bolt of fear pass through him. Over the last few days he had almost forgotten the subject, and here was Adnan taking him back to Hell again. Adnan looked like a child in a strange city who had lost his parents, and feelings of tenderness and guilt swept over Hisham at once.

"I told you, everything's fine," he said with a pretence of calm, trying to look composed and forcing a smile to his lips. "A lot of days have gone by without anyone enquiring about us. If they were after us, they'd have arrested us ages ago with the others, wouldn't they?"

"Do you think so?"

"Yes; and anyway, whatever happens to us is only what God has preordained," Hisham said, walking towards the street. But Adnan walked with him silently, without his being able to stop him.

"What have you made up your mind to do?" Adnan asked in a flat, dull voice, at the point where the alley joined the main street.

"I'm going to go to Riyadh to apply to the faculty, maybe in a week, or ten days at the most. What about you?"

"I don't know, I really don't."

They were now very close to Hisham's house and he was afraid that Adnan would come even further, obliging Hisham to invite him in. He stopped.

"Sorry, Adnan," he said. "I've got to finish doing some things for my father, so I'll have to leave you now. We'll meet up another time." Hisham went off in the direction of his house.

"Doing some things for your father, or doing some things with Juliet, eh Romeo?" called Adnan, with the cheerful spirit of the old days. Hisham smiled and waved to him from a distance as he hurried off. Adnan stood there, watching Hisham gradually disappear from sight.

❧ 60 ❧

Noura was just about to leave when Hisham got home. Before going in he heard his mother say goodbye to her from the other side of the door. Instead of going inside Hisham quickly hid behind the wall parallel to the alleyway that led to Noura's house. Moments later Noura appeared, carrying the empty milk pail. Hisham suddenly emerged from his hiding place, giving Noura such a fright that she dropped the pail. Hisham snatched it up and handed it to her. "Tonight," he said hastily, and they each walked away quickly in opposite directions.

Hisham went home. His mother was in the garden, trying to catch something of a breeze, with all the heavy humidity in the air. He went up to her cheerfully and greeted her, kissing her on the head uncharacteristically.

"God bless you, God bless you," she said. "You're back early," she went on with surprise. "That's not like you even on school days, so how come you're home so soon when it's the holidays now?"

Instead of answering, Hisham simply smiled, and his mother smiled back as he went to his room. The air there was unbearable, but all he could feel was how happy he was. A few moments later his mother came in with a glass of milk in which she had put some ice.

"Drink this. It might relieve the heat a bit," she said.

"Milk!" he replied, feigning astonishment. "Noura must have been here?"

"Yes. She only left a few minutes ago. She's a very clever girl."

"In what way?"

"She saw your father's car in front of the door this afternoon and realised we were back; clever girl. And beautiful too, and from a good family." His mother looked at him with a smile. He knew what she was getting at and smiled back, before drinking the milk in one go and then sucking an ice cube without commenting. His mother went out, warning him about sucking ice cubes and the effect it would have on his tonsils.

"She certainly is a clever girl ... very clever," Hisham said to himself, smiling wickedly as he pictured his tryst with her that night.

❧ 61 ❧

Hisham was fervent with desire when he went to meet Noura that night, and so was she. And yet, the moment he entered her house, all that desire, all the heat he had been wrapped in, suddenly evaporated, like a hungry person who, for no apparent reason, has indigestion .... When she jerked him by the hand over to their usual corner, she was the one to begin kissing him with an audacity he had never come across in her before.

"I hadn't imagined I was so madly in love with you," she was saying as she kissed him, gluing her lips to his almost painfully. He returned her feverish kisses with a coldness he himself had not thought possible. Her lips were as hot and soft as could be, and yet he did not experience the sensation that usually swept over him when he met her, and which he always longed for. Noura noticed the frigid passivity in his lips, despite all the fireworks she was giving off herself and pulled away in bewilderment.

"You don't love me any more, Hisham," she said, lowering her eyes. "There's another girl, isn't there?" With her big eyes she gave him a flirtatious look tinged with worry.

Hisham smiled wearily. "No," he said, looking at nothing in particular, "I love you more than love itself, but …" He did not finish his sentence; he did not know what the matter was with him.

"So what's wrong?" she said with gentle reassurance, leaning towards him and taking his clammy palm in hers. She gave him a quick, gentle kiss. "You know I'm crazy about you," she said softly. "You're the light of my life. For Heaven's sake, tell me what's wrong." Words like these were normally guaranteed to make his head spin and set his soul ablaze, but he felt nothing now. He did not want to worry her, and smiled as he drew her to him; without hesitation she flung her arms around his neck, fixing her mouth to his with her eyes closed. Yet once again he could not respond, and she drew apart, gazing at him with suspicion. There was a silence disturbed only by the chirping of the crickets in the garden.

"Have I told you?" she said after a pause, looking at him with a smile, "I've bought a new petticoat. Would you like to see it?" Without his answering she began to lift up her dress, showing first her calf and then her lower thigh. Even in the faint light he could make out her ripening body. "Isn't it pretty?" she said, taking hold of the hem of her red petticoat, which was embroidered at the bottom. Hisham knew she wanted to get his attention. She had never done this; she would never let his hand reach up to those forbidden regions. He looked at her with pure love and smiled, and then took hold of her dress and pulled it down over her leg and gave her a long embrace, smelling her hair with pleasure. He kissed her and then suddenly got up.

"They must be wondering where I am," he said. "I'd better be off." Without waiting for her to answer, he left. She watched him go, wrung with confusion, astonishment and frustration.

❖ 62 ❖

After greeting his father and mother Hisham went to his room and lay on his bed, thinking about what had happened. He loved Noura; now, at this moment, he longed for her and wished he could go back. Only a few moments earlier she had been before him. But he did not know the reason for what had happened. He went over to his bookcase and soon lost himself with Freud in *The Future of Fantasy*.

He wanted to find an explanation for his words to Adnan that evening, automatically and without thinking about it: 'Whatever happens to us is only what God has preordained.' He thought he had settled this matter long ago, when he embraced Marxism as the only scientific thought capable of reaching truth and predicting the future with any accuracy. There was no such thing as coincidence or fate, he told himself; life was not a drama in which one already knew the beginning and the end and where the only difference was in the details, which in any case had been determined beforehand. Everything had a cause and nothing was preordained. That was the philosophy he had pledged himself to. He was under threat of arrest because he had belonged to a clandestine organisation; if he had not belonged to it, he would not be under threat. If one of the others betrayed him, he would inevitably be arrested, and if they did not betray him he would not. Causality was the essence of existence. He had rejected metaphysics the moment he had found what he had been looking for in Marxism, so how and why had that expression escaped him?

His thoughts led him to the conclusion that in times of need a person became a helpless child again, searching for a father to protect him and a tender mother, and God was the supreme example of the omnipotent father figure. He recalled a saying of Voltaire's: 'If God did not exist it would be necessary to invent Him'. Man wanted someone to be responsible for him in times of need, when everything was in danger; when the need disappeared, he wanted to be directly responsible for himself ... and become God himself. It was all a comforting fantasy, but a fantasy nonetheless. This conclusion put Hisham at his ease and satisfied his questions. He felt he had reached a scientific deduction in keeping with his faith. 'Dialectical materialism' and 'historical materialism' crossed his mind; weren't they also forms of inevitable 'predestination'? But he dismissed these thoughts under the pretext that he had not explored Marxism deeply enough, which was why he needed to study it starting with its fundamental principles; this was what he was going to do, and no doubt there were convincing scientific answers to questions like this. Marxism was as far as scientific thought could go in terms of programmatic development. With that Hisham went off contentedly to sleep alongside his parents in the television room with the air–conditioning on.

❧ 63 ❧

During the next few days the preparations for his journey to Riyadh progressed at full throttle. He received his papers from the school, had three new robes made in one go, and bought new headdresses and skullcaps, new shoes and some socks. His father gave him some expensive Nejdi shoes he had had made by a famous cobbler in Qusaim during their last trip there.

Hisham's mother was not happy about him travelling to Riyadh; she would have preferred him to go to the College of Petroleum and Minerals in Dhahran and stay near her, but he insisted on studying economics and politics, and politics was not taught at the College of Petroleum. In the end his mother left matters in God's hands, reassured by the fact that Hisham would be living in his uncle's house and would come to see them every holiday, and he promised to write often.

The day of his departure came. His mother made him a special breakfast, including eggs with tomatoes, baked beans, watermelon jam, yellow and white cheese, homemade bread, fried and boiled eggs. She sat with him for a long time, giving him bits of advice about steering clear of shady company and suspicious places and bad habits and politics and all the things God had forbidden, all the while saying over and over that she knew he was a 'sensible boy' who would never do anything foolish, but that she had to warn him all the same. After breakfast she gave him one hundred riyals as a good-luck present.

Shortly before midday Hisham's father returned from work to take him to the train station. His mother was quite calm as she said goodbye to him. She kissed him on both cheeks and he kissed her on the forehead and left, carrying his huge black suitcase and imagining the prayers of his mother that he could not hear. Adnan and Abd al-Karim were already at the station when he and his father got there, and everyone was fighting to get to the ticket desk. On the platform the crowds were even worse. Abd al-Karim would not let him push and shove with all the others, but instead took the money from Hisham's father and threw himself into the throng by the ticket desk. Minutes later he returned with a second-class ticket; he was smiling, his headdress having fallen off and his face shining with sweat.

Hisham's father gave him three hundred riyals' spending money to last him until he got his first grant from the faculty. Hisham was thrilled. With a fortune like this he would be able to buy whatever he wanted, especially now that he would be responsible for purchasing his own food and drink and paying for his accommodation. He put his suitcase in the luggage carriage, and kissed his father on the forehead, embraced his friends and boarded the train. He shoved his way through crowds of people with their distinctive smells, which the humidity made somehow different from any other smells anywhere else. Once he had fought his way to a seat and sat down, he looked out of the window to where his father and his friends were standing. As the train moved off, he waved goodbye to them; he took a long look at his father, who was watching the train carry his son away into the future, and perhaps into the unknown, though in reality there was no difference ...

Through the window of the train from Dammam the buildings of Riyadh began to appear, vague and indistinct like a dream on a summer afternoon. The heat haze of that August day mingled with sandstorms, whipped up by the breath of genies from the al-Dahna desert, giving Riyadh the appearance of …